READ HERRING HUNT

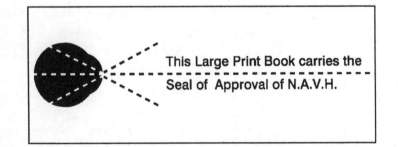

A MYSTERY BOOKSHOP MYSTERY

READ HERRING HUNT

V. M. BURNS

WHEELER PUBLISHING
A part of Gale, a Cengage Company

GALE
A Cengage Company

Farmington Hills, Mich • San Francisco • New York • Waterville, Maine
Meriden, Conn • Mason, Ohio • Chicago

Copyright © 2018 by Valerie Burns.
A Mystery Bookshop Mystery.
Wheeler Publishing, a part of Gale, a Cengage Company.

Wheeler Publishing Large Print Cozy Mystery.
The text of this Large Print edition is unabridged.
Other aspects of the book may vary from the original edition.
Set in 16 pt. Plantin.

LIBRARY OF CONGRESS CIP DATA ON FILE.
CATALOGUING IN PUBLICATION FOR THIS BOOK
IS AVAILABLE FROM THE LIBRARY OF CONGRESS

ISBN-13: 978-1-4328-5474-4 (softcover)

Published in 2018 by arrangement with Kensington Books, an imprint of Kensington Publishing Corp.

Printed in Mexico
1 2 3 4 5 6 7 22 21 20 19 18

*In loving memory of Coco Chanel
for 17 years of love and cuddles*

ACKNOWLEDGMENTS

Special thanks to my agent, Dawn Dowdle, at Blue Ridge Literary; Mary Lasher for capturing my fur babies so well and providing such great cover art for the original publisher's edition; Kristen Lepionka for answering my S.O.S. and providing great promo support and social media graphics; and the wonderful staff at Kensington Publishing, John Scognamiglio, Paula Reedy, and Michelle Addo.

Thanks to Anthony Cameron (aka Trooper Tony) and Eric Haskin for answering my questions related to police procedures. Thanks to Dave "Moose" Mitchell (aka Missouri Man) for allowing me to pick your brain regarding college football rules and regulations; and Chris Siriano for assistance with the House of David. Special thanks to my friend, Cassandra Morgan, for taking pity on me and allowing me to benefit from your social media expertise.

I appreciate all of the support I've received from '17 Scribes and fellow unicorn Kellye Garrett. Thanks to my SHU Tribe (June 2012) and especially Jessica Barlow, Lana Ayres, and Michelle Lane. I am so incredibly blessed to have such a fantastic training team (Deborah Hughes, Grace Dixon, Jamie Medlin, and Tena Elkins). Thanks for helping to make my days easier so I can spend my nights pursuing my dream. You guys rock!

My dream of writing a book and getting published would not be a reality without the love and support of friends, family, and really good friends who have become my family. This includes my dad, Benjamin Burns; my sister, Jacquelyn Rucker; my niece, Jillian Rucker, and nephew, Christopher Rucker; and good friends Shelitha Mckee and Sophia Muckerson. You have all been there throughout all of the ups and downs on this entire roller-coaster ride. Thanks for always having my back.

CHAPTER 1

"Did you see the getup that little floozy had on?"

"Shhhh." I glanced around to make sure the "little floozy" was out of earshot. Tact wasn't Nana Jo's strong suit.

"Don't shush me. I've seen Sumo wrestlers wearing more fabric."

Nana Jo exaggerated, but not by much. Melody Hardwick was a supermodel thin, heavily made-up college senior who had attached herself figuratively and literally to my assistant, Dawson Alexander.

"Surely that boy knows she's nothing more than a little gold digger." Nana Jo had taken an instant dislike to Melody.

"You don't know she's a gold digger. You just don't like her." I locked the door to the bookstore. "Besides, it's not like Dawson has any money."

"He may not have a pot to pee in now, but the boy has PEP." Nana Jo wiped down the counters and bagged the trash.

"What's pep?"

"Potential earning power. That boy is the best quarterback MISU's had in at least a decade. They're undefeated and if things keep going like last week, they have a shot at a bowl game and maybe a championship."

My grandmother had always been a sports enthusiast, but ever since the Michigan Southwest University, or MISS YOU as the locals called it, quarterback started helping out in my bookstore, she became more of a fanatic.

"He was embarrassed. Did you see how she clung to him?"

"Dawson's a big boy. He can make his own decisions."

Based on the look she gave me, she wasn't convinced. Frankly, I wasn't convinced either. I was concerned about him too. School was a challenge for Dawson. At the end of his freshman year, he was placed on academic probation. Thanks to a lot of hard work and tutoring from me and Nana Jo throughout the summer, he'd raised his grades, avoided academic suspension, and turned his life around. He didn't have to work at the bookstore anymore. His football scholarship covered room and board. I never wanted to charge him for staying in the studio apartment I created in my garage, but student athletes had to pay the going rate for housing and get paid fair market wages for work.

"Girls like that ain't nothing but trouble. You mark my words. Just like Delilah, she'll come after him with a pair of scissors first chance she gets. That woman is nothing but trouble."

Nana Jo's words broke my reverie and brought back the worry I thought I'd eliminated. I tried to shake it off, but it lingered at the back of my mind.

We cleaned the store and then she hurried off for a date with her boyfriend, Freddie.

I took a quick tour around the store. I looked at the books neatly stacked on each shelf. It was still hard for me to believe I owned my own mystery bookstore. Market Street Mysteries had been a dream my late husband and I shared for years. After his death over a year ago, I was finally living our dream. I walked down each aisle and ran my hands across the solid wood book-shelves that still smelled woodsy and fresh and shined with the oil polish Andrew, my Amish craftsman, gave me. After six months, the store was doing well and I still got a thrill walking through and realizing it was mine. My four-legged companions on these strolls trailed along behind, toenails clicking on the wood floors. Toy poodles, Snickers and Oreo, may not share my love of mysteries, but they definitely approved of the baked goods that made their way under tables and counters.

The back of the bookstore was enclosed to provide a yard for privacy and an area for the poodles to chase squirrels and bask in the sunlight. As fall hit the Michigan coastline, the weather had turned cool. The leaves were starting to darken from bright shades of yellowy green to deeper, rich hues of amber, burgundy, and russet. Lake Michigan was also undergoing a change from the deep blue calm of summer to the pale blue that blended into the horizon and was only discernible from the sky by the choppy white swells that danced across the surface and pounded the shore. Autumn was my favorite time of year, and I lingered outside and enjoyed the sunset until Snickers reminded me she hadn't been fed by scratching my leg and ruining my tights. I needed to remember to make an appointment with the groomers first thing tomorrow or give up wearing skirts.

When my husband, Leon, and I dreamed of the bookstore, we planned to make the upper level into a rental unit to offset the cost. After his death, I sold the home we'd lived in and turned the upper level into a two-bedroom loft for me and the poodles. Nana Jo moved in after a dead body was found in the back courtyard, but she still had her villa at a retirement village. I never dreamed how much I'd enjoy living in the space.

Next week would be one year since Leon's death. The pain was less crippling. The bookstore kept me busy during the day. But the nights were still difficult. I started writing to help occupy my time and my mind. Six months ago I'd finished the first draft of a British cozy mystery and spent the last few months editing. Nana Jo wanted me to send it out to an agent, but that would involve allowing someone besides me and my grandmother, who loved me, to read it. I wasn't ready for that type of humiliation and rejection yet. Besides, in the unlikely event that a publisher was interested in my book, they'd want to know what else I had. What if one book was all I had in me? The only way to find out would be to try again. So after dinner, I made a cup of tea and headed to my laptop.

Wickfield Lodge, English country home of

Lord William Marsh–November 1938

Thompkins entered the back salon where the Marsh family was having tea and coughed. "I'm sorry, but the Duke of Kingfordshire is on the telephone."

Lady Daphne was in her favorite seat by the window. She started to rise but was stopped when Thompkins discreetly coughed again.

"His Grace the duke asked to speak to your ladyship." He turned toward Lady Elizabeth.

Lady Elizabeth Marsh glanced at her niece Daphne, noting the blush that left her cheeks flushed. She placed her teacup down and hurried out of the room. In the library, she picked up the telephone. "Hello, James dear, is there —"

"Thank goodness you're home. I'm sorry but I don't have time for pleasantries. Time is of the essence." Lord James FitzAndrew Browning, normally calm and composed, had a slight tremor in his voice, which reflected the urgency of his call even more than his words and lack of propriety. The duke took a deep breath and then rushed on. "This is going to sound strange, but I need you to trust me. You're going to get a call from the Duchess of Windsor asking for permission to move her hunting party to Wickfield Lodge this weekend. It's vital she be allowed to do so."

Whatever Lady Elizabeth expected, it hadn't

been this. She stood frozen for a moment before recovering herself enough to respond. "Well of course, James. We . . . we have no plans this weekend."

James released a huge sigh, and she could almost see him wiping his brow.

"James, you know we're happy to help any way we can, but you mentioned this was 'vital.' Vital to whom?"

James hesitated a moment before responding. "Vital to England. The Crown. Maybe the entire world."

CHAPTER 2

Saturdays were busy days at the bookstore, and I was thankful my nephews, Christopher and Zaq, were home from college for fall break and helping out. The twins were invaluable in getting the bookstore up and running over the summer. The boys were twenty and while they were identical, their personalities were so different it was very easy to tell them apart. Both were tall and slender. Christopher was business oriented and preppy, while Zaq was technology inclined and edgier. Neither was a mystery lover, but they each had their own gifts, and I was thankful they were willing to spend time helping out their aunt and earn extra pocket money.

Nana Jo was a mystery lover and was great at helping match customers with authors and mystery subgenres like hard-boiled detective stories, cozy mysteries, or police procedurals.

Today was a home football weekend for MISU and a bye week for the twins' school, Jesus and Mary University, or JAMU to the locals. When Dawson started working at the bookstore, I toyed with the idea of putting a television in the store so we could watch him play on Saturdays. However, a television in a bookstore seemed paradoxical. I compromised by foregoing the smooth jazz I normally piped in and tuned into the sports channel instead, at least for MISU and JAMU games. I expected complaints from people who liked to sit and read in peace and quiet. But so far the comments were all positive. I suspected the lack of protest was due to the customers' desire to support a hometown boy combined with their affection for Dawson's baked goods. They were willing to give up a little peace and quiet to support someone they knew.

Thankfully, Dawson and the MISU Tigers had today's game well in hand with a healthy lead of three touchdowns. Home team wins made for happy customers, and happy customers spent more money. As locals discovered Dawson lived and worked here, I'd noticed an increase in traffic. Many were football fans who wanted to congratulate him, talk sports, and get autographs for wide-eyed kids. The others were infatuated young girls who glanced shyly at him when he was working and then hid behind books, giggling whenever he looked at them. Regardless of the reason, the extra traffic was good for business.

MISU won handily and I had a very good day in sales. The twins had dates and hurried out immediately at closing.

"You should go to the casino with me and the girls," Nana Jo said.

"Thanks, but I think I'll stay home. I want to get some writing done." We reshelved books and cleaned the store.

"Great. You started working on the next book in the series? You know, I'm really proud of you. But you still need to start sending your book out to agents. I hear getting published is a long process. I read somewhere Agatha Christie was rejected for five years before she got her first book deal."

"I know. I —"

The alarm system I'd installed this summer startled me and I dropped the books I was shelving. The alarm buzzed whenever a door or window was opened, even if the system wasn't armed. Nana Jo stepped around to see who had entered and I picked up the books I'd dropped.

I placed the books on a nearby table and headed for the front of the store. I could have sworn I'd locked the door. Just as I came around the corner, I heard Nana Jo.

"We're closed."

"Oh, I know. I just thought I'd wait for Dawson."

I struggled to recognize the voice. As I got to the main aisle, I saw Dawson's scantily clad girlfriend, Melody. Today's ensemble included more fabric than the one she wore yesterday, but not by much. A short black skintight miniskirt with a deep V-neck mesh cut top with fabric that barely covered her breasts and red, six-inch heels that Nana Jo's friend Irma called hooker heels.

"Lord have mercy. What're you wearing?" Nana Jo stared openmouthed.

The shocked expression wasn't lost on Melody, who laughed and twirled to insure Nana Jo got the full effect. "You like?"

"Is someone watching your pole?"

Melody flushed and cocked her head and took a step forward as though she were about to say something insulting.

Younger people often thought of the elderly as feeble and weak. However, my Nana Jo was close to six feet, two hundred pounds, held a green belt in aikido, and could shoot a bat off the top of a building at three hundred yards. *Don't ask me how I know that.* Despite the difference in their ages, in a fight, my money was on Nana Jo.

"Dawson isn't here and the store is closed." I stepped in between the two women. "If you're looking for Dawson, I suggest you try campus."

For a moment, Melody looked at me as though I were gum she'd scrapped from the bottom of her shoe.

"What's going on?"

I was so intent on preventing an altercation between Nana Jo and Melody I hadn't heard Dawson enter through the back door.

Apparently, Melody hadn't either. "Dawson. How long have you been there?" She smiled big.

"Long enough." The chill in his words made me turn to look at him. His eyes were hard and his face was set like granite. "What're you doing here, Melody? I told you we were finished yesterday."

Melody kept her smile in place as she sauntered around me. "I knew you couldn't really mean that. We both said things we didn't mean yesterday." She stood inches from Dawson and placed her hands on his chest and leaned close. "Let's go up to your room and talk things over."

Dawson didn't move for several seconds, but I could see the vein in the side of his forehead bulge with each breath. Finally, he grabbed Melody by the wrist.

She winced in pain. "Ouch. You're hurting me."

Dawson turned and walked out the way he came, dragging Melody by the wrist along with him.

"I guess he was smart enough to see through that little cheap hussy after all," Nana Jo said. "I think that's the last we'll see of her."

I hurried to secure the front door. Something in the way Melody looked and a flutter in my spine told me Nana Jo was wrong.

Normally, Sundays were spent with my mom. Church, lunch afterward, and girl time. This Sunday was no different. Today we were shopping in downtown South Harbor.

Unlike North Harbor, South Harbor had a bustling downtown with picturesque cobblestone streets and brick storefronts that sold everything from fudge and truffles to overpriced coffee. Mixed between quaint soda shops and antique stores were clothing stores with shoes that cost more than a month of my salary when I was a teacher.

"Honey, isn't this cashmere sweater lovely? It would look great on you." My mom held up a bubblegum-pink garment that looked as though it might fit one of my thighs.

"Mom, I couldn't fit my imagination in that sweater."

"They have larger sizes, dear. I really think you need to upgrade your wardrobe. Everything you own is black or brown. You look like you're still in mourning." She placed the fluffy concoction up to my neck.

I glanced at the tag and nearly choked. "Are you joking? That sweater costs more than my house payment."

"You really should put more effort into your appearance. You've really let yourself go since Leon died. I think you're hiding behind your mourning and it's time you started living again, and maybe dating."

I stared openmouthed. "Not all of us can live the life of a princess. I don't have the time or money to waste getting my nails and hair done and buying overpriced sweaters. I have a business to run."

The salesclerk, who had walked up with a bright smile on her face, turned and walked away.

My mom sighed and replaced the sweater. She walked to the back of the store. That sigh spoke louder than any words could have. Obviously I had disappointed her again. I stood there for a moment and then sorted through the rack of sweaters, looking for one that would fit over my head without making me look like an overstuffed sausage. I could afford the sweater. That wasn't the problem. Finances had always been tight when Leon and I were working. A cook and an English teacher didn't buy cashmere sweaters. But I'd sold the house and used the insurance money to buy the building. The bookstore was doing well, not *Fortune* magazine worthy, but thanks to low overhead, frugal spending, and hard work, it was making a profit. One cashmere sweater wouldn't break me, and it would make my mom happy. But, as a grown woman in her mid-thirties, I shouldn't have to buy a sweater I didn't want to make my mom happy. I wished Nana Jo had come with us today. She would have understood and helped intercede between me and my mom.

My mom was so very different from Nana Jo; it was hard for me to imagine my grandmother gave birth to her. They were polar opposites. Josephine Thomas was tall and hardy. My mom, Grace Hamilton, was five feet, less than one hundred pounds dripping wet, and delicate. My mom was like a dainty porcelain figurine you keep on the tallest shelf behind a glass door, locked away from harm for fear of breaking it. Nana Jo blamed my grandpa, who always called my mom his little princess, for planting the "princess seed" in her head. In her mid-sixties, my mother had never had a job outside of the home. She'd never paid a bill until after my dad died. She was the princess.

I dropped my mom off at her South Harbor condo and headed back over the bridge to North Harbor, where I belonged. I glanced at the pink shopping bag on the seat that contained a white cashmere sweater I would be too afraid of spilling anything on to ever wear and swung my car into the parking lot of a nearby liquor store. I glanced at my watch. Thankfully, it was after twelve, when alcohol could be purchased. I looked at the license plates of the cars parked in the lot, noting the majority were Indiana residents who had escaped across the state line into Michigan, where they could buy alcohol on Sunday. We were all escaping from something, but I didn't have the time or energy to figure out what at the moment. A bottle of wine would have to substitute for therapy for now.

During the summer, I saw quite a lot of Dawson. When the fall semester started, we barely saw each other, despite the fact he lived in the apartment over my garage.

Twice daily football practices, weight training, and classes took up a lot of his time. But Dawson loved baking and he was really good at it. His apartment was a tiny studio with only a one-burner stove, which made it challenging to bake on a large scale. Dawson had gotten into the routine of using my kitchen to bake enough goodies to get us through the week at the bookstore. So, when I entered through the back door, I smelled a sweet, delicious aroma wafting down the stairs to greet me.

I climbed the stairs without my normal escorts. Snickers and Oreo usually heard the garage door and bounded to the bottom of the stairs to greet me. However, the possibility of a cookie or treat dropping to the floor was a greater enticement than seeing me.

I placed my pink bag on the counter with less care than I used for the bottle of wine. Dawson had his back to me as he lifted a tray of cookies out of the oven and placed them on a rack on the counter.

"What an amazing smell." I breathed deeply and allowed the smell of vanilla, almonds, and sugar to fill my senses.

"Thanks. You're just in time to try one." Dawson turned to face me.

"Oh my God! What happened to your face?"

He didn't say anything, merely hung his head. I hurried around the counter and turned his face toward the light to get a closer look. Three red scratches trailed across both cheeks. There was a gash under his left eye and a bruise on his forehead. His eyes were bloodshot and dark circles underneath indicated he hadn't slept.

He tried to turn away, but I held his chin and forced him to look at me.

"What happened to you?"

We stood like that so long I didn't think he would answer.

Eventually, the silence grew too much for him. "I'm fine."

I snorted. "Well, you sure don't look fine."

Dawson shrugged. "It's nothing." He forcefully, but gently, pulled my hands away and walked to the back of the kitchen. He leaned against the wall and folded his arms, providing a barrier.

I took a deep breath and tried to steady my breathing. "Was it your father? Is he out of jail?"

He shook his head.

"Then who?"

He hung his head. "Let's just say Melody didn't take our breakup well."

26

"You should go to the doctor. Those scratches look deep, you —"

He was shaking his head before the words were out of my mouth. "If I go to the doctor, the newspaper might find out."

Sad that at nineteen you had to be concerned about the newspapers running a story about a girl who lashed out when her boyfriend broke up with her. But this season the MISU Tigers were getting a lot of publicity, Dawson in particular.

I went to the bathroom and got a cold compress and mercuric acid. He didn't balk when I made him sit at the dining room table and didn't say one word when I started to treat the cuts. "Newspapers are the least of your worries. Wait until Nana Jo finds out!"

He winced, but I wasn't sure if it was the mercuric acid or the thought of what Nana Jo would say.

"What an unusual request. James didn't have any other information?" Lord William asked as he absentmindedly broke off a piece of his scone and fed it to Cuddles, the Cavalier King Charles Spaniel positioned at his feet.

"Not that he told me. Although, I'm sure he'll fill us in when he gets here." Lady Elizabeth picked up the knitting she kept nearby, which she said helped her think clearly.

"Is Lord Browning coming too?" Lady Daphne Marsh picked at an imaginary string on her skirt and avoided making eye contact with her aunt.

"Well, I suppose so, although I didn't ask him. I just assumed he would." Elizabeth looked at her husband. "You don't mind do you, dear?"

"No. No. Of course not." Lord William tossed the remains of the scone down to the dog and pulled out his pipe. "I'm sure James wouldn't have asked if it wasn't important."

"My thoughts exactly." Lady Elizabeth resumed her knitting.

"I don't suppose you know anything about this?" Lord William asked his niece.

Lady Elizabeth Marsh sighed. Sometimes her husband could be rather slow to read the signs or he would have noticed his niece, Daphne, had said very little since Lord James Browning's name was mentioned. The two met six months ago when he came to help out his friend and old classmate Victor Carlston, Earl of Lochloren, who was accused of murdering one of Daphne's beaux. At the time, Victor believed he was in love with Daphne and chivalrously stepped in to protect her by allowing the police to believe him guilty of murder. Lord James helped to reveal the true killer and ensured his friend's freedom. Victor was now living in wedded bliss with Daphne's sister, Penelope, down the road at his family estate, Bidwell Cottage. The Marshes hoped another announcement of marriage would be forthcoming as Lord James and Lady Daphne seemed destined for the altar. However, the duke's visits of late had been fewer and far between.

"No. I haven't spoken to James . . . ah, the duke in nearly two weeks," Daphne said almost in a whisper.

"I suppose you better tell Thompkins and the rest of the staff to prepare for guests," Lord William said.

"I would, but I think I want to wait until we're sure," Lady Elizabeth said. "Technically, she hasn't asked yet. I don't even know how many people to expect."

"Do you suppose David will come too?" Lord William asked.

Lady Elizabeth knitted. "I have no idea. The last I heard, he was in France."

"I don't suppose there will be a problem with the Queen Mother and the rest of the family?" Daphne asked.

"Well, I guess that depends on what type of problem you mean." Lady Elizabeth knitted silently for a few moments. "Bertie and Elizabeth are still very angry and the Queen Mother

29

is disappointed in David. I still feel rather badly that none of the family attended the wedding."

Lord William sputtered. "But really, how could we attend? It would have been a sign the family agreed with his abdication to marry a divorced woman — an American." Lord William waved his pipe while he spoke, flinging ashes across the sofa.

Lady Elizabeth looked up and shook her head. The sofa was starting to show bare patches from the maids brushing off tobacco. It would have to be recovered soon. "Well, I don't know if the fact she was twice divorced or an American was the objectionable part. I might have considered attending if the wedding were one day earlier or one day later."

"I agree. It was as though they were thumbing their noses at the family by getting married on King George's birthday," Daphne said. "Really, his own father's birthday."

"Bad form." Lord William refilled his pipe.

"Regardless of the circumstances, David and Bertie are brothers, and I believe they'll work things out in the end," Lady Elizabeth said. "Besides, James said it was vital to the Crown that she hosts her hunting party here. So, that must mean the king is at least aware of the event."

Lord William nodded and puffed on his pipe.

"At any rate, it doesn't appear we'll find out

how the Crown feels about things. The duchess hasn't called. What if she's found another place to hunt?" Daphne asked.

Thompkins entered the room silently and coughed. "Her Grace, Wallis Duchess of Windsor is on the telephone for your ladyship."

CHAPTER 3

Nana Jo's response when she saw Dawson's face was loud and littered with old-fashioned words like "floozy," "harpy," "tart," and "shrew." When she calmed down, she mixed up a concoction with aloe vera gel, honey, vitamin E oil, and baking soda. Dawson looked like he had leprosy most of the day Sunday, and he had to fight off Snickers, who kept trying to lick off his mask, but Monday his face looked so much better, it was like night and day. The scars were still there. Only time would truly heal them, but the improvement was amazing.

"Mrs. Thomas, you're a miracle worker." Dawson kissed Nana Jo on the cheek.

"Well, you need about two more days before the scars will disappear completely." Nana Jo stared at her handiwork. "But at least you don't look as though you've been in a catfight."

"You never cease to amaze me," I said

after Dawson hurried off to campus.

Nana Jo and I sat at the breakfast bar and drank coffee.

"Where on earth did you learn to mix up your healing paste?"

Nana Jo smiled as she sipped her coffee. "I grew up on a farm. There was always some kind of accident that happened on a farm and most people were too poor to go riding off miles to a doctor. My grandmother used to be the local midwife and, well . . . medicine woman. She mixed all kinds of things up in her kitchen and grew herbs for healing everything from the croup to rheumatic fever."

"I never knew that." I stared at my grandmother. I'd known this woman all my life and she was still able to surprise me.

Nana Jo shrugged. "I never thought it worth talking about. Most of those old remedies would be considered nothing more than old wives' tales nowadays."

"Scientists are discovering that a lot of those old remedies actually worked. I read an article recently that chicken soup really does help with a cold. Although scientists aren't sure if there is some ingredient in the chicken soup itself or if it's in the person's mind. Whatever the reason, it works."

We sat for a few moments and talked

about poultices, plasters, and herbal teas. Then we went downstairs to the bookstore.

I had a lot of fears when I quit my job as an English teacher and opened the bookstore. Would I be able to handle things alone? Would I be able to make enough to support myself? Did people still read books? The answer to all of those questions was yes. Recently, an old friend I hadn't seen in over twenty years asked if I found working in a bookstore monotonous and boring. I didn't even need to think before I answered. Market Street Mysteries was a lot of things, but monotonous and boring certainly wasn't one of them. New people came in every day. Boxes of books arrived weekly. Some boxes included books from writers I'd read for years, which were like old friends. Familiar series from Victoria Thompson, Emily Brightwell, Jeanne M. Dams, and Martha Grimes sent a thrill of excitement through my body as I gazed at the bright covers and anticipated the joy of figuring out whodunit. There was also the joy of discovering new writers and wondering which ones would be added to my list of favorites. On those rare moments when the store was quiet, I sometimes went for a walk in downtown North Harbor and stepped into shops owned by my neighbors. The bookstore had helped me through one of the worst times of my life, the death of my husband and best friend. I'd created a new life for myself with new friends and I hoped a new career as a writer, one day.

A few doors down from Market Street Mysteries, a new restaurant had opened. I stood in front of the window and stared at the menu taped on the door. I looked at my watch and realized it was after two, and my stomach growled as I read the menu. I stepped inside and waited while my eyes adjusted to the darker interior.

"I'm glad you decided to come in." A man with salt-and-pepper hair and beard, cut close in the style worn by the military, soft brown eyes, and a big smile came out from behind the bar.

I must have looked puzzled because he motioned to the window. "I saw you outside."

"Oh. Yes. Sorry."

"No need to apologize. That's why I put the menu up. I was hoping it would entice people to come inside."

"Well it worked." I laughed.

"How about a nice table by the window?"

I nodded and took a seat in the chair he held out for me.

"I have a lovely white wine from a local

vineyard."

"Oh, no. Just water with lemon, please."

When he left, I looked around. The restaurant was clean and decorated with an urban edge. Exposed brick walls, stained concrete floors, and iron fixtures created a modern, hip atmosphere. Televisions lined the wall behind the bar. My waiter returned with a glass and a carafe of ice water with lemon.

He smiled as he placed the carafe of water on the table. "You own the mystery bookstore a few doors down, don't you?"

I took a sip of water and nodded.

"I thought so. I've been trying to meet all of the other store owners around here. I'm Frank Patterson."

He held out his hand and we shook.

"Samantha Washington, but you can call me Sam."

"Sam, I'm pleased to meet you. How long have you been down here?"

I knew he was asking about how long my bookstore had been open. I looked at him and started to respond when my attention was caught by the picture on the television behind him.

Melody Hardwick's picture filled the screen. Then it was replaced by pictures of a body covered by a blanket.

I gasped.

The words that scrolled across the bottom of the screen said Melody's body had been found by early morning joggers. The police believed her death was the result of "foul play." The picture that next filled the screen and nearly stopped my heart was of Dawson getting into the back of a police car.

I didn't remember the walk back to the bookstore. Nana Jo said I came in looking like a whirling dervish. I did remember marching into the South Harbor police station with Nana Jo. The brick two-story building was downtown and not far from my bookstore. North Harbor and South Harbor shared the same Lake Michigan coastline. The two towns were separated by the St. Thomas River that zigzagged through northern Indiana and southern Michigan for over two hundred miles and ended as it wrapped around North Harbor in a U and flowed into Lake Michigan.

The county police station and courthouse were attached and comprised a sprawling complex located on an area that sat on a small street in between North and South Harbor. Other than field trips as a child, I had only been to the complex as an adult when I was summoned for jury duty. My memory of the facility was prior to 911 and didn't include security cameras and metal detectors that would rival those at the nearby River Bend airport.

I was so concerned about Dawson I didn't remember a number of things from the time I saw his face on the television to the moment I walked into the police station. However, the memory that would live with me until my death would be when Nana Jo set off the metal detectors and we were instantly swarmed by police officers with guns drawn, all shouting for us to raise our hands and lay down on the floor. I remember the officer who pulled my wrists behind my back and the feel of the cold metal handcuffs as he placed them on my wrists. I looked over at my grandmother as she lay by my side, also cuffed and on the ground. My heart raced and my blood pounded in my head. Yep. That was a memory that would stay with me forever.

Thankfully, my nephews hadn't been idle after we left the bookstore. One of them must have called their mother. Never had I been so happy to see and hear my sister, Jenna, as I was at that moment.

"What do you think you're doing?" Jenna said in the cold, steely voice I dreaded. "You have ten seconds to get my sister and grandmother off that floor or as God is my witness, I will sue every last one of you." Jenna was a criminal defense attorney well-known by the police for her tough, no-nonsense attitude. I'd once heard that the district attorney's office referred to her as a pit bull and I had to say, as her sister, I thought it was pretty accurate.

"You know these women?" One of the officers stepped up from the pack.

"I just said that, didn't I? And you have two seconds to lower your weapons," Jenna said between clenched teeth. Then she turned her back to the officers and looked directly into the camera that was positioned over the door. "As you can see, these imbeciles have my sister and elderly grandmother handcuffed and laying on the cold concrete. Obviously they aren't a threat, yet these officers continue to point their weapons."

The officers put away their guns. One of the officers helped me to a standing position. It took two of them to help Nana Jo to stand.

"Your 'elderly' grandmother set off the metal detector." He turned Nana Jo's purse upside down and all the contents flew across the floor. His cocky smile turned into a sneer as he looked at Nana Jo's iPad, phone, notebook, brush, holster, makeup, and about twenty other items lying on the ground. He kicked the empty holster and looked around the floor. But there was no weapon.

"Hey, Barney Fife, you break my iPad and you're buying me another one," Nana Jo said.

Jenna smiled and continued to address the camera. "No weapon, just an empty holster. And if she had brought her weapon, you'd find her permit to carry in her wallet."

The smirk vanished as the officer looked at the wallet and found the permit. He returned the wallet and other belongings to Nana Jo's purse and nodded to the officers holding us and the handcuffs were removed.

"I guess it was the iPad that set off the detector. Anyway, she should have announced she had a weapon and shown her carry permit immediately," he said as though he were educating a child — bad mistake.

"I'll keep that in mind the next time when I actually have a weapon. Of course, you would have known that if you nincompoops would have waited a minute before Wyatt Earp and the rest of the posse drew their guns like they were about to shoot it out at the O.K. Corral." Nana Jo snatched her purse away from the officer.

"I intend to subpoena the videotapes, so

make sure nothing happens to them. If my sister or grandmother is injured due to this incident, you will be hearing from me."

The officer looked as though he wanted to say something, but the look in Jenna's eyes showed him silence would be his best defense.

"Now, where have you taken Dawson Alexander?" Jenna's question brought me back to the reason for our visit.

We were escorted to a reception area. We signed in and were then led to a small conference room. Jenna was allowed to go with the police officer, but Nana Jo and I were left to wait. I wanted to protest, but the look in Jenna's eyes convinced me silence was my best defense as well.

Still flustered from the experience of being handcuffed and having guns pointed at me, I was glad for an opportunity to sit down. I hadn't realized how nervous I was until I poured myself a cup of water from the pitcher on the table and my hands shook so badly I spilled most of it on the table.

"Are you okay?" Nana Jo grabbed some napkins from her purse and helped me clean up the water.

"No," I answered truthfully. "But I will be. That was scary."

Nana Jo smiled. "That was pretty nerve-racking. I'm sorry, honey."

"I'm glad you thought to leave your gun at home."

She smiled. "I didn't."

"What?"

She shook her head. "Honestly, I was as surprised as that policeman. I must have left it at home, but it was an oversight. I was so upset about Dawson I didn't even think about my peacemaker."

"Lucky for us." I smiled and leaned across the table. "I'm pleasantly surprised to know you have a permit to carry."

Nana Jo grinned. "Well, we can thank Jenna for that too. To be honest, I've been carrying a gun for more years than you've been alive. But after everything that happened in the summer, Jenna convinced me I needed a permit."

We waited for what felt like an eternity but was only twenty minutes. Jenna returned with Detective Bradley Pitt. Detective Pitt had been the lead investigator in the murder of Clayton Parker, a realtor who was found in the backyard of my building over the summer. He was an unpleasant man with a knack of jumping to the wrong conclusion, like when he thought I murdered Parker. Detective Pitt was short with a bad comb-over and polyester pants that were too short and a bright, flowered polyester shirt that was too tight. His certainty that I was a murderer forced me, Nana Jo, and her friends from the retirement village to become sleuths to figure out who murdered Parker.

"Stinky Pitt, I should have known you'd be behind this debacle. Once again you've got everything bass-ackward, upside down sideways." Nana Jo taught Detective Pitt in elementary school and loved to embarrass him by using his childhood nickname.

Detective Pitt's jaw clenched and his ears got red. "I wish you would remember that no one calls me that anymore." He glared at Nana Jo, who contrived to look innocent.

She loved to goad him and knew exactly what she was doing. But she was careful never to call him Stinky Pitt around other police officers.

"Look. Dawson Alexander is *absolutely* not a killer," I said. "You've arrested the wrong person."

"We haven't arrested anyone *yet*. We just brought him in for questioning." Detective Pitt walked around the small conference table. "But, that's not to say we won't be pressing charges. We've barely had time to talk to him."

"And from now on, you won't be talking

to him without legal counsel present," Jenna said. "Now, I want to talk to my client."

Detective Pitt looked as though he wanted to comment but, to his credit, he kept silent. He merely shook his head and mumbled something about lawyers meddling or muddling, I couldn't really tell, under his breath as he left.

"Wow. You're tough," I said with more than a little awe.

Jenna laughed. "They don't call me pit bull for nothing. I earned that title."

We waited for several minutes and then the door opened and Detective Pitt returned with Dawson.

Detective Pitt looked as though he intended to stay and listen, but Jenna wasn't having it.

"Thank you, Detective. I'll let you know when we're done."

His only response was to turn and leave, but the door did seem to close with a bit more force than I remembered him using previously.

Dawson looked as though he'd aged ten years since this morning. Could it only have been a few hours? His eyes looked tired and the scars that seemed faded this morning looked more prominent now; although I might have been more attuned to them, given our current situation.

"Dawson, I've told Detective Pitt I'm your legal counsel. However, you don't have to accept me. If there's someone else that you —"

"No. I really want you to represent me. I was just too embarrassed to ask." He hung his head and looked up sheepishly. "I don't know how I'm going to pay you."

"Pshaw. Don't worry about that. I don't charge family."

Dawson looked surprised and misty-eyed.

I was a bit misty myself. Dawson was like family. Leon and I were never blessed with children, but Dawson had come into my life during a time when I was in need of someone to focus my attention onto. He'd allowed me to mother him and had slid into one of the holes that Leon's death had opened up.

"Now, I need to know, what have you told them?" Jenna looked at me and Nana Jo. "Normally, I wouldn't do this in front of you. Conversations between a client and an attorney are privileged."

"That means you can't tell anyone what he says to you, right?" I asked.

"Pretty much. It's complicated, but that's the general idea. Legal counsel is charged with giving the best advice possible. However, if someone comes to a lawyer for advice, they need to feel free to communicate everything without fear anything he says will be used against him. If he holds back, because he's afraid, I can't give the best advice." She looked at Dawson. "Do you understand?"

He nodded.

"Now, understand, only the conversation between an attorney and a client is privileged. If Sam and Nana Jo stay, they could be compelled to reveal it. That's why I would recommend they leave."

Nana Jo and I both started talking at the same time, but Dawson overrode us. "It's okay. I didn't kill her. I don't have anything to hide. They can stay."

"I don't care what the law says. I'd never tell them anything," Nana Jo said.

"Neither would I."

Jenna merely shook her head. "Am I the only law-abiding citizen in this family?" She smiled. "My family would apparently lie under oath." She shook her head.

"For someone I care about, I'd lie like a rug," I said.

"Darned straight," Nana Jo agreed. "That's why we keep you and your husband, Tony, around. Two lawyers in the family come in pretty handy."

Jenna shook her head, then turned her attention to Dawson. "I need you to tell me everything you've said to the police."

"I didn't really say anything. They kept me waiting in a room for almost an hour. Then Detective Pitt showed up. He started asking me a lot of questions, but I'd had a lot of time to think when I was waiting." He paused and then shook his head. "My dad didn't teach me much, but he always said, 'Never say nothing to no cops, boy, not without a lawyer. They've gotta give you a lawyer in this country. Ain't America great?' That's what he would say." He looked around at us. "So, I didn't say anything. I just said I wanted a lawyer."

Jenna breathed a sigh of relief.

"Attaboy," Nana Jo said.

Dawson smiled. "I didn't think they'd do it. Detective Pitt kept saying I didn't need an attorney because I wasn't under arrest. When that didn't work, he said innocent people didn't need attorneys. If I wasn't guilty of anything, then I should want to help them." He looked at Jenna. "I have to admit, I was starting to crack. If you hadn't come, I probably would have started talking."

Jenna looked as though she wanted to spit nails. She got up and started pacing around the small room. "Why, that no-good dirt-bag. I'll have his badge," she mumbled. After a few minutes, she sat down again and smiled at Dawson. "I'm sorry you had that experience. In this respect, your dad was right. If you ask for an attorney, they are supposed to stop and immediately call for a public defender." She sighed. "However, now on to business. Do you have a dollar?"

Dawson looked puzzled but didn't question Jenna's request. He pulled out his wallet and took out a dollar and handed it to her.

She took the dollar. "Thank you. This is my retainer. That means you are retaining me to represent you and be your lawyer. I'll write you a receipt and have you sign a document to that effect. Okay?"

Dawson nodded.

"Okay. Now, you are not to talk to the police at all unless I'm with you. Understand?"

Dawson nodded.

"I called your coach on my way here. He's aware of the situation. He doesn't know the university's position yet. But I'm guessing the university will want to distance themselves from you until this whole mess is cleared up. There's been so much negative publicity about football players and other athletes getting arrested, I'm sure the university counsel will recommend they take a neutral stance. But we'll deal with that hurdle when we get there."

Jenna pulled a notebook, tape recorder, and pen out from her briefcase. "Normally, I wouldn't do things this way. But I need to know everything. Start from how you met Melody to today." She turned on the tape recorder.

He paused and took a couple of deep breaths before beginning his tale. "I met Melody on campus. One day she came up to me in the quad and asked for my cell phone. When I gave it to her, she put her number in my contacts and handed the phone back. She told me to call her."

Nana Jo whistled.

"Shush. I'm willing to let you two stay, but you need to be quiet and let him finish," Jenna said.

We nodded.

She looked at Dawson. "Go on."

"Well, she was hot and she was a senior and . . . she was *really* hot."

"We get the picture. She was hot and easy and you got involved. Is that right?" Jenna asked.

Dawson nodded. "Yeah. We were involved."

49

"How long?"

"Only a couple of months. The season started in late August, and she came up to me in September."

Nana Jo made a sound that sounded like, harrumph. "Figures. MISU was on a winning streak, and your picture was on the front page of the *River Bend Times*. She saw her chance to latch on to a meal ticket and she took it."

"Nana Jo, please." Jenna looked irritated. "Stop interrupting."

"It's okay. She's right. At first I was flattered. Guys looked at me different when I walked around campus with Melody on my arm. Girls too. But she didn't really care about me. She only wanted to be seen with me. She just wanted to go to parties and have her picture taken. She wanted me to move out of my apartment." He glanced at me shyly. "She went to the owner of Harbor Point Apartments and convinced him to rent the penthouse apartment to me."

"Harbor Point?" Despite Jenna's warning, I couldn't stop myself from interrupting. "Those units are really expensive. They look right out on Lake Michigan. The penthouse must cost a fortune."

"Normally, they lease for three thousand a month."

Nana Jo whistled, and I nearly choked.

Even Jenna seemed surprised. "How could you afford that?"

"I can't. The owner is a big MISU fan and a friend of hers. She said he was willing to lease it to me for two hundred a month."

Jenna looked as though she could barely believe her ears. "Two hundred? That's ridiculous. Sam could get more than two hundred a month for the garage studio. Why would he do that?"

Dawson shrugged. "I don't know, but it seemed shady. I didn't like the guy. He seemed slimy. He was older and wore polyester shirts with all these gold chains. He had really dark chest hair and big fake-looking hair that looked like a toupee. I just didn't trust him." Dawson looked down.

After six months, I knew Dawson pretty well. Nana Jo and I exchanged glances. There was more to this. Jenna hadn't spent nearly as much time with Dawson as we had, but her instincts must have kicked in because she remained quiet and waited. Most people didn't recognize the power of silence and tried to fill it in quickly. As a former teacher, I can honestly say silence generated more results than anything else I'd ever said or done. It worked this time too.

"He reminded me of my dad. I knew there would be something in it for him later. One night I was playing pool with some friends by the old HOD."

"The HOD?" Jenna stared. "That trailer park owned by the House of David?"

Dawson nodded.

The House of David was a religious commune that flourished in North Harbor during the early twentieth century. At one time, the area thrived with an amusement park, baseball stadium, and fruit and vegetable market. Practically all their businesses had closed long ago when their founder, Benjamin Purnell, was tried for fraud and accused of child molestation. The molestation charges were never proved, but the rumors did plenty of damage. Purnell died not long after the trial and the House of David split into two factions.

"I saw him there. Virgil Russell was at the bar, drinking."

Either Dawson had learned to read my mind, or I'd let my thoughts show on my face, because he hurried to add, "I wasn't drinking. I just like to go there and shoot pool. It's quiet. No one there talks football or knows who I am." He hung his head.

I hadn't realized how much pressure he was under. I thought his biggest worry was keeping his grades up and staying on the team. I hadn't realized how much the pressure of the media and the fans was weighing on him. As I scanned his face now, I saw what I hadn't before.

"So, you saw this Virgil Russell at the pool hall," Jenna continued. "Did he see you?"

"No. I snuck out as soon as I saw him. But, he looked like he was waiting for someone. I don't know why, but I waited in the car until he came out. When he came out, he wasn't alone."

Dawson's voice got very soft. He was obviously reluctant to continue, but he took a couple of deep breaths and plowed forward. "That's when I saw them. Melody and Virgil were together."

Jenna looked at me.

I shrugged. Obviously she knew Virgil since she introduced Dawson to him. Again, my face must have revealed my confusion.

Dawson fidgeted and refused to make eye contact for several seconds. Then he looked at me. "Don't you see, they were *together.*"

Finally, it dawned on all of us at the same time.

"It was disgusting. He had to be old enough to be her father. He had his hands all over her, and she was wrapped around him like a . . . like a . . ." Dawson struggled

53

to find the right simile to describe what he'd seen.

Nana Jo didn't have any trouble conjuring up the right comparison. "Like an octopus."

"Yeah. That pretty much says it all."

I studied Dawson's facial expressions and body language, and I knew there was more. He was holding something back. But I refused to entertain the thought he murdered that girl.

Jenna took a couple of deep breaths. "Okay, so you saw your girlfriend with another man. Did that make you angry?"

Dawson seemed to think about the question before answering, "Maybe for a few seconds. But, honestly, I think I felt relieved."

"Relieved? Why relieved?" Jenna asked.

"I knew things wouldn't work between Melody and me. I knew she didn't care about me. This gave me the excuse I needed to end things with her. And that's what I did. I broke it off."

"When was this?"

He was silent for a few moments. "Friday night, right after the pep rally."

"How did she take it?"

Dawson rubbed his face. "Not so good. At first, she tried to deny it was her. Then, when that wouldn't work, she said I was mistaken about their relationship. She claimed they were just friends." Dawson shook his head. "She must think I was the biggest hayseed on the planet. There is no way I mistook their relationship when he had his hands all over her. He was groping her like a . . . like a . . ."

"Like a blind man at a produce stand." Nana Jo again came to the rescue.

"Nana Jo." Jenna was not amused, and her voice said, *either be quiet or you'll have to leave.*

Nana Jo used her hands to indicate she was zipping her mouth shut and throwing away the key.

Jenna turned back to Dawson. "Okay, so three days ago, you broke up with her. She didn't take it well. What happened next?"

"Saturday was the football game. Later that evening, she came by the bookstore. She said she wanted to talk. I took her up to my apartment. We got into an argument."

"Did you hit her?" Jenna asked.

Dawson shook his head. "No. I never hit her. Although she hit me several times. She scratched me. I had to grab her wrists to protect myself." He held up his hands to show how he had grabbed her. "She kicked and spit and lashed out with everything she had. I held her down on the sofa until she calmed down. Then I picked her up and put her out. She screamed and cussed and beat on the door for a while. I was afraid she'd wake up the whole neighborhood, but I never opened the door. She finally must have gotten tired and left. That was the last time I saw her."

"Sounds like she really made a big racket." Jenna looked at me. "Did you hear it?"

I shook my head. "No. I didn't hear a thing." I turned to Nana Jo. "Did you?"

Nana Jo shook her head.

Jenna sat and stared. "Dawson, is there anything else you want to tell me?"

He paused and eventually shook his head. "No. That's everything."

"What about yesterday? Did you see her Sunday?"

"No. I stayed home. I baked."

"That's right. I was there with him," I said eagerly.

"But you weren't there all day. You went to church with Mom yesterday. I know because she told me. You went to church and dinner and then shopping."

"Well, yeah, but he was home baking when I got home."

Jenna didn't look relieved. "What about you?" She turned to Nana Jo.

"Ruby Mae's granddaughter sang a solo

56

at their church. I went to hear her and then I went to brunch with the girls."

The girls were Nana Jo's friends from the retirement village. They were feisty, active, and sweet each in their own way.

Jenna frowned. Then she got up and paced. "I'm going to be honest. It doesn't look good. We need to find out when she died. The police will most likely arrest you."

Dawson looked terrified and, I have to admit, something clutched my chest that seemed to be restricting my airway and forcing tears to my eyes. "But he's innocent."

"I know, but he has a really good motive. Plus, he had an altercation with the deceased. It's just a matter of time before they find Dawson's skin cells under her fingernails. Even a fool like Detective Stinky Pitt could get a conviction with that."

The thing clutching at my heart made it hard to speak. With effort, I managed to squeak out, "But what are we going to do?"

"I'm going to work on a defense."

Nana Jo stood. "And we're going to figure out who killed that floozy."

CHAPTER 4

It was dark when we finally made it home. Jenna kicked us out hours earlier. She wanted to go over Dawson's testimony with him again without interruption before they talked to the police. Nana Jo and I waited for them in the waiting room. Three hours later, we saw Jenna on her way to the restroom. She didn't think they were going to charge Dawson today, but there were still hours of more questions. She suggested we go home, and she promised to call if there were future developments. I hadn't eaten much more than stale peanut butter crackers from the vending machine, and I was starving. Neither Nana Jo nor I felt like cooking, so we left and picked up a pizza on the way home.

Christopher and Zaq kept things going at the bookstore while we were out. When we arrived, everything was clean and locked up tight. Crumbs on the rug in the kitchen and no other surprises told me Snickers and Oreo had been fed and let out to take care of business. I needed to remember to give my nephews each a bonus.

Nana Jo and I finished off an entire pizza that included, according to the menu, everything except the kitchen sink, along with a bottle of wine. Afterward, the lethargy hit and neither of us felt like talking. Before Nana Jo went to bed, she sent a text to the girls. We were scheduled to have dinner on Tuesday night at Randy's Steak House.

My body was exhausted, but I couldn't shut off my mind. I tossed and turned so much even Snickers decided the tidal wave was too much and hopped off my bed in exchange for her cozy little dog bed in the corner. Oreo was too excitable to be allowed to roam free at night. If he stepped on Snickers one time too many, he'd learn her bite was as bad as her growl. For his own safety, I crated him at night. When I finally gave up trying to sleep and turned on the light, Oreo barely glanced at me. Snickers got up, circled her bed three times, and laid down in a tight ball with her back to me. I grabbed my laptop and decided to force my mind to wind down. Escaping to the British countryside would be just the trick.

■ ■ ■ ■

"A shame 'er ladyship 'as to entertain the likes of that American upstart?" Mrs. McDuffie pursed her lips as though she'd just tasted something sour.

Thompkins, the Marsh family butler, stood erect and, without saying a word, looked with disapproval at the stout freckled housekeeper.

"Her ladyship is not one to shirk her duty." Thompkins looked down his long bony nose at the housekeeper.

"Well, o' course not." Mrs. McDuffie's face turned almost as red as her hair at the very idea anyone would imply she was criticizing her ladyship. Mrs. McDuffie might not be the most highly educated of servants, but loyalty to the Marsh family, and her ladyship in particular, she had in abundance. "I never said she did."

Thompkins had shared the news of the hunting party with the other servants and asked if anyone had questions.

" 'Ow many is comin'?" Gladys, the latest addition to the household staff, asked softly. She was still relatively new and a bit in awe of the butler.

"Her ladyship said we should prepare for a weekend hunting party to include between twelve and fifteen guests." Thompkins removed an invisible speck of lint from his immaculate sleeve. "The duchess wasn't exactly sure."

Mrs. McDuffie snorted. "Not sure? 'Ow can she not know 'ow many people are comin' to 'er own bloomin' party?"

Gladys and the two footmen had the decency to suppress their laughter. Millie and Flossie were day help and didn't have the same training.

Thompkins could remember a time when servants were a noble breed who took pride in a life of service to the great families of Britain. In his early days with the Marsh family, there was a large staff of more than fifty servants. Most lived on the grounds in the servants' quarters. Now there were only seven full-time servants who were live-in. Himself, Mrs. McDuffie the housekeeper, Gladys the housemaid, Mrs. Anderson the cook and her daughter, Agnes, the undercook, and Frank and Jim the footmen all lived on the grounds. The term footman was rather misleading. The two men weren't footmen in the traditional sense of the word. Basically, they helped with heavy lifting and did whatever was needed around the house and estate. Frank was the son of the groundskeeper and lived with his dad in the groundskeeper's cottage at the back edge of the property. The two new housemaids, Flossie and Millie, came in daily from the village. The Marsh family didn't entertain often, so the smaller staff saw to the family's basic needs. Thompkins used a temporary staffing service when additional help was needed, which thankfully wasn't often.

He looked at the staff waiting for his instructions and cast aside thoughts of the old days. Thompkins wasn't delusional. He knew the "good old days" weren't good for everyone, especially servants. Many servants were ill-treated by their masters and poorly paid. They worked fourteen or more hour days and retired to tiny shared rooms where they roasted in the summer and froze in the winter. He'd grown up serving the Marsh family, and while the previous duke was a kind man, the conditions were less than ideal. Fewer servants meant everyone at Wickfield Lodge had their own room, something that would have been given to only the privileged few in days past. The wages were decent, modern conveniences made the work easier, and the Marshes treated their servants with respect, allowing them to have lives outside of service and encouraging them to better themselves through education. No, Thompkins didn't long for the way things were so much as he longed for the work ethic and pride in a job well done and the respect.

Flossie looked at Thompkins in wide-eyed delight. "Mr. Thompkins, sir, do you know if Her Royal Highness will be bringing any servants, like a lady's maid? I'd be more than happy to —"

Mrs. McDuffie snorted. "Bloody 'ell. 'Er Royal 'Ighness indeed. I'll not be bobbing and curtsying to that little American piece of —"

"Mrs. McDuffie." Thompkins, the normally calm, cool, and collected butler prided himself on always maintaining an even demeanor and not allowing any hint of emotion to show, trembled with the effort to maintain his calm. He took several deep breaths and regained his composure. He turned to the maid. "You will address the duchess as *Her Grace,* or *Duchess of Windsor,* or simply as *duchess.* The king has not awarded the duchess the title of Her Royal Highness. We therefore shall not refer to her as such." Thompkins looked sternly at all the servants but lingered on Flossie, who turned red and dropped her gaze.

Flossie was a good girl, obedient and well-mannered. Her biggest flaw was an affection for the cinema and American actresses. He had once caught her dancing around the kitchen, pretending she was Miss Ginger

Rogers. He'd told Mrs. McDuffie, who gave her a stern talking-to. She took the correction well, without any sulking, and he'd never caught her dancing again. With any luck, this tendency toward star worship was a phase she'd outgrow in time. He looked kindly at her now. Her demeanor was composed and respectful, but her eyes still held a spark which indicated she was still starstruck.

"I believe the duchess will bring her own maid, but I do not know about any other staff. I will meet with her ladyship later this afternoon and find out what the staffing needs are." Thompkins turned to the cook. "Mrs. Anderson, her ladyship will want to go over the menu with you for the weekend. I believe the Duchess of Windsor is very concerned about her weight and some . . . modifications may be requested."

Mrs. Anderson sniffed but nodded her head. She was a good cook but could sometimes be a bit touchy about anyone who interfered with her reign over the kitchen. Even Thompkins walked a fine line when it came to the cook. He took a deep breath, relieved she had not taken offense at the request.

"Is that all?" Mrs. McDuffie looked at the butler as she rose from the table.

Thompkins nodded.

"Then come along, girls. We better get busy

airing out the bedrooms."

Mrs. McDuffie and the maids got up and headed up the back staircase to make sure all of the guest rooms were properly aired and ready for their guests.

Frank and Jim stood and turned to Thompkins. Frank, tall, blond, and good-natured, was solid, with an athletic build. He was well liked, especially by the local girls, but was getting a reputation for his prowess on the rugby pitch.

Jim was also tall and athletic, but with more grace and panache. He too enjoyed rugby but was also a very good bowler on the regional cricket team.

"Sir, I was wondering if you want me to fetch me dad," Frank asked.

Frank's father, Hyrum McTavish, had been the Marsh gamekeeper for the past fifty years and lived in a cottage on the property.

Thompkins was grateful he wouldn't have to make the long trek out to find the gamekeeper, who could be anywhere on the large estate, although Lord William mentioned he believed the man was checking on an injured muntjac fawn. Just as he was about to respond, Lady Elizabeth entered the room.

"M'lady." Thompkins stood straight and bowed his head slightly. He was happy to notice the two footmen were also standing at attention in a respectful manner.

"Thompkins, I'm so glad I found you. I just got off the phone with the Duchess of Windsor. Our earlier conversation was so hurried I didn't get to ask very many questions about the guests, and Lord William was particularly curious about the hunting."

Lady Elizabeth was usually very refined, but Thompkins couldn't help noticing she seemed annoyed.

"Yes, m'lady."

"Well, it turns out the gentlemen won't be hunting after all." She sighed. "They want to *shoot.*"

Thompkins understood her ladyship's annoyance. "Excuse me, madam, but I thought . . ."

"Yes, so did I. Lord Browning definitely said a hunting party and the duchess also said hunting. When I called, however, she talked about how much Count Rudolph was looking forward to the pheasant. That's when I realized we weren't talking about the same thing." She sighed. "I guess it's one of those language differences between America and England. Apparently, hunting and shooting is the same thing in the States."

Thompkins scowled slightly but quickly removed all traces of distaste from his countenance and nodded. "Very good, your ladyship. I was just about to send Frank out to notify his father about the hunting." He turned to Frank. "Please inform Mr. McTavish to prepare for a *shooting* party. He can hire beaters and whatever additional help he will need." Thompkins turned to her ladyship, who nodded her approval of the orders.

Frank nodded. "Yes, sir."

Frank and Jim nodded to her ladyship. They turned and left.

"Thompkins, I do hate springing this on you with such short notice. Please call the staffing agency and get whatever additional help is needed."

Thompkins nodded. "Yes, m'lady." Thompkins coughed delicately. "May I ask if the duchess had a firm idea of the number of guests we should expect?"

"Oh, yes. I almost forgot. That was one of the main reasons I called." Lady Elizabeth handed Thompkins a list of names. "These are the people that were invited."

Thompkins looked over the list. When he was done, he looked up.

"Yes. I know what you're thinking. I was as surprised as you are." Lady Elizabeth's brow creased, and her normally happy expression was replaced by one of worry. "Lord William is furious. He's upstairs smoking at a furious pace." She sighed. "Neither of us likes to dabble in politics, especially now. Things are

so uncertain in Europe and the slightest mis-
step could send England spiraling into another
world war."

"Perhaps it would be better to decline . . ."

Lady Elizabeth sighed. "I wish I could, but
I've already said we would do it." Lady Elizabeth stood up straight and pushed her shoulders back. "Besides, Lord Browning will be
here. I don't believe he would have asked us
to host the party unless it was vitally important.
We shall just have to trust in providence and
Lord Browning to keep an eye on things."

"Yes. M'lady."

CHAPTER 5

I don't remember exactly what time I went to bed, but it was late. Normally, I dreaded the sound of my alarm clock. However, this morning, I awoke before it went off, thanks to the amazing aroma that infiltrated my room.

I yawned and reached over to turn off my alarm and shuddered as Snickers licked me at just the right moment. I used my blanket to wipe off my tongue and the inside of my mouth and opened my eyes to find her inches from my face, awaiting another opportunity to clean my face. I sat up and scrubbed off my early morning dog kiss and hopped out of bed, eager to get dressed. Thanks to the glorious aroma of cinnamon rolls and coffee coming from my kitchen, I knew Dawson was home and my breakfast would consist of more than coffee and cold cereal.

I'd never timed myself, but I suspected I

could complete my morning routine 50 percent faster when I knew bacon or coffee was waiting for me. Showered and dressed, I hurried to let the poodles out so I could dig into breakfast and find out how Dawson was doing.

Nana Jo beat me to the kitchen and was perched on a barstool enjoying cinnamon deliciousness. I think I heard her moan as I passed.

Dawson placed a plate on the counter, along with a mug of steaming hot coffee. "You eat. I'll take the dogs out."

I didn't argue.

Dawson grabbed two dog biscuits from the canister on the counter and Snickers and Oreo followed him downstairs like lemmings. My poodles were loyal, but they would sell their souls for dog treats.

Nana Jo and I ate in peace until Dawson and the poodles returned.

"You look like you've been rode hard and put away wet."

I kicked Nana Jo. "Why don't you tell him what you really think?"

"I'm not sure I know what that means, but I get the general idea." He smiled.

"How are you?" I asked, although if the dark circles under his eyes and the haggard look of his face were any indication, he hadn't slept.

He confirmed my thoughts. "I couldn't sleep, so I gave up and decided to make cinnamon rolls."

"They're delicious." I licked icing off my fingers.

"Thanks." He took a deep breath. "I'm going to pack a bag and stay on campus. Mrs. Rutherford said I'll probably be arrested soon." He hung his head.

I gasped and tried to stop the tears that came to my eyes from falling. "But they can't. You didn't do it. Jenna knows that."

He held up a hand to stop my tirade. "She does know it, and it means a lot to me that you believe in me."

"We both do," Nana Jo said.

He nodded. "Thanks. But she said the case against me is pretty strong. There's a lot of circumstantial evidence and the district attorney wants to show the community he's tough on crime."

"Why that two-bit, lily-livered, attention grabbing, snake oil salesman," Nana Jo sputtered. "He'd arrest an innocent man just to get his name in the paper. I've got half a mind to march down there and give that young whippersnapper a piece of my mind. I —"

Dawson held up both hands. "Whoa.

Hold on there, Mrs. T." Dawson fought back a smile. "I appreciate the sentiment, but I don't think making the district attorney mad is going to help."

"He's right. As much as I hate to admit it, he's just doing his job."

Nana Jo wasn't one to go down without a fight. "No, he isn't. His job isn't to arrest innocent people. His job *should be* to get to the truth. I guess that's just too much for those pea brains."

Something Dawson said had been niggling at the back of my mind. "Wait, why are you going to stay on campus? I don't understand."

He avoided eye contact. "If I'm going to be arrested, I think it would be better someplace else."

At first I thought he was saying he would be embarrassed if Nana Jo and I were there to see him arrested by the police, but something in his eyes told me there was more to the story. "Dawson, I can't lie and say it wouldn't make me sad to see you arrested. But knowing you're innocent makes it easier. If you're worried about me and Nana Jo, please don't be. We're a lot tougher than we look."

"Darned straight," Nana Jo added.

Dawson still avoided eye contact and

shuffled his feet around. "It wouldn't look very good for the bookstore to have one of your employees arrested."

I got up and walked around the counter and lifted his head so he looked me in the eyes. "Dawson, I appreciate your concern, but I don't give a flying fig what people think. This is your home and you don't have to leave it for fear of what people might say."

His eyes filled with water, and he looked like he wanted to say something but wasn't able to find the right words.

I gave him a hug, and he put his head on my shoulder and wept.

We stood there for several moments and then he stood up straight and wiped his face with a dishcloth. "Thank you, Mrs. W. Thank you both."

Nana Jo had been weeping into a handkerchief. She wiped her eyes and blew her nose. "Now that we've gotten that off our chests, it's time to get busy. If the authorities won't figure out who killed that . . . girl, well, then, I guess we'll just have to do it for them." She took another sip of her coffee.

As much as I hated to admit it, Nana Jo was right. Jenna would do everything she could to protect Dawson legally. However, the police and Detective Pitt weren't going to look for another murderer when there was so much evidence against Dawson. Unless we stepped in and found the killer, an innocent man would go to jail.

The rest of the day went by in a daze. My mind was only half engaged on books. The other half of my brain scrambled to think through what I knew about Melody Hardwick. Several months ago, when the realtor who listed this building for sale was killed in the back courtyard and the police thought I was the murderer, Nana Jo and her friends from the retirement village helped me find the real killer. The girls used their vast collection of family and friends to get information to solve the crime. I wondered, was it merely luck that helped us put the pieces together or could we do it again. We were scheduled to meet for dinner tonight, so time would tell.

Tuesday was Senior Citizen's Day at Randy's Steak House. Half-priced meals, at least for my grandmother and her friends, had become a ritual. The host knew us by name. I was only in my thirties and didn't qualify for the discounted meal, but I racked up frequent diner points and was only one meal away from a free dinner.

"Alright, ladies. You know why we're here. Let's get this party started." Nana Jo took one last bite of her hot banana pudding and pulled her iPad out of her purse. "Why don't I start?" She looked around and saw no opposition. "I called Freddie and filled him in on the situation."

"He's a hottie, that Freddie. I'd sure like to fill him in on a thing or two." Irma Starczewski broke into a coughing fit. Irma was a petite woman in her mid-eighties. Her voice was deep and raspy from decades of chain-smoking and she had a mouth like a sailor.

Nana Jo looked over her glasses and down her nose at Irma. "I'll bet you would. Fortunately, he has better taste. Now, if I may be allowed to continue."

Irma stuck her tongue out before another coughing spell hit. She looked around discreetly, then pulled a flask out of her purse, and took a swig.

"As you all know, Freddie's son, Mark, is on the state police. He said the little gold digger had a record a mile long, and Melody Hardwick wasn't her real name."

"*Nana Jo.* Just because you never liked Melody . . . or whatever her name was, doesn't mean we want to jump to conclusions. We have to try and be as open-minded and fair as possible."

Nana Jo looked at me with the innocence

of a babe. "I don't know what you're talking about. I'm merely reporting the facts."

I smiled. "So, you're telling me Mark really called her a 'gold digger'?"

"Well, I might have added that bit myself, but you're missing the important part. Melody Hardwick isn't her name."

"I wonder if Dawson knew." I looked at Nana Jo, who shrugged.

"Are you going to tell us what her real name is? I've got a hot date tonight with a guy who used to work at MISU and I intend to ask about her." Dorothy Clark was six foot, three hundred pounds, and looked like a linebacker for the Chicago Bears. She was also a helpless flirt with a black belt in aikido. She had a way with men and they melted at her feet. She could give classes. If there was any information to be gotten out of her date, I had no doubt Dorothy would get it.

Nana Jo scanned her iPad. "Elizabeth Mae Simpson."

Dorothy took a pen and wrote the name on a napkin and passed it to Irma and Ruby Mae.

"Apparently she used different aliases too. Beth, Lizzy, Bessie. Twenty-two, brown hair, brown eyes, and one hundred fifteen pounds."

"What did she get arrested for?" Ruby Mae pulled her knitting out of the bag she always carried. Ruby Mae was my favorite of Nana Jo's friends. She was a soft-spoken African-American woman. I thought she was in her eighties, although her skin was so smooth it was hard to tell. She was born and raised in Alabama and she spoke with a southern accent, even though she'd spent most of her adult life in Chicago, where she single-handedly raised her nine children after her husband walked out on them.

"He called her a grifter," Nana Jo said.

Ruby Mae frowned. "What's a grifter?"

"I googled it and, I quote, 'a grifter is a con artist who swindles people out of their money through fraud.' "

"Well, I'll be d—"

"Irma!" everyone yelled.

"Sorry." Irma put her hand over her mouth and burst into a coughing fit.

"Sounds like that little girl was up to no good." Ruby Mae knitted. "Looks like our boy, Dawson, dodged a bullet." Ruby Mae looked up from her knitting. "I'm sorry. Poor choice of words."

"We know what you meant." Nana Jo patted Ruby Mae's hand. "And for the record, I agree. He definitely dodged a bullet."

"What about the other guy you told us

about?" Dorothy asked.

Nana Jo put her reading glasses back on and went back to her iPad. "Oh, yeah. Virgil Russell. Mark didn't have time to look him up."

"I've got a call into my great-grandson, Ernie. He's a realtor. He knew about this Virgil Russell person. He's a bad mother —"

"Irma!"

"Sorry. Ernie says he's a slumlord."

"Did he have any details?" Nana Jo typed into her iPad.

Irma coughed. "I'm having lunch with him tomorrow. He said he'd ask some of his associates. I'm sure he'll have some information for me."

"Great." I was always amazed at how quickly these ladies could spring into action and tap into their connections to get information.

"How is Dawson holding up?" Ruby Mae asked.

I got teary eyed, but now was no time for weakness. We had a job to do. I took a deep breath and told them what Dawson told us this morning.

Ruby Mae sniffed and dabbed her eyes. Irma swore under her breath before breaking into another coughing spell that required a swig from her flask. Dorothy looked stoic and determined.

"Well, things don't look good, but we can help. We need to get as much information as possible." Nana Jo spoke like a general rallying her troops.

"I'm going to call Jenna," I said. "I'm hoping she can tell us whether the autopsy is done. There might be some useful information in there."

"Good idea." Nana Jo typed. "I'm going to check with Freddie and see if there is anything else Mark can tell us about Virgil and his business dealings."

"My granddaughter, Jillian, goes to MISU," Dorothy said. "I don't know if she knew Melody or Elizabeth Mae."

"I think it'll be easier if we continue to refer to her as Melody." I glanced around and received nods from everyone. "It'll be less confusing."

"Good. I'll ask my granddaughter about Melody. If she didn't know her, maybe she knows someone who did," Dorothy said.

"Sam, I can see your wheels turning," Nana said.

She knew me so well. "I'm going to the campus too. I want to talk to the athletic director about Dawson." I looked down. "It would be horrible if he lost his scholarship because of this. I thought I'd go to the student center and look around too."

Nana Jo stared. "What for?"

I took a moment to formulate my thoughts. "Remember when that foreign exchange student drowned in the Thomas River last year? There was a memorial service on campus. Lots of students came together and set up a makeshift memorial with flowers and keepsakes."

"I remember. The newspapers and television cameras interviewed all those kids," Dorothy said. "There were some really sad stories about his life in Kenya and how his family had such high hopes for him."

"I was thinking there might be something like that for Melody. If so, maybe I could talk to some of her friends, find someone who knew her really well."

Nana Jo nodded. "Good idea."

"Well, it looks like we have a plan of attack." Dorothy started to rise. "I've got to get ready for my date."

"Just one more thing," Nana Jo said. "We've got to work fast on this one."

We all looked at Nana Jo with puzzled expressions.

"MISU has a bye week this Saturday, but if we're going to a bowl game, we need to clear Dawson before the next game."

CHAPTER 6

After dropping Nana Jo and the girls at the retirement village, I swung by Jenna's house. My sister and brother-in-law were both successful attorneys who chose to live in North Harbor, rather than in a South Harbor Mc-Mansion. At one time, North Harbor was the place where the elite showed off their wealth, with large Victorian mansions set back from the street with expansive lawns behind wrought iron fences. When the lucrative automotive jobs moved south, so, too, did the wealthy. Those who stayed left their older homes and moved to working-class South Harbor.

Jenna and Tony bought an older, dilapidated Victorian mansion for one dollar from the city and lovingly and painstakingly renovated it. The house was large, at close to four thousand square feet but felt warm and cozy inside. My sister turned the front turret into her home office with a curved desk and one of the house's seven fireplaces; it was a cozy space which overlooked a lovely rose garden. When I pulled in front of the house, the light in the turret showed my sister at her desk. Jenna must have seen me. By the time I climbed to the top of the porch, she was waiting with the door open.

"Come in."

I laid my purse on the table inside the door and followed my sister into her office. "Where are Tony and the twins?"

"Tony had to work late and the twins went to a poetry reading."

I must have looked as surprised as I felt because Jenna laughed.

"I know. I was as surprised as you look. Quincy Troupe is doing a reading and they have dates."

"Ah . . . okay, that explains it."

I didn't read a lot of poetry, but I was familiar with Quincy Troupe. He wrote a biography on jazz musician Miles Davis and a poem about former basketball hall of famer, Magic Johnson. If the twins went to a poetry reading, Quincy Troupe would be the poet.

She returned to her chair behind her desk, and I sat on the Victorian love seat we'd picked up at a yard sale and she'd reupholstered. Every time I saw that love seat, I smiled at the memory of Jenna and I trying to cram it into the back of my SUV without damaging it more than time and generations of wear and tear already had. The ornately carved mahogany wood with its overstuffed velvet seat, tufted back, and rolled arms wasn't my taste, but it fit the house and room perfectly.

"I would ask what brings you here, but I'm sure I can guess."

"I just came from dinner with Nana Jo and the girls. Any updates?"

She looked at the papers on her desk. "Things don't look good." She picked up a file. "She was strangled."

"Do they know how?"

"Based on the bruising, the killer probably used his hands."

"Which means . . . ?"

Jenna nodded. "It was probably a man or a very strong woman."

"When?"

"The coroner believes her death occurred between midnight and two thirty Monday morning. Dawson claims she banged on his door until midnight, although the police won't take his word for that."

"Does the medical report say anything else useful?"

Jenna shook her head. "Not really. She'd

eaten last around eight." Jenna scanned the document. "She had sex with someone within the past day. The police are going to want a DNA sample from Dawson."

"He was her boyfriend. That doesn't mean he killed her."

Jenna looked down. "No, but once we give the DNA sample, they'll know it's his skin cells under her fingernails and only Dawson's word for it she was alive afterward." She nodded. "They'll arrest him."

I took several deep breaths to steady my breathing.

"I'm going to take Dawson tomorrow for the cheek swab. We'll wait downtown. Most likely, they'll arrest him shortly afterward. The district attorney was a classmate of mine. He's not the sharpest tack in the box, but he's no fool and owes me a favor. We'll have a bond hearing tomorrow afternoon."

"Do you need any money?"

She shook her head. "No. I've got a bail bondsman I work with a lot. He's going to take care of everything."

No matter how much I blinked, I couldn't stop the tears from streaming down my face.

Jenna reached behind her desk and pulled a box of tissues from a shelf and brought them to me.

I took the tissue, wiped my eyes, and blew

my nose.

"Sam, I'm sorry. I know how much Dawson means to you, but I want you to be prepared. This is going to get worse before it gets better."

I looked up. "What do you mean?"

Jenna paced. "The media have already started calling. They'll show up at your bookstore and stick microphones and cameras in your face. Some may try to follow you. I can prevent them from entering, but I can't prevent them from setting up their cameras outside on the street. I recommend you don't make a statement. Let me handle all of that."

I nodded. "Is there anything we can do?"

"Yeah. Find out as much as you can about her. Normally, I work with an investigator, but he's knee-deep in other higher-priority cases." Jenna smiled at me. "Besides, I'm pretty sure even if I told you to stay out of it, you wouldn't."

I smiled. "You're right."

Jenna looked serious. "Sam, be careful. There's a murderer out there. Don't go off on your own. Normally I don't condone guns, but Nana Jo should keep her 'peacemaker' ready. Whoever murdered Melody thinks he's gotten away with it. He won't take kindly to anyone who gets too close."

Jenna's words stuck with me throughout my drive home. At home, I let Snickers and Oreo out and stood in the courtyard and watched while they sniffed for the appropriate places to do their business. I noticed Dawson's light on in his apartment. I found that light comforting and couldn't help wondering how many more times I'd see it. The tears started again, and I had to shake myself to prevent a breakdown.

When I went back inside, my mind was restless and I knew sleep would be elusive. I avoided the struggle and distracted myself with a trip to the British countryside.

Thompkins entered the library of Wickfield Lodge and stood very stiff and straight in the doorway. He coughed and then announced, "The Duke of Kingfordshire, Lord James Fitz-Andrew Browning."

James entered the library.

"Excellent. You're just in time for tea." Lady Elizabeth looked to the butler, who nodded, stepped back, and closed the door.

James was a freckled, fair-haired, good-natured man with broad shoulders and a stocky build. The Marshes met him six months ago when he came to help his longtime friend Victor Carlston avoid swinging for a murder he didn't commit. After the real killer was apprehended, he was best man at the wedding of Victor and Lady Penelope Marsh. Since then, he'd made many visits to Wickfield Lodge and had become very attentive to Lady Daphne.

"James, I'm so glad you've finally come. Now maybe you can tell us what this whole thing's about," Lord William announced in his loud, but good-natured tone.

Lady Elizabeth shot a glare at her husband. Lord William frowned and pulled out his pipe.

Lady Elizabeth waited and watched.

James glanced at Daphne sitting in the window seat. He strode across the room to her and reached down for her hand.

Daphne nodded, gave a brief smile that didn't reach her eyes, extracted her hand, and returned to the view out the window.

Lady Elizabeth noted her niece's cold greeting and added more warmth into her voice. "James, we're all so glad you've arrived."

Thompkins rolled in a tea trolley filled with tea, sandwiches, scones, and tarts. He rolled the cart beside Lady Elizabeth and bowed.

"Wonderful, Thompkins. Thank you," Lady Elizabeth said to the retreating figure, then grabbed the silver teapot and poured. "James dear, would you like tea or perhaps you'd prefer something stronger?"

James accepted the teacup. "No, tea will be fine. Thank you." He looked over at Daphne before taking a sip.

Once the tea was distributed, Lady Elizabeth turned to James. "Now, maybe you can tell us what you've gotten us into?"

He took a deep breath and placed his cup on the table. "First, I want to thank you for agreeing to host the duchess's hunting party. We were at our wits' end trying to figure out what to do."

"Of course we're happy to help out, but it seems so strange," Lady Elizabeth said.

Lord James nodded. "I dare say it does." He paused. "I appreciate your trust, but I'm afraid I must ask you to trust me a little longer." He looked at Lady Daphne, who was engrossed in her cup of tea and didn't make eye contact with him.

"Unfortunately, I can't put forward an explanation, at least not yet. I hope to be able to explain at some point, but I can't right now. In fact, I must ask that you not even mention the fact I rung up to ask. It's imperative the Duchess of Windsor not know I had any involvement in this. As far as she or anyone else outside the family is concerned, I'm merely an invited guest, a friend of the family." James looked again at Daphne.

Lady Elizabeth stared in puzzled amazement. "But how can she not know? I mean, I've never even met Wallace before. Surely someone had to suggest Wickfield Lodge as an alternative location. I can't believe she came up with the idea on her own."

"Ah . . . that. Well, all I can say is someone the duchess respects suggested the location. The fact that you're a favorite cousin of the king and could prove beneficial in smoothing the way with her royal relations was an additional enticement." James smiled briefly. "However, I can't stress enough how important this is."

Lady Elizabeth looked to her husband, who puffed on his pipe and absentmindedly fed bits of his sandwich to Cuddles, sitting attentively at his feet.

James looked uncharacteristically nervous. The 15th Duke of Kingfordshire always exuded a casual, easygoing manner, common for young men of his station. A wealthy, privileged, aristocrat without a care in the world was the image he presented. However, closer inspection showed intelligence, a keen mind, a purposeful chin, and a determined jaw. If eyes were the window to the soul, then his soul showed a depth of conviction and courage.

Lady Elizabeth nodded her ascent.

"Dashed secretive." Lord William looked from his wife to his niece. After a pause, he nodded.

Attention turned toward Daphne. Lady Daphne sat in her favorite seat in front of the large picture window that looked out onto the back terrace. Framed by the large window, she gazed outside. The sun shone through the window and illuminated her beauty with a brilliance that was dazzling. Golden hair and piercing blue eyes which sparkled like the sun on the ocean in the early summer. She was stunning. She turned her head toward James and lifted her long dark lashes. Her glacial gaze caused Lord James to gasp and Lady Elizabeth shivered involuntarily.

"What are you asking?" Her words hung in the air like a cloud of smoke.

Lady Elizabeth placed her teacup on the table and stood. "Darling, I think we need to have another talk with the servants." She picked up the knitting bag she kept at her feet.

Lord William stared after his wife.

"Are you coming, dear? I really think we both need to talk to them."

After a few moments, Lord William's eyes registered the secret message his wife was sending and hoisted himself from the sofa, dislodging Cuddles, and followed his wife to the door, mumbling, "Servants, yes. Have to talk to the servants. Tricky business."

"Wait," Daphne said. "There's no need for you both to leave. His Grace can't have anything to say to me that can't be said in front of both of you."

His Grace looked as though he had a lot he'd like to say. However, he set down his teacup and walked to the seat next to Daphne.

Daphne turned to face him and an invisible veil immediately closed over her eyes and provided a barrier to her thoughts.

"Daphne, I think you know I care about you deeply. The past few months have been rather busy and I apologize for not being more attentive. However, my feelings are —"

"Oh, dear." Daphne laughed. "I think you've mistaken me. I wasn't asking you for a profession of love. We both know that would be phony."

James snapped back as though he'd been slapped.

"I was merely asking how far you want to go with this charade you've arranged. Are you merely an old family friend, my brother-in-law's dearest friend? Or are you supposed to mean something to the family."

"Daphne." Lady Elizabeth couldn't stop the shock that registered in her voice.

Daphne looked innocently at her aunt. "I'm

sorry if I shocked you, Aunt Elizabeth. I was merely trying to determine how much of an actress my part required."

James's eyes flashed and his jaw clenched. "I wouldn't want to tax your acting ability. Let's just say I'm a friend of the family."

"Fine with me." Daphne turned back to her window.

"Fine." James stood and took his pipe from his pocket and moved to the mantle.

Lady Elizabeth and Lord William looked at the two young people and then quietly slipped out of the room.

Victor and Penelope walked the three miles from their home to join the family for dinner, which helped to remove some of the strain.

Daphne and James were excessively kind on the rare instances when they spoke to each other, which increased, rather than decreased, the tension. Daphne also showed a deep interest in all of the details of Penelope's housekeeping dilemmas, even going so far as to offer to help interview maids. For his part, James remained in a daze. He was silent, only speaking when spoken to. After dinner, the family retired to the back parlor for coffee.

Lady Elizabeth pulled out her knitting and looked around. She gazed at her niece Lady Penelope and smiled. After nearly four months of marriage, it was obvious the couple was blissfully happy. Victor had believed himself to be in love with the fair and beautiful Daphne for most of his young life. Six months ago he'd realized Penelope was his heart's true desire. Lady Elizabeth glanced at her new nephew with fondness.

Victor sat in a chair in front of the fireplace with his legs outstretched, completely at home. He smoked while Lord William reminisced about his days in His Majesty's service. Knowing glances were exchanged between Victor and James. Daphne retreated to her seat by the window and engrossed herself in a magazine. However, Lady Elizabeth was sure she hadn't seen her turn a page in nearly thirty minutes.

Penelope leaned toward her aunt and whispered, "What's with the Ice Queen?" She inclined her head slightly toward her sister.

Lady Elizabeth sighed. "She's hurt. I think she genuinely cares for James."

Penelope glanced across at her younger sister. The two young ladies were so different; a casual observer wouldn't have guessed they were sisters. Daphne was petite, fair-skinned with blond hair and blue eyes; traits she inherited from her father, Peregrine Marsh. Penelope looked more like their mother, with dark hair and eyes. In the summer, if she wasn't careful, her skin tanned to a dark brown, very similar to their mother, Lady Henrietta Pringle. The loving couple died in a car accident not long after Daphne was born. Lord William and Lady Elizabeth raised the two girls and couldn't help looking upon them as the daughters they never had.

"I believe James genuinely cares for her too." Penelope glanced at the duke. "What happened?"

Lady Elizabeth placed her knitting on her lap. "He hasn't been around much in the past couple of months. Then he comes and, after arranging this elaborate weekend, he doesn't confide in her what's going on."

"Maybe he can't."

Lady Elizabeth looked at her niece. "I was hoping he'd confided to Victor?"

Penelope shook her head. "If he has, Victor hasn't said, but I'm sure he wouldn't have asked you to do it if it wasn't important. I've never seen his estate, but according to Victor, James's family home makes Buckingham Palace look like a nice cottage. If it was just a matter of needing a large estate for the shooting, he certainly could have hosted it himself."

"He doesn't want anyone to know he is anything more than an invited guest, a family friend." Lady Elizabeth frowned.

"What's the matter? You seem upset."

94

Lady Elizabeth knitted a few stitches. "I just have a very bad feeling about this whole thing. After seeing the guest list, I have to say, if anyone other than James had asked me to do this, I would most certainly have declined. Your uncle hates getting involved in politics, and there's been so much negative publicity about people like the Cliveden set in the papers that I'm worried."

Penelope scowled. "The Cliveden set?"

"You know, dear, that group Lady Nancy Astor invites to Cliveden House. The newspapers have been full of how they are trying to appease Hitler and, well, all kinds of things."

"I've read about them, but I'm rather surprised you have."

"One must stay up on current events." Lady Elizabeth knitted. "It's so distressing. I don't know what's worse. To think we could be so close to war again" — she stopped knitting and looked at her niece — "or to sit back and do nothing while Germany takes over Europe. If he's left unchecked, he won't stop at the Channel."

Penelope reached across and patted her aunt's hand. "I pray it doesn't come to that. But, try not to worry. This is just a weekend shooting party and Victor and I'll be here as much as possible. We'll help in any way we can."

Try as she might, Lady Elizabeth couldn't shake off the feeling in the pit of her stomach of trouble ahead. She could tell she was upsetting her niece, so she smoothed the frown creasing her forehead and smiled. "Thank you, dear. I know it will be a tremendous help." She then turned to the others in the room. "Would anyone care for more coffee?"

CHAPTER 7

I'd always loved Wednesdays, especially when I was a teacher. My coworkers started the week looking forward to Friday and the weekend. That meant five whole days of classes and grading papers. If I focused on Wednesday, instead of Friday, the week went much faster. This Wednesday changed that forever. This Wednesday, Dawson submitted to a DNA check and then waited patiently for the police to arrest him, which they did.

I was determined to be strong and not permit myself to cry. I didn't want to make things worse for him by breaking down. I was the last thing he needed to worry about. I closed the bookstore so Nana Jo and I could go to the police station with Dawson and Jenna.

First, Jenna took Dawson to the North Harbor Clinic, where he was escorted to a private room.

"Why are you having this done here? I thought the police took care of this," I asked while we sat in the waiting room.

"The state lab is backlogged. It'll take them at least six months before they get to us."

"Wouldn't that be better? I mean, they can't arrest him without the DNA evidence, can they?"

"Oh, yes they can. Plus, I don't want to take the chance the state loses or contaminates the sample. They have some good people, but they're overworked, and when you're overworked, mistakes happen. Besides, I work with this lab all the time. They'll have the results back in a few hours."

"But in six months, we will have figured out who the killer is."

Jenna turned to face me. "Sam, murder is a felony. If Dawson is arrested for a felony, he'll be suspended until his case is resolved. Trust me. I would prefer more time too, but ultimately the decision is his."

He returned before we could discuss things further. The entire process took less than ten minutes.

I followed Jenna and Dawson to the police station and thought over what Jenna said. Six months wasn't a long time, but faced with less than two weeks to find a killer, it seemed like an eternity. Football meant a lot to Dawson. It was the vehicle that enabled him to get away from his abusive father and to get a good education.

This time Nana Jo had her gun, but she stopped at the metal detectors and held up her carry permit. She also announced loudly she was packing an iPad in her purse. The police officer manning the metal detector remembered us from two days earlier and didn't look amused. He looked through her purse carefully and handed back her wallet and purse and ushered us through. Our entry was unheralded and low-key.

Jenna notified Detective Pitt we were coming beforehand and he waited for us at the desk.

My sister was bossy, opinionated, and annoying. She was also hardworking, dedicated, and super organized. These skills came in handy as an attorney. To minimize the amount of time Dawson sat in a jail cell, she had reviewed the judge's schedule and talked to the district attorney. Dawson was arrested, fingerprinted, photographed, and arraigned all before three. The bail bondsman was good to his word and waited for us at the courthouse. By three thirty, we were back at the bookstore. Dawson hadn't slept well last night, so he made pie dough.

Not my idea of fun, but to each his own.

Jenna, Nana Jo, Dawson, and I sat at one of the bistro tables in the back of the store, drank coffee, and ate apple pie à la mode, drizzled with salted caramel. It was a delicious muddled mixture of warm spicy comfort which almost buried my sadness. For several minutes, we sat and ate in silence. It was a glorious few minutes.

"That pie was great. You could enter a baking contest." Nana Jo licked her spoon.

The tips of Dawson's ears were red. He still got embarrassed when people complimented him, even though he loved to watch people enjoying his creations.

"What happens now?" I asked Jenna.

"Dawson's officially suspended from school."

"Looks like you'll have plenty of time to bake." Nana Jo patted his shoulder.

"Is there a way he can get his assignments?" I asked Jenna. "Nana Jo and I can tutor him so he doesn't fall behind when he goes back in a couple of weeks."

Jenna smiled at me. "That's a great idea."

Dawson looked misty eyed. He looked like he wanted to say something but couldn't find the words. Eventually, he stared at his plate and mumbled, "Thank you."

"So what are your plans for today?" Jenna asked.

"I'm going to the campus." I looked at my watch. "I better get a move on."

Jenna looked very serious. "Sam, I know I don't have to tell you this, but there may be reporters there. It would be best if you leave all of the comments to the press to me."

"Don't worry. I have no intention of talking to anyone from the media."

We both turned to stare at Nana Jo.

"What're y'all looking at me for?" She looked indignant.

"Nana Jo, this is important. I —"

"I know. I know." She zipped her lips and folded her arms over her chest.

Jenna sighed. "I'm not trying to insult you. I know you would never do or say anything to deliberately hurt Dawson or our case. But the media can turn your words inside out and before you know it, we've got a big media mess on our hands. We need all of the goodwill and public opinion we can get."

At that moment, Jenna's phone rang. While she was answering, Nana Jo got a text message. Then Dawson's phone rang.

Jenna listened to the caller for a few seconds and then her face underwent a transformation. She went from relaxed to panicked in less than five seconds. "Turn on the television. Quick!"

I didn't have a television downstairs in the bookstore, so we hurried upstairs.

At the top of the stairs, Jenna said, "Turn on the news."

I grabbed the remote and turned to one of the local news stations. I couldn't help but gasp at what I saw on the screen.

Standing atop the courthouse stairs was A-squared, Alex Alexander, Dawson's father. There were at least three microphones shoved in his face. Greasy hair, dirty jeans I felt sure were once blue, and a faded-out, greasy shirt that read, BEAM ME UP, SCOTTY. THERE'S NO INTELLIGENT LIFE DOWN HERE.

"Turn it up," Jenna demanded.

Nana Jo and I exchanged glances, but I complied. We'd run into Dawson's father before when he broke into the bookstore. The last time I saw him, he was handcuffed and getting into the back of a police car.

"Police brutality and discrimination, that's what this is. My boy didn't kill that girl. The cops is trying to frame him. They don't like it when a local boy gets a chance to make it outta this hellhole of a town. They just wanna push you back down," A-squared ranted.

One of the reporters tried to steer the

conversation into something more productive than the current tirade. "Mr. Alexander, there's a lot of evidence against your son. How can you be so sure he didn't kill her? Have you talked to him?"

"Nawh, I ain't talked to him. I been in jail. Just got out. Don't need to talk to him. I know he didn't kill nobody, specially not that little tramp. Fine piece of [bleep]. But that's all she was." He made a hawking noise and then spit something brown on the ground.

I cringed, grateful the network sensors were working and bleeped out the foul language. This was a disaster, but try as I might, I couldn't stop staring at the television. Just like a train wreck, I couldn't turn away.

"She was asking for what she got."

Jenna groaned and put her hands to her face.

"Are you saying Melody Hardwick deserved to be murdered?" one of the reporters questioned.

"[bleep] right. She wadn't no saint. I can tell you that. But it wadn't my boy that done killed her."

"How can you be so sure?"

" 'Cause I know who did kill her." A-squared stared into the cameras.

This sent the reporters into a frenzy. They flung out questions at the speed of light. But A-squared merely grinned at the cameras, tapped his forehead knowingly, and winked.

Detective Stinky Pitt must have been standing nearby because the next thing we saw was him pulling A-squared away from the cameras.

We stared at the screen for what felt like an hour afterward, but he never reappeared. When it was clear nothing more would be shown, I flipped to the other news stations. The same A-squared circus played on all of the news stations, but none of them had more than what we'd already seen.

Jenna hopped up and began to pace around the room. I'd seen my sister mad before, but nothing compared to this. Her face was red, and she kept mumbling, "Oh my God. Oh my God."

Dawson's jaw was set in such a way I was certain he was grinding his teeth. He clenched and unclenched his fists. He looked mad enough to spit nails, as Nana Jo would say.

Nana Jo was the only one who looked to be enjoying herself. There was a twinkle in her eyes and her shoulders shook in silent laughter. After a few seconds, she finally burst out laughing.

Jenna spun around and stared. "What's so funny? God knows I need a good laugh right now. That moron just insulted women, implied Melody Hardwick deserved to be murdered, and announced to the world he knows who murdered her. Oh, and he just got out of jail. People will think like father, like son. We need people to like Dawson and to believe him innocent. Most people will be so repulsed by that idiot, they may convict Dawson in the public's eyes without a trial."

Nana Jo wiped a tear from her eyes. "You were worried Sam or I would say something to the media to ruin your case. Looks like we're the least of your worries. We could hardly make a bigger mess than that fool just did. Beam me up, Scotty, indeed."

We stared at her and then each other.

Nana Jo smiled. "Nothing you can do about it now anyway. What's done is done."

Dawson had been tight-lipped throughout the news report. "What are you going to do now?" he asked Jenna.

"I'm going home and have a nice long bath, a good dinner, and a glass of wine . . . maybe a bottle. Then I'm going to bed. Tomorrow, I'll figure out what to do about your dad. I need to figure out a way to distance you from him." She grabbed her keys. "I'll talk to you in the morning," she said to Dawson.

He nodded.

"Please, don't make this any worse than it already is." She looked at me and Nana Jo.

We crossed our hearts and held up three fingers in the Girl Scouts' honor and watched her leave.

My stomach growled and Nana Jo and Dawson acknowledged they were hungry too, so we scanned the cabinets for something to eat. Dawson discovered my stand mixer not only mixed dough but could also make pasta. Leon had bought several of the attachments that made everything from ice cream to sausage. The company that manufactured the stand mixer was headquartered in North Harbor, so accessories weren't hard to come by. I promised myself one day, when things settled down, I'd take a class and learn how to use the attachments I already had. That day never came. Now, Leon was gone. I wiped away a tear and hoped Nana Jo would chalk it up to the onions I was chopping. Thankfully, there were videos for virtually everything on the Internet. Dawson watched a five-minute crash course on making pasta, then took flour, salt, and water and made spaghetti.

Nana Jo made a spicy marinara sauce and I chopped and grated. The end result was delicious.

Spaghetti, a salad, and garlic toast gave me the final push I needed to head out to the campus in search of answers. Surely there was someone else besides Dawson who wanted to see Melody Hardwick dead. I prayed I could find that person before Dawson paid for a crime he didn't commit.

CHAPTER 8

I really should have gone to campus earlier or waited until tomorrow, but time wasn't on my side. I didn't have a plan as I parked in the visitor lot and walked to the student union.

MISU was on a beautiful, sprawling campus with acres of rolling lawn manicured to perfection. The campus sat on the outskirts of North Harbor with views of Lake Michigan from its western side. Ivy-covered brick buildings dotted the landscape and presented a peaceful backdrop. The university was founded in the early twentieth century with an emphasis on agriculture and teaching. Later, as the automotive industry grew in North Harbor and Detroit, the university expanded to include engineering and finally, a liberal arts school was added. The large trees that provided shade and shelter were centuries old.

I enjoyed walking across MISU's campus

because there was so much beauty to be seen. I wasn't sure where to look for a memorial for Melody Hardwick, but I started at the student union.

On the first floor there was a bookstore that sold everything from textbooks to macaroni and cheese. There was a cafeteria and an entire wall set aside for event flyers, jobs, and protests. I spent fifteen minutes scanning the board. The only thing I found close to a memorial was a MISU Students for Peace candlelight vigil to be held next week to mark the anniversary of the Kristallnacht or Night of Broken Glass. Kristallnacht, November 9, 1938, was the date the Nazis torched synagogues, vandalized homes, schools, and businesses of Jewish citizens, and killed close to one hundred people. Students of all races, nationalities, and religions were invited to a peaceful vigil on campus to mark the date and pray for peace. I was touched that students in a small Midwestern university wanted to remember an event from more than seventy years ago. I felt a moment of nostalgia for my teaching days. As a high school English teacher, I met and, I hoped, influenced some of these caring people.

"Sam."

I was so absorbed in my thoughts I hadn't

seen or heard Dorothy Clark's approach and jumped when she touched my shoulder. "Dorothy. I'm sorry. I didn't see you there."

She stood next to me, holding a large bouquet of flowers. "I know. I called your name several times. What's got you so engrossed on that board? Or are you just woolgathering."

"I was looking for some type of notice about a memorial for Melody, but I can't find anything." I looked at Dorothy closely. "You look nice. You must have a hot date?" I smiled and sniffed her flowers.

"I had a date, but the professor had to cancel at the last minute." She frowned. "If he'd given me a little more notice, I would have gotten a replacement. But, oh, well." She looked around. "Hey, you wanna join me? My granddaughter is performing at the new Hechtman-Ayers Center for Performing Arts tonight. I've got an extra ticket so it won't cost you a thing."

I protested, but Dorothy was persistent.

"Look, you're not going to find out anything that'll help Dawson tonight from that board, and it's too late to go wandering around campus by yourself, anyway." She grabbed me by the arm. "You look as though you could use a little culture in your life, anyway. Besides, afterward, we'll take

Jillian out for coffee and you can pump her for information."

"But I'm not dressed for it."

"You look fine. You won't be the only person there in jeans. You'll look just like the other students."

Dorothy's intention was to place my mind at ease, but her words reminded me of my mom's criticism of my attire earlier in the week. I thought I had shoved those thoughts into my internal sea of forgetfulness. Dorothy's words brought the feelings back to the surface. I looked at my jeans, black T-shirt, and black hoodie. It was a lot of black. I thought about what I'd worn yesterday and the day before and briefly thought of my closet. It was full of blue jeans and dark shirts. I could hear my mom's voice in my head, *". . . hiding behind mourning."*

I shook myself to get my mom's voice out of my head.

"Are you cold, dear?" Dorothy asked.

"No. I'm just . . . never mind. I'm fine. I'd love to see your granddaughter perform."

We walked the short distance to the new performing arts building. Dorothy had excellent seats near the front. Once we were seated, I looked around. She was right. I wasn't the only person wearing jeans.

However, I refused to head down that road again. Instead, I focused on the beautiful building. Unlike the majority of the buildings on campus, the Hechtman-Ayers Center wasn't the traditional ivy-covered limestone box but was a light and bright, modern, concrete and glass shell. The school now offered everything from sculpture and metal-smithing to painting and dance studios, along with three performance spaces.

The performance tonight was *Giselle,* a classic ballet. According to the program book, Giselle was a frail but beautiful peasant girl in love with a count pretending to be a peasant. The count was already engaged and when his duplicity was revealed, Giselle dropped dead and became a spirit who trapped men and forced them to dance to death. Dorothy's granddaughter had the lead role, and she looked and performed beautifully.

When the performance was over, she received a standing ovation and there were very few dry eyes in the building. I hadn't attended very many ballets. I'd seen the *Nutcracker* and *Swan Lake* in person, but this was amazing.

I walked around the art gallery in the lobby while Dorothy went backstage and congratulated her granddaughter. Dorothy's son and daughter-in-law were out of the country and she wanted to make certain Jillian had family present for her performance. The lobby was a multipurpose space. In addition to showing off the lovely architecture of the building, with its tall walls and glass ceiling, it was also a marquee for advertising future performances and an exhibition space for sculptures and artwork. I didn't understand all of the art exhibited, but I appreciated the creativity and intelligence needed to create it.

Dorothy and Jillian were back long before I'd finished perusing all of the art, but maybe I'd come back another day. The three of us walked to the student union. They had a small River Bend Chocolate Factory café that served chocolate, treats, and beverages. Most of the ballet patrons must have had the same idea because the small shop was packed, but Jillian and I snagged a table in the corner while Dorothy ordered.

"You were amazing. How long have you studied ballet?" I asked while we waited for Dorothy.

Jillian was tall with a slender, dancer's body. She had large expressive dark eyes, and her hair was pulled back in a tight bun at the back of her neck.

"Thank you. I started ballet when I was three." She beamed. "I love dancing."

"Do you do other dancing besides ballet?"

"Jazz, tap, hip-hop, ballroom, Latin, you name it."

"Wow. So, are you a dance major?"

She looked sad. "No. I'm majoring in business with a dance minor." She shrugged. "My dad thought I needed to major in something that would provide a stable income."

"It's good advice, although I recommend studying what makes you happy and obviously for you, that's dance. But business skills are always handy."

"I agree. I don't dislike business; in fact, I've been thinking I might like to have my own dance studio one day, but business classes aren't the thing that gets me revved up every day. I have lots of interests. In fact, I think we have one of them in common."

I smiled but must have looked puzzled.

She laughed. "Grandma said you own a mystery bookstore. That must be cool."

"I do, and I enjoy it a lot. Do you like mysteries?"

"I love to read. I read some mysteries, but mostly I like romance. Grandma said you're investigating who killed Melody Hardwick.

That sounds pretty cool."

"Well, I'm not sure about cool, but I don't believe Dawson killed her and the police don't seem to be looking for anyone else."

"Of course. I totally get it. How can I help?"

"Did you know Melody?"

"She was supposed to be in my history class, but I don't think I ever met her. She was a senior and I'm just a sophomore, and we didn't run in the same circles. But I do know her roommate."

"Supposed to be?" I asked.

Jillian looked away. She was trying to decide whether to share something. I remained quiet and waited to see what she did. Eventually, she continued. "She was on the student list, and she gets grades . . . but I never met her."

I must have looked confused.

"We can see the grades online, so we know how everyone did on their quizzes and tests. It helps to know how you're doing in comparison to the other students." She shrugged. "Weird thing is, she's getting A's, but I've never seen her in class, not one time — not even for quizzes."

"But she has an A in the class?"

Jillian nodded.

"That is strange. What class is it?"

115

"History of Cults. The professor is nice. He's a little odd, but he's British, so his accent is nice. I think he's some kind of expert on the House of David."

"Interesting."

Dorothy arrived with coffee for herself and tea for Jillian and me. There were also three slices of cheesecake, which looked divine. Jillian allowed herself one taste then declined the rest, stating if she ate the rest, her dance partner wouldn't be able to lift her. Dorothy and I were forced to eat her slice too.

We chatted until Jillian recognized some of her friends and said she had to get back to the dorm. Before she left, she agreed to meet me at the student union tomorrow at eleven, in between classes, and would introduce me to Melody's roommate.

I offered to drive Dorothy back to the retirement village. She had taken a taxi here, which must have cost a small fortune. We walked to the parking lot and, even though it was dark, I felt safe. Whether my feeling of safety was due to well-lit walkways with emergency police call boxes placed along the path or the fact Dorothy had a black belt in aikido, I wasn't sure. I suspected it was probably due to Dorothy's presence. I hoped her six-foot stature would deter anyone with malicious intent. If not, I'd witnessed her martial arts skills up close and she was definitely no one to be trifled with.

I drove to the retirement village.

As she got out of the car, she said, "I should have some information for you tomorrow afternoon. Tell Josephine I'll call her."

I promised to relay the message, waited until she was safely inside, and drove home. Since Dawson's studio apartment was immediately above my garage, he knew when I was home. As soon as my engine was off, he opened his door and Snickers and Oreo ran down to meet me. They took care of business and we went upstairs. Drained didn't even begin to tap the surface of how I felt. Every muscle in my body felt tense and wound as tight as an alarm clock. I needed to relax, so I took a shower and, while the hot water pelted my skin, I thought about why I felt like a rung-out dishrag. A lot had happened in one day. From Dawson's DNA test, arrest, and arraignment to the A-squared media debacle, it had been one crazy day. We'd gone through a lifetime worth of life's worst events in less than eighteen hours. I didn't want to upset Dawson, so I'd held my emotions in check all day. Without a release, I felt like I would explode. As the heat from the hot water massaged and loosened my muscles, I cried. I started out with just a few tears but ended up sobbing into a washcloth until I had no tears left to cry. When I was spent, I felt hollow and hungry. I dried off and put on my pajamas. When I opened the bathroom door, I noticed a light in the kitchen and smelled coffee and apple pie.

In the kitchen, Nana Jo sat on a barstool with a cup of steaming coffee and a plate of apple pie.

"The last slice of pie is in the fridge."

"I shouldn't eat this. I just ate one and a half slices of cheesecake with Dorothy a couple hours ago."

"You've had a shock. You're supposed to eat sugar when you're in shock. Isn't that what they always do in those British cozies you read?"

I laughed. "They drink tea with sugar. They don't eat cheesecake and pie."

"To-may-to. To-mah-to."

I took my pie to the microwave.

"Twenty seconds gets it hot enough to melt ice cream without making the crust rubbery."

I punched the time on the microwave and got the vanilla ice cream out of the freezer.

Apple pie and ice cream were great, but Nana Jo's coffee seemed like the perfect accompaniment. If I drank coffee this late at night, I'd be awake for hours. However, something in my body desperately needed that caffeine. So, I took an individual coffee packet and placed it in the single-serve coffee maker. The smell of the coffee, heated apples, and spiced, sugary goodness was divine.

Nana Jo was right. My ice cream melted atop my pie and created a swirl of vanilla bean with the spiced apples, and when I took a bite, I moaned.

"Told you so."

We ate in silence for a few moments.

"You feel better?"

Without saying a word, I knew Nana Jo was referring to my breakdown in the shower. Either she had ears like a bat or I was a lot louder than I thought. My money was on bat ears. Teachers learned to hone their senses after decades in the classroom. She had the ability to hear a gum wrapper in the back of a large classroom.

"You heard me?"

She nodded as she used her spoon to scrape the last bit of ice cream from her plate and then licked it clean before putting it in her coffee cup.

"Actually, I do feel better."

She nodded. "Sometimes you just need a good cry and apple pie." She smiled. "It helps to release the pent-up anxiety. Cry too much and you end up with a headache. Too little and you still feel tense."

"I guess it just all sunk in. I know Dawson didn't kill Melody. But unless we figure out who did, he could go to jail." I stared at my bowl. "Or worse."

"Don't think about that. We have to stay focused. Now, Sherlock, what have you learned?"

I smiled. "Well, Watson, I didn't find out much." I told Nana Jo what I learned from Dorothy's granddaughter, such as it was.

"Let's recap what we do know. It might help to get your 'little gray cells' working."

Nana Jo loved mysteries as much as I did, so I knew she knew the "little gray cells" were a reference to Hercule Poirot and not Sherlock Holmes. So, I didn't correct her.

"We know Melody was a con artist, and I don't believe leopards ever change their spots. Once a con artist, always a con artist."

"You think she was playing a con on Dawson?"

"Yep. I think she planned to get that boy to marry her. I'll bet you my last plug nickel when she looked at him all she saw was dollar signs. That whole penthouse thing was just the start."

"But why?"

"To get him away from us."

I stared. "What do you mean?"

"It's what cults do. They have to get their victims away from friends and family so they can start the brainwashing."

"How do you know that?"

"There was a lecture at the Village a month or so ago about the House of David. Ruby Mae and I went. It was pretty interesting stuff. I even bought a book on them since they were local."

Nana Jo and I talked for a while, until she said she needed her beauty rest if she was going out sleuthing tomorrow. I delivered Dorothy's message and she went off to bed.

I was still pretty alert from the coffee and decided writing might help to organize my thoughts.

Thompkins was kept busy greeting the guests and showing them to their rooms. Lord Charles and Abigail Chitterly were the first to arrive at ten on Thursday morning. Lord Charles was a portly man with thinning hair who was known for a hardy appetite for wine, women, and rich foods. His wife was a mousy

American whose only distinctive feature seemed to be her affection for jewelry. She looked like a walking jewelry advertisement, wearing rubies, emeralds, and diamonds in every shape and size. They were followed by the Polish ambassador, Józef Lipski, a short, thin man with weak eyes, large spectacles, and a stammer. The French ambassador, Georges Brasseur, an arrogant, hawk-nosed man was next. Thompkins showed both gentlemen to their rooms as the footmen, Jim and Frank, took care of the luggage.

The German emissary, Count Rudolph Heigel, was tall, with slightly thinning blond hair and vacant blue eyes. He was a bit of a dandy, with immaculate attention to attire. He was a model of Aryan fervor who wore his role as an aide to the German secretary of state, Joachim von Ribbentrop, like a medal. Geoffrey Fordham-Baker, editor of the *London Times* was one of the last to arrive. Fordham-Baker was the fourth son of Henry Fordham-Baker, 2nd Viscount of Lampton. Short, fat, and bald, Fordham-Baker dressed in a slovenly manner and left a trail of crumbs in his wake. Cuddles followed him like a living Hoover, cleaning up the trail. Thompkins escorted each of the guests to their room and made sure everyone knew what time lunch would be served.

Since no one was exactly sure when the entire party would arrive, lunch was a cold buffet, allowing guests to eat whenever they arrived. This made serving a lot easier for the staff and Thompkins was able to keep an eye on the guests, without maintaining a constant presence in the dining room. Additional staff would arrive later once everyone arrived. The Marsh family wasn't on intimate footing with any of the early arrivals but did their best to make their guests as comfortable and welcome as possible.

Thompkins was grateful for the extra staff in the evening. Wallis, the Duchess of Windsor, arrived with her maid, Rebecca, and an American socialite, Virginia Hall, an hour before dinner. Rebecca was a dark-haired, dark-eyed vixen, who winked, smiled, and flirted with every male she encountered. Similar to Wallis, she was tall and slender but was curvaceous in areas where Wallis was not. The duchess had a vast amount of luggage, which required two extra footmen and the maid to organize. Virginia Hall was much more interesting, with less baggage. She was an intelligent, well-spoken woman with an infectious laugh, thick dark hair, light green eyes, and a wooden leg. She spoke freely about her accident as Thompkins showed her to her room. A hunting accident in Turkey required the amputation of her left leg from the knee down. Despite the wooden appendage, she exuded an air of confidence and determination.

Lady Elizabeth held dinner, to allow the duchess time to freshen up and change. It was, therefore, after nine when the party sat down to eat. Chitterly and Fordham-Baker were well on their way toward intoxication before they tasted their first bite of dinner. Fordham-Baker made an indelible impression on Thompkins by requesting to have his port glass filled while the duck consommé was served. Thompkins halted momentarily but quickly recovered. A glance to Lady Elizabeth was acknowledged by a slight nod, and Thompkins was back to his stiff, proper self.

Wallis, the Duchess of Windsor, was neither beautiful nor brilliant, yet she carried herself in a way that made people almost believe she was. Her dark hair was pulled back in a severe bun at the nape of her neck and emphasized her gaunt frame. She barely ate more than a few spoonfuls of the delightful dishes Mrs. Anderson prepared, despite the hours Lady Elizabeth and the cook spent planning a menu that was satisfying to men who'd spent the day shooting and a woman reported to be overly conscious of her weight. Wallis had a raspy voice and a loud, obnoxious laugh. She flirted shamelessly with Victor, Count Rudolph, or Count Rudy, as she called him, and Brasseur.

After dinner, the group retired to the parlor for coffee. Lady Elizabeth knitted and watched the spectacle. Lord William had been attempting to engage Geoffrey Fordham-Baker in conversation, but the editor had fallen asleep while nibbling on a biscuit. Cuddles, who had just finished consuming crumbs from the cuff of his pants, attempted to climb into his lap to gain access to the biscuit. Thankfully, Lord William caught him and removed him from the room and further temptation.

Lady Abigail had taken a seat near Lady Penelope and was pretending to ignore her husband's attention toward Daphne.

Daphne looked a bit strained as she removed Lord Charles's hand from her knee for the third time by Lady Elizabeth's count.

Virginia Hall and Lord James laughed and talked amiably with the Polish ambassador, Józef Lipski.

Wallis, Count Rudolph, and Brasseur were huddled in a corner near the fireplace. A word of French occasionally escaped the confines of their circle and was quickly followed by a laugh or wink from the duchess. The conversation was obviously meant to be private and no one ventured into their circle. Victor stood nearby but didn't attempt to infiltrate their conclave.

Thompkins silently entered the parlor and hurried to Lady Elizabeth. He whispered in her ear. She paused for a second but quickly nodded.

Thompkins left and, after a brief pause, he opened the door again and announced, "Miss Rebecca Minot."

Thompkins stepped aside and in waltzed a slender raven-haired beauty that appeared to have just stepped off the screen of a Hollywood picture.

The maid smiled large as she entered the room. "Ah, I am sorry for zee lateness. Zee butler he is so . . . how do you say" — she paused — "he is very proper." She stood very straight and stiff in a pose to impersonate Thompkins. She laughed. "He must get zee permission for me to come. Ah . . . but I am here now."

Rebecca sauntered over to the duchess.

"Yes, Rebecca, you're here now. That's all that matters. I couldn't entertain all of these handsome men without you here to help me." The duchess glanced at Lady Elizabeth. "You don't mind that I invited Rebecca to join us, do you? She's more like a companion than a maid, anyway."

Lady Elizabeth smiled. "Of course I don't mind."

"I knew you'd understand. You're not the least bit stuffy and stuck-up like Cookie, your cousin." She tilted her head back and used a finger to push her nose up in the air. Then she looked down her nose and sniffed.

Rebecca and Wallis laughed.

Lord William blustered. He looked as though he wanted to speak but eventually pulled out his pipe and filled it with tobacco, dropping most of it on the carpet.

Lady Elizabeth couldn't hide her confusion. "Cookie?"

Wallis laughed. "That's what I call her. Elizabeth looks just like a Scotch cook."

Lady Elizabeth took a few deep breaths to calm herself. "No. I can't say that she does. I have always found Her Royal Highness to be elegant, graceful, and refined."

"I daresay we British must seem very silly to outsiders, but thousands of years of tradition are hard to forego." Daphne smiled. "Did you really find Her Royal Highness stuffy and stuck-up? That's odd. I've never thought so. But then, she has made quite a few changes over the past year. I'm sure as she acclimates to her new position, she'll adapt."

Victor nearly choked on his drink, and Penelope had to walk over and pat him on the back. "I'm fine now. Thank you, dear."

A brief flash in her eyes and flared nostrils were the only indication Wallis recognized the snub. She quickly recovered and gave a hollow laugh before pulling Rebecca over to join the French and German contingent.

James looked at Daphne with pride and respect in his eyes before returning to his conversation with Virginia Hall and the Polish ambassador.

"It's very dull here. How about zee music and dancing?" Rebecca shimmied, which gained her the attention of Lord Charles and several other men.

Victor flipped the switch for the wireless and tuned into the Seager's Good Mixers program featuring Oscar Rabin and his Romany band. Rebecca pulled Lord Charles to the center of the floor, where she tried to teach him the Lambeth Walk.

"Come on, dance with me, Rudy?" Wallis turned to the count.

Rudolph Heigel's face was extremely red. His eyes bulged and he stood very erect. "I will not defile myself with such things."

The duchess looked confused. "But you dance so well." She turned toward the others. "Rudolph used to be in pictures. He was an actor before he joined the military." She looked at the count. "What's the matter?"

"Oscar Rabin is a Jew," he spat.

Lord William's face turned beet red, and he sputtered, "Abominable manners. Rude. Raised in a barn."

Lady Elizabeth managed to relay her displeasure in a single withering glance, which sent a flush up Count Rudolph's neck and made his ears look like beacons. A contrite look crossed his face briefly before he turned away toward Wallis.

Józef Lipski watched near the fireplace. When he heard Count Rudolph's comments, his face grew red. He breathed heavily and clenched his hands into fists. The look in his eyes was one of murderous rage. He started toward Count Rudolph but was intercepted by Virginia Hall.

"Come on and dance with me and Cuthbert."

Józef Lipski halted. He looked puzzled. "Cuthbert?"

"That's what I call my constant companion." She patted her wooden leg. "Cuthbert isn't the best of dancers, but I think we can manage a slow twirl if you won't mind."

Lipski gave Count Rudolph a scowl then turned his attention to Virginia. "I would be honored." He bowed and the two of them swayed to the music.

Daphne looked relieved when Lord Charles abandoned her for the maid's company. For several minutes, she sat comfortably, without having to dodge unwanted hands.

Lady Elizabeth strolled over to her niece. A few seconds later, Penelope joined her sister in the seat vacated by Lord Charles, leaned over, and whispered, "Well done."

Daphne smiled. "Thanks, but I doubt she even noticed the snub."

Lady Elizabeth smiled. "Trust me. I've heard she and David are livid over being denied the title of 'Her Royal Highness.' She noticed." She raised her cup in salute. "Nicely done."

Daphne looked around. "This all seems like such a bizarre farce."

"What do you mean, dear?" Lady Elizabeth asked.

"The world is on the brink of another war. Representatives from all of the nations currently in conflict are assembled at one house, our house." She inclined her head toward Count Rudolph. "Twenty years ago all of the nations represented here were at war. Now here we all sit, dancing, drinking, and making merry."

Penelope looked at her sister with surprise. "I never knew you were concerned with foreign affairs."

Daphne smiled. "Surprised I care about more than my clothes and hair?"

"Well, honestly, yes."

"I admit I've been pretty self-absorbed and shallow, but things are different now." She glanced across the room at James. "There's a lot at stake, not just for England, but for the world. I sure hope James knows what he's doing."

Lady Elizabeth stared at her niece. "So do I, dear. So do I."

CHAPTER 9

Coffee late at night, combined with too many hours spent writing into the wee small hours of the morning, left me sleep deprived and cranky Thursday morning. Not even the smell of bacon soothed the savage beast. I sat at the bar and drank three cups of coffee before I even spoke to anyone. It was the safest plan. That way, no one got hurt.

Dawson hadn't baked anything, which left me unreasonably irritated. He didn't have to bake every day. There were plenty of treats for the customers, even though we weren't charging for them. I hadn't bothered to get the certificate from the Health Department to allow us to sell food, but no permit was needed to simply offer them and leave a container for donations.

"You better now?" Nana Jo asked after I finished my third cup of coffee and started to eat my bacon sandwich.

"Hmmm," I mumbled.

"Good. Jenna called. She'll be here any minute."

Right on cue, the doorbell rang. Snickers and Oreo were momentarily torn between heading downstairs to bark at the newcomer and waiting for bacon to fall to the floor.

"I'll go." Dawson grabbed two biscuits from the jar on the counter and headed downstairs.

The poodles followed the biscuits downstairs.

Dawson let Jenna in and took the dogs out.

Jenna joined us upstairs. She had a cup of tea from one of those high-priced coffee shops that had sprung up all over town and a white box. She hopped onto the seat next to me and grabbed a piece of bacon from my plate.

"Ten minutes ago, that move might have cost you a limb," I growled.

"What's wrong with her?" she asked Nana Jo.

Nana Jo shrugged. "Woke up on the wrong side of the bed."

"I wish you would stop talking about me like I'm not here." Maybe three cups of coffee weren't enough. I poured myself another one and pretended I didn't see the looks Nana Jo and Jenna exchanged.

Dawson and the poodles made their way back upstairs.

"So, I've had some time to think about how we should proceed after the unfortunate events of yesterday." Jenna smiled at me and slid the box toward me.

I knew my sister. If she brought me treats, she was working herself up to say something I wouldn't like.

I stared at the box pointedly for several seconds and then looked at my sister and raised an eyebrow.

"Aren't you going to open it?"

"Beware of geeks bearing gifts," I said.

"It's Greeks, not geeks." Jenna wasn't always the brightest bulb in the pack, but she eventually got the joke and groaned. "Just open the box."

I opened the box, which contained half a dozen strawberry tarts from my favorite bakery, A Taste of Switzerland. The tarts glistened with a sugary glaze under the lights in my kitchen, and I swore I heard them whisper my name.

Nana Jo reached in and grabbed a tart. "Hmmm. This must be a biggie if you're softening the blow with ten dollar pastries."

A Taste of Switzerland's pastries weren't quite ten dollars each, but they were pricey. I wanted to be strong and hold out until I heard what Jenna was leading up to, but after Dawson and Jenna each grabbed tarts, there were only three lonely looking tarts left in the box. My willpower fled. I grabbed one. I bit into the flaky crust and my eyes rolled back into my head as the sugary goodness seeped through my body. I might have moaned because I heard laughter and when I opened my eyes, Nana Jo, Dawson, and Jenna were all staring at me with silly grins on their faces.

"Shut up." I licked the gooey strawberry filling off my fingers.

"I guess that must have done the trick," Nana Jo said.

"I know my sister." Jenna wiped her hands on a napkin.

"Alright." I wiped my mouth and took a swig of my coffee, swishing it around in my mouth to make sure every delicious crumb made its way to my stomach. "What do you want?"

"I want to use the media to our advantage. I'd like to invite some of the media here to the bookstore and have them interview Dawson. I want them to see he's nothing like his dad. He isn't a killer. He's just a kind, honest kid who plays football, bakes, works hard, and goes to school."

"I thought you didn't want us talking to

the media?" I tried to avoid sounding whiney and deliberately flattened the scowl I felt developing on my forehead.

"Yeah, well, that was before Dawson's dad went on television and in one fell swoop insulted the police, the victim, and all women everywhere." She looked at Dawson. "No offense."

"None taken," he mumbled.

"Here's what I want. One of Tony's fraternity buddies is the producer for WJMU. He's agreed to an exclusive interview. I get to see all of the questions in advance and I'll be right there the whole time. I can pull the plug if he goes off script and, trust me, I will."

Dawson looked uncertain. "I don't know . . ."

"You can't be shy. You've done interviews after football games. It'll be just like that."

"After a game, I talk about football. I can talk football all day. What am I gonna say to this guy?"

"You'll tell him about growing up without your mom and how you were raised by an abusive, alcoholic father."

Dawson shook his head. "I don't wanna talk about any of that."

Jenna looked down. "Unfortunately, some of it's going to come out anyway. I talked to a friend at the *River Bend Times,* and some of the information from child protective services has already been leaked."

Nana Jo and I were indignant.

I asked. "Aren't juvenile records supposed to be confidential?"

Jenna shrugged. "Dawson's records are, but his father's aren't."

"Well, I'll be . . ." Nana Jo said.

"This will be your chance to show the public who you are. There's been so much negative publicity in the news about athletes behaving badly and getting away with it, the public may not be supportive."

"Jenna's right." Nana Jo turned to Dawson. "This is your chance to show them you're just a poor kid trying to pull yourself up by your jockstrap."

I nearly choked on my coffee. "I think the phrase is bootstrap."

"Whatever." She rolled her eyes. "Show them how you bake to unwind. Heck, let them taste your cookies."

Dawson groaned. "I'll never live this down. When the guys on the team hear I like to bake, they'll never stop raggin' me."

Nana Jo patted him on the back. "Honey, I hate to break this to you, but the guys on the team are the least of your problems right now."

Jenna and Nana Jo were right, but I was still reluctant. Agreeing to this could expose Dawson to public ridicule, and there was no guarantee anyone would believe him. "This seems risky to me."

My sister wasn't someone who took risks. There was more to this than she was revealing.

"What aren't you telling us?"

Jenna sighed. "Okay. I've talked to a friend in the DA's office. He wants to be seen as tough on crime, so he plans to come down hard on you, just to show how tough he is."

Nana Jo mumbled something that sounded like weasel.

"But what about my dad? He said he knew who the real killer is."

Jenna paused for a moment. "Frankly, no one is taking him seriously."

I exchanged a glance with Nana Jo.

Jenna took a deep breath. "Your dad could be facing more jail time. He's been trying to extort money."

"From who?" I asked.

"Anyone . . . everyone. The media, the police, the district attorney, you name it. He says he knows who the killer is, but he won't talk unless he gets a quarter of a million dollars."

Nana Jo whistled.

Dawson stared openmouthed but then dropped his head and looked away.

"My source at the police station doesn't believe he knows anything, but they'll investigate, provided he gives them something."

We discussed the interview for a while longer. Finally, Jenna looked at Dawson. "Well, what do you think?"

Dawson looked at Nana Jo and me. "Do you think I should?"

Nana Jo nodded. "I do. I think it will be your chance to tell your story. Plus, if you want, I'll be there to support you."

Everyone looked at me. I stared in my empty coffee cup, then took a deep breath. "I think you should do it too. But, it's totally up to you. You have to follow your gut. What do you think?"

Dawson took a moment before responding. "I don't really want to do it —"

I started to interrupt, but he held up a hand to stop me. "But I think I should. Mrs. Thomas is right. It will give me a chance to tell my side of things."

Jenna exhaled. "Great. I was hoping you'd agree, especially since I already told them to come around noon."

Dawson looked as though he was mustering up his courage to speak. Finally, he said,

"I'll do the interview." He turned to Jenna. "But can you do me a favor, please?"

Jenna said, "Sure, if I can."

Dawson took a deep breath. "Can you please help my dad? I know he's a big jerk and he's done some bad things, but he's still my dad."

Jenna stared at Dawson for a moment. "Dawson, I don't know if I can help your father. He —"

"But he really needs someone —"

"Wait. It's not that I don't want to help. I may not be able to help. I have to be careful there's no conflict of interest. I'm your lawyer, and I have a responsibility to represent you to the best of my ability."

Dawson hung his head. "I understand. I just thought maybe you could talk to him."

Jenna stared at him. "Okay. I'll talk to him. But, I can't promise anything. I have to check with his PD. And as long as she's okay with it, I'll talk to him. Okay?"

"Great. Yeah. That's great." He perked up and smiled. "Thanks."

We talked for a bit and decided we didn't all need to hang around for the interview. Since I'd already made arrangements to go on campus and meet Jillian, I'd let Nana Jo and Jenna handle the media.

Jenna left not long afterward.

I did some paperwork for the bookstore until the twins arrived to help. I would miss them when fall break was over and they went back to school. They were such a great help.

I met Jillian at the student union as arranged. She was dressed in a miniskirt with leggings and a sweater with ballet flats. Last night her hair had been slicked back into a bun. Today it was thick and wavy and loose.

"I like your hair."

"Thanks. It takes a lot to get it under control for performances." She laughed.

She took me to Melody's dorm. The door was slightly open, but we knocked and were instructed to come in.

"Mrs. Washington, this is Emma Lee." Jillian turned to Emma. "This is . . . Mrs. Washington."

"Please, call me Sam." I extended my hand.

The dorm room was small, about the size of my bedroom at home. Small bedrooms are fine when it was just one person and all you needed to do was sleep in the room. However, this room was shared by two people. So there were twin beds, two desks, two dressers, and two closets. One side of the room had posters, family pictures, and a colorful comforter on the bed and looked homey. The other side was barren with nothing except a nondescript blue coverlet to prove anyone lived there.

Emma Lee was petite. She might have been five feet and one hundred pounds if she wore weights. She was Asian with dark almond eyes and long dark hair, which she wore pulled back into a ponytail. She looked uncertain, but good manners always showed and she stepped forward and shook my outstretched hand.

Jillian went to Emma's bed and sat.

Emma pulled out her chair for me and I sat. She sat in the other chair and waited.

"I wondered if you could answer a few questions about your roommate for me."

Emma was silent.

I intercepted a look between the two girls. Jillian nodded as if to say "she's okay."

"Fine. But I'm not sure how much help I can be." Emma spoke with a distinct southern accent, which made me smile to see that southern belles came in all different shapes, sizes, and colors.

I couldn't hide the surprise on my face and I heard it in my voice. "As her roommate, you must have gotten to know each other pretty well."

Emma shook her head. "I hardly ever saw her."

I looked at the bare side of the room.

"Melody rarely used this room." She went to the closet and opened it. "She kept a few items of clothing here, but that's about it."

"But if she didn't stay here, where did she stay?"

Emma shrugged. "Beats me."

"Do you know if she had any family?"

She shook her head. "I have no idea. When we met, I tried to ask the normal questions, like 'where're you from?' I tried to get to know her. But she shut me down so fast it made my head spin."

"How long were you roommates?"

"Only since the start of the semester."

"Is there anything you can tell me about her?" I got up and walked over to Melody's side of the room. "Mind if I look?"

"Help yourself, but there ain't much to see. When I realized she wasn't planning to stay, I took a peek." Emma got up and joined me.

There were three sweaters, a warm leather bomber jacket, and a pair of tennis shoes in the closet. The dresser had two pairs of underwear, a bra, a nightshirt, and a small bag of toiletries.

"Is that it?" I closed the last drawer.

"Yes, ma'am."

I stood in the room and looked around, mentally comparing Emma's side of the room with Melody's. "But where are her school items?" I walked over to the desk and opened the drawer. There wasn't even a pencil.

"Beats me." Emma shrugged.

I stared at her. "Did the police remove anything?"

"No one from the police came by. Well, not while I've been here at least." She looked confused. "That's odd, isn't it?"

"Yes. I would have expected someone would have come by."

A sudden thought made Emma gasp. "Sweet Jesus, you think they notified her family?"

"I'm sure someone from the school has if the police didn't," I said with more confidence than I felt.

It must have been enough to put Emma at ease, because she breathed a sigh of relief. "Well, thank the Lord for that."

"Did you have any classes with Melody?"

Emma shook her head. "No, ma'am."

"What was her major?"

She shrugged. "Beats me."

I was confused. "But she was a senior. That means she'd be graduating in a few months. Surely she mentioned what she was getting her degree in?"

"All I know is she transferred here from the East Coast. Melody wasn't talkative."

Jillian mumbled, "At least not to women."

"Help me understand." I looked from one of them to the other.

Emma said, "She didn't talk much, but from what I gathered, she was majoring in M-r-s."

"Excuse me?"

Emma smiled. "You know, M-r-s." She pointed at her ring finger.

"You mean she was just here looking for a husband."

They nodded.

I turned to Jillian. "But aren't you in the same class?"

"Supposed to be, but that's what's weird. I've only seen her there once all semester." Jillian pulled her laptop out of her book bag, typed something, and navigated for a few seconds. When she was finished, she turned the laptop to face me. "Here's the online link to our class. We use a program called Canvas."

"I'm familiar with Canvas. I used to be a teacher."

Jillian smiled. "Great. From here, anyone enrolled in the class can see the syllabus, the homework assignments, and exams, pretty much everything."

I looked at the familiar site.

Jillian navigated to the grades section.

"I can see all of my grades because I'm logged into the system. But, if I click here" — she clicked on a link on the navigation bar — "I can see everyone's grades in the class. That way, I can see how I stack up against everyone else."

I stared at the screen. "But there are no names listed, only student identification numbers. How do you know which one is Melody's?"

"They do that for privacy," Emma added.

"True. But, it doesn't take much to figure out who's who." Jillian looked sheepish. "Process of elimination. Look. This is me." She pointed to a line on the screen. "There are only fifteen people in this class and the rest of us talk to each other."

"They tell you their grades?" I asked.

"Sometimes. But you can pretty much figure out who got what. Last month, Martin was complaining about getting a low grade. He said he had a perfect score up until then. So that has to be him." She pointed at a line on the screen. "Eva had a family emergency and had to go home. So the incompletes for the last two assignments are hers."

Emma added, "Regina was telling every-one how she aced the last test, which made up for her getting low scores on the two previous ones."

"Based on what people have said, and through the process of elimination, I know this" — she pointed at one line — "has to be Melody. No one else has gotten a perfect score through the entire course."

I stared at the screen and then at Jillian. "You're amazing. You'll be a fine detective."

She grinned. "Must run in my genes."

"I'll bet if we could find out her student number, we could confirm her grade," I said. "Although, I'm not sure what that will tell us."

"She's getting a perfect score in a class she never attends," Jillian said.

"Seems fishy to me," Emma added.

"Me too."

I offered to take the girls to lunch to thank them for their help. Thursday was Emma's short day for classes, but Jillian had a lab and wouldn't be free until after two. We agreed to meet at the student union at two fifteen.

MISU wasn't a large campus, but it could be quite confusing to get around, so I had to ask for directions to the administration building. I hadn't held out much hope they'd provide information to a total stranger. The Family Educational Rights and Privacy Act of 1974, or FERPA, made it impossible for anyone to get student educational information without written permission from the student. Parents couldn't even get their son's or daughter's grades, so I wasn't surprised when they refused to provide them to me.

As I left the administration building, I ran into Peter Castleton, MISU's athletic director. He'd been very supportive of Nana Jo and me tutoring Dawson over the summer.

"How's Dawson?"

Castleton was about five ten, two hundred pounds. He was bald with the lean, muscular physique of a runner.

"As well as can be expected. He's worried, and he misses football."

Castleton nodded. "I'm sure, but the policy is very clear. Any athlete charged with a felony must be suspended from all academic and athletic activities until the situation is resolved."

"I know."

Castleton stared at me pointedly. "You understand I'm in a bit of a difficult situation here. I like Dawson. I think he's a good kid with a very bright future if . . ."

"If he doesn't get convicted for murder?"

Castleton nodded. "I'm really sorry. We try to warn the boys."

"Warn them?"

Castleton squirmed. "Against honey traps."

"What's a honey trap?"

Castleton rubbed the back of his neck. "Some young people enter college with the sole intention of finding a spouse, preferably a wealthy one or someone with the potential to become wealthy — a meal ticket."

"You think Melody's only interest in Dawson was as a meal ticket?"

He waved his hand. "I don't know anything about her personally, and I don't want to speak ill of the dead, but some of the players talk."

"Can I talk to them?"

He stared at me.

"We're trying to figure out who else might have wanted to kill her. The police are stuck on Dawson and aren't looking for anyone else. I'm hoping maybe some of the players may have seen or heard something that might help."

Castleton seemed to think that through. "The players will be watching a film at six tonight in the athletic center's media room."

He pulled out a piece of paper and an envelope from his back pocket and wrote on it. "Show this and your driver's license to the guard and he'll let you in." He handed me a note which granted me permission to enter, basically a permission slip.

"Thank you."

I still had about thirty minutes before I was to meet Emma and Jillian at the student union, so I made my way to the history department. After asking around, I found a long, narrow closet with Professor Harley Quin's name on the door. The door was open.

Jazz drifted from inside, which made me stop. I peeked inside. A blue-eyed Sean Connery pretended to play the piano along with the music.

I must have moved because he glanced my way, smiled, and turned down the music.

"I'm sorry. I didn't mean to interrupt."

"Caught in the act." He not only looked like Sean Connery, but he spoke with a British accent.

"That's one of my favorites."

I could tell by the skeptical look on his face he didn't believe me. "Really?"

"I love David Benoit."

Surprise and a small amount of awe played across his face. "Ah . . . but what's the name of the song?"

I smiled. " 'Linus & Lucy.' "

He smacked his leg. "Brilliant. Nine out of ten people would have said, 'Peanuts.' You really are a fan. Come in. Welcome to my closet." He made a grand sweeping gesture with his arm and pushed a pile of papers onto the floor. He had on brown tweed pants and a white shirt with a bow tie. He looked like Sean Connery in *Indiana Jones and the Last Crusade*.

I walked into the room, which couldn't have been more than five feet wide. I could literally reach out and touch both walls at the same time. There were books and papers on practically every surface.

"Now, what can I do for you? You're not one of my students. I certainly would have remembered you."

I grinned at the compliment. "Well, I was hoping you could help me. I have some questions about one of your students."

He looked puzzled. "I'll try." He turned in his seat so he faced me.

I was finding it very hard to look him in the eyes without smiling like a lovesick schoolgirl. I needed to pull myself together. I took a deep breath. "Can you tell me about Melody Hardwick?"

He looked puzzled. "Melody Hardwick . . .

Melody Hardwick, I'm afraid I don't . . . you don't by any chance mean the girl who was strangled by that football player, do you?"

Nothing could have cured my lovesick attitude quicker. I squinted my eyes and my blood pressure rose. "Dawson Alexander is a fine young man, and he did *not* kill anyone." I enunciated when I was angry, and I was angry now. "And, in this country, people are innocent until proven guilty." I rose and turned for the door.

"Whoa. Wait. I'm sorry." He jumped out of his seat and grabbed me by the arm. "I'm sorry. I didn't mean to offend you. Please forgive me?"

Hearing someone accuse Dawson of murder made me furious.

"Please. Won't you sit down?" he begged.

I took several deep breaths and returned to my seat.

"I'm very sorry. I didn't mean to insult you or Mr. Alexander. I was merely repeating what I'd heard. Now, how can I help you?"

"Melody Hardwick was one of your students. I was hoping you could tell me something about her."

He shook his head. "I wish I could, but I've only been here a semester and I'm afraid I don't really know many of the students yet. I saw her picture in the newspaper, but honestly, it didn't ring a bell with me. Are you sure she was in my class?"

I nodded. "Yes. She was in History of Cults."

He thought for a moment and then shook his head. "I'm sure you're right, but I don't remember her. I guess she didn't make much of an impression on me."

He smiled in a way that implied I was making an impression. I felt nervous and uncomfortable. It had been a long time since anyone flirted with me. I was out of practice and began to fidget so much I dropped my purse.

"I know one of the other girls in the class, and she tells me Melody never attended class but she had a perfect grade."

"Well, that's odd. Let's take a look." He turned to his computer and tapped away for a few minutes. "Now I remember. It's the name that threw me. I have an Elizabeth Mae Simpson."

"Yes, that's her. She was using an alias."

"How odd." He scanned the computer screen. "Miss Simpson is showing a perfect score. You say she never attended class? I'll certainly have to look into it. Must be a mistake." He turned to face me. "This computer system is different than the one I'm used to back in England. I must have made a mistake." He smiled. "I'm sure I would have found it before the end of the term."

It sounded reasonable.

"Now, is there anything else I can help you with?"

"Actually, there is something else, but it's rather personal." My face heated.

"Now this sounds promising." He settled back and fixed an inquiring look on my face.

"I'm writing a book."

"Wonderful."

"Thank you. It's a mystery set in the British countryside. I was wondering if maybe you could help me with some research," I stammered.

"I'd love to. I'll be happy to answer any questions I can. Perhaps we can discuss it over dinner say, tomorrow night?"

"Mrs. Washington?"

I turned, thankful to see Jillian standing in the doorway. "Yes. Tomorrow night will be fine."

"Why don't you leave me your number and I'll call you with the details."

"Okay." I hurriedly wrote my cell number on a sheet of paper and rushed from the room, remembering at the last minute to turn and say, "Thank you."

"No. Thank you."

Outside, Jillian rushed to keep up with me. "Hey, I'm sorry, Mrs. Washington. I didn't mean to interrupt. I had to drop off a book with one of my professors. I didn't mean —"

"It's okay. You didn't interrupt anything. He's just going to help me with some research for a . . . a book I'm working on."

"Granny told me you've written a book. That's great."

Dorothy Clark certainly had a big mouth. I'd have to be careful what I told her, but none of this was Jillian's fault. "Come on. We better get over to meet Emma."

CHAPTER 10

Emma was waiting for us at the student union. Both girls in tow, I headed to downtown North Harbor. They asked to see my bookstore and I was rather curious about Dawson's interview, so I headed home.

The interview had just wrapped up and the reporters were loading equipment into a large van in the back parking lot.

Dawson looked tired, but no other signs of distress were present. Nana Jo wasn't waving her peacemaker and there were no dead bodies, so I assumed all went well. I was a bit anxious to watch it.

There were a few patrons in the shop, but my nephews had things under control. The twins rushed to offer assistance to my two young friends. Boys would be boys.

I walked over to Dawson. "How'd it go?"

He shrugged. "Okay, I think." He rubbed the back of his neck. "I hate talking about myself, but Mrs. Rutherford said it was good."

I patted his shoulder. "Then I'm sure it was fine." I stared at him. "You look tired. Have you eaten?"

He shook his head.

"Why don't you come with us?" I looked around. "Melody's roommate, Emma, and Dorothy's granddaughter, Jillian, helped me earlier, and I promised them lunch." I looked at my watch. "Although it's almost dinnertime."

"Where are you going?"

"I thought I'd try that new restaurant that opened up a few doors down. I started to eat there the other day, but I never actually got to eat." That was Monday, when I'd seen the police had picked up Dawson for Melody's murder and rushed to the police station. Definitely a day I'd like to forget.

Nana Jo joined us. "He did a real fine job. Real fine."

I could tell by the raspy sound in her voice, Nana Jo had fought back tears.

"I was just inviting Dawson to lunch."

"Good. I'm hungry enough to eat an entire heifer. Let me get my purse."

Nana Jo ran upstairs and by the time she returned, I'd arranged for Jillian, Dawson, Zaq, and Emma to go down and secure seating. Christopher agreed to stay and keep things going in the bookstore in exchange for a burger and fries.

"I called the girls while I was upstairs. They're on their way. We were supposed to meet for the book club."

"I totally forgot about the book club meeting today."

The Sleuthing Seniors Book Club formed over the summer, and Nana Jo and her friends met at the bookstore on the first Thursday of every month to discuss mysteries.

"Maybe I should go tell everyone there will be four more coming for lunch." I started toward the door.

"No worries. I already sent a text message to Jenna."

Nana Jo looked like she wanted to talk, so I waited.

"That boy has really had a tough time." She shook her head and swallowed hard in an effort to keep her emotions in check. "I knew things were hard, but I never knew everything."

"He doesn't like talking about his dad or his life as a kid. Remember when we found him hiding out in the bathroom of the bookstore?"

Nana Jo nodded. "His father got drunk as

a skunk and beat the crap out of him. He ran away with nothing but the clothes on his back."

I patted Nana Jo and tried to keep from getting teary eyed as I thought back. "I'm so glad he came here."

"Sometimes I wonder what would have happened if he hadn't been working at that country club."

I laughed. "And if I hadn't drank four glasses of champagne on an empty stomach and made a spectacle of myself at the funeral reception for Clayton Parker when I puked and needed help getting home."

Nana Jo laughed. "Clayton Parker was an evil man, but if it weren't for him, we might not have Dawson with us now. Maybe he wasn't so worthless after all."

Clayton Parker's death wasn't a reason for rejoicing, but I understood what she was getting at.

When the girls arrived, we walked to the restaurant. Two tables had been pushed together at the back of the restaurant. Dawson sat at the end with Jillian and Emma on either side of him. Zaq was next to Emma and Jenna sat next to Jillian. I sat next to Jenna and across from Dorothy. Nana Jo seated herself at the head of the table and Irma and Ruby Mae were on her sides.

When the waitress arrived to take our drink orders, Nana Jo took a look at her watch and ordered a Wild Turkey, neat. She pulled out her iPad and put on her glasses. She waited until all the drink orders were placed. "Now, we're under a time crunch, so I suggest we move forward with our meeting." She looked around.

No one disagreed.

"Who would like to start?" She looked around the table.

Irma coughed and raised her hand. "I talked to my great-grandson, Ernie. He's a realtor." She coughed. "He said Virgil Russell was a shady character and a slumlord. Apparently, he applied for a grant from the government to build that high-rise on the lake. Said he was building low-income housing for minorities and senior citizens so he got a super low interest rate. But then he made those units the smallest units he could. Ernie says he rarely rents to low-income folks unless they pay him under the table."

"What do you mean, pay him under the table?" I asked.

"If they have a section eight voucher, they pay a reduced rate to their landlord and HUD pays the difference. The landlord is supposed to make repairs, but Ernie said

Virgil Russell stalls on the repairs."

"What's HUD?" Jillian asked.

"The Department of Housing and Urban Development," Ruby Mae added.

"Why would anyone put up with that?" Dorothy asked.

Ruby Mae looked up from her knitting. "They put up with it because they don't want to make trouble." She looked around. "I found out quite a bit on that scoundrel, but I'll wait my turn. I don't want to interrupt." She nodded to Irma. "Go ahead, honey."

Irma continued, "Ernie said Virgil Russell is a sleazy, low-life slumlord who can't be trusted any farther than he can spit." Irma then turned and spit on the floor.

"Irma!" everyone said.

Irma coughed and then took a swig of the whiskey the server placed in front of her. "Sorry."

Nana Jo turned to Ruby Mae. "Perhaps you would like to go now."

Ruby Mae stopped knitting long enough to take a sip of her coffee. "What I found out confirms what Irma said. Virgil Russell is a slumlord. My niece's boy, Robert Earl, works downtown at the County-City building. They've been trying to clean up a lot of the run-down housing in North Harbor. He said a lot of the worst properties are owned by absentee landlords, but Virgil Russell owns over one hundred rentals, basically shacks. Most of them need to be torn down."

"Roach motels is what Ernie called them." Irma burst into a coughing fit.

Dorothy smacked Irma on the back. "You need to build up your immune system. You're just a wreck." She reached in her bag and pulled out a bottle of tablets. "Here, you need to take these air immune tablets. They're wonderful." Dorothy handed two tablets to Irma.

Irma looked at the tablets and then popped them both in her mouth and started to chew.

Dorothy looked stricken and then shouted, "What are you doing? You don't just put them in your mouth. You have to dissolve them in water."

Irma coughed and then began foaming at the mouth. She reached for a glass of water. With each gulp of water, more foam came from her mouth.

Restaurant patrons began to stare.

The manager came over. "Is everything okay? I'm trained on the Heimlich."

Irma shook her head but then realized he was making his way toward her. Finally, she reached in her mouth and pulled out her teeth. She took her napkin and wiped her tongue and mouth.

"Blech. Dorothy, what the h—"

"Irma!"

Irma grabbed her drink and tossed it back, then grabbed Nana Jo's drink and took a long swig. Then she swished the liquid around in her mouth and swallowed.

We all stared for several seconds and then burst out laughing.

The manager looked around like he didn't know what to think of us. He eventually joined in the laughter too.

When we finally pulled ourselves together, Jenna wiped her eyes. "Oh my goodness."

Zaq and the younger crew continued laughing.

Irma smiled and picked up her teeth and wrapped them in her napkin, which got everyone started laughing again.

Nana Jo said, "Irma, what made you take your teeth out?"

Irma said, "Once that stuff got in my teeth, I tried using my tongue to work it out. I guess it agitated the darned things with my saliva and I started foaming. Then when I drank the water, it got worse. Since I couldn't get it out of my teeth, I decided to get rid of the teeth." She grinned and everyone laughed again.

Nana Jo said, "Ruby Mae, I think it's safe for you to continue now."

"Well, as I was saying, Virgil Russell is a slumlord."

Emma tentatively raised a hand. "Excuse me. I just think that's awful. Why do people put up with that?"

Ruby Mae continued, "The wait list for low-income housing is long, especially for more than two bedrooms. When I was in Chicago, after my husband left, I was on the wait list for five years for one of those Section Eight housing vouchers that helps low-income people afford decent housing. By the time I finally got to the top of the wait list, my cleaning business had taken off and I didn't qualify anymore, and I'm thankful for that. Lord knows I'm thankful. Some of those places were awful. I would have just as soon slept outside." She shook her head. "There was a lady at my church who was living in one of Virgil Russell's run-down shacks. I've never seen such filth. She complained, and he made her life miserable. He wouldn't make repairs. Her toilet was out for almost six months, and he wouldn't repair it. He wouldn't collect the trash. It was bad."

Emma looked appalled. "But that's horrible. Why did she stay?"

"Where else is she gonna go, baby? She had three small children and no other family. She didn't have the money to get the repairs done herself." Ruby Mae leaned in. "But here's the worst part. You know that filthy little heathen had the nerve to tell her she could pay in *other ways.*" Ruby Mae raised her eyebrows in a suggestive manner.

Everyone got what Ruby Mae was talking about except Emma, who had a puzzled expression on her face.

Irma leaned over and patted her hand. "She's talking about sex, honey."

Emma's face turned bright red, and her expression went from puzzled to shock to revulsion in less than ten seconds. "Eww." She shook herself. "That's just . . . eww."

"That's illegal, isn't it? How was he able to get away with doing that?" Jillian turned to Jenna.

"Yes, it is illegal. Unfortunately, a lot of people won't report it for fear of repercussions, also illegal."

"But doesn't someone inspect these homes to make sure they're fit to live in?" Jillian asked.

"They do. Sometimes that just plays into the landlord's hands. The government only pays so much for the apartment rent, whatever the average market rates are. The benefit to the landlord is they can get a low interest loan as long as they designate a certain amount of units for low-income residents. If the landlord accepts the Section Eight housing certificate, he's guaranteed to get his money from the government. Then he doesn't do repairs. The renter reports the landlord. He's given an ultimatum. Either do the repairs or he'll be removed from their list of approved rentals." Jenna paused and looked around. "He doesn't do the repairs and is removed as a valid Section Eight landlord. They remove their tenants. The landlord can now do the repairs and raise the rents."

"And he's gotten the low interest loan." Nana Jo pursed her lips and scowled.

Jenna nodded.

"That sounds sordid, but . . ." I tried to put my thoughts into words.

"But does it make him a killer?" Nana Jo asked.

I nodded.

"Unless, maybe Melody knew something about it and she threatened to turn him in?" Jillian asked hopefully.

I shook my head. "No. More likely she knew about it and was helping him." I looked tentatively at Dawson, but he didn't seem to be bothered by talk of Melody.

"What happened to your friend?" Emma asked Ruby Mae.

"Once our church found out what was going on, we packed up her stuff and moved her in with one of the members. Things worked out well, and now she's got one of those Habitat homes." She smiled. "That's all I was able to find out."

We turned to look at Dorothy.

"My date did know a little bit about this Melody person, but he was a bit grabby, so I didn't get as much information out of him as I would have liked." She winked. "I may have to go out with him again to see what else I can get out of him."

"Way to take one for the team," Nana Jo said sarcastically.

"I aim to please." Dorothy smiled, then got serious. "Turns out Melody was in a special program in New Jersey for troubled teens or at-risk kids." She rummaged in her purse and pulled out a sheet of paper. "Higher Ed Restart or some such thing. The way I understand it, some of these kids are really smart but keep getting in trouble. This program gives them an opportunity to go to college. The hope is they'll get a good education and redirect their energy so they use their brains for good rather than evil."

"I think I've read about this program," I said. "When I was a teacher, there was a lot of information floating around about how it's cheaper to send kids to Harvard for four years than it is to prison. Plus, they can learn a skill that's useful and hopefully not end up back in their negative environment. But, I didn't know they were doing it here in North Harbor."

"That's dangerous, isn't it?" Emma asked tentatively.

"Harvey said they had very strict criteria," Dorothy reassured her. "No one with a history of violence. No rapists. No murderers. No arsonists. No child molesters." She continued to scan her paper. "He said MISU only took two. Both were older than the traditional students. Melody was one and the other was a guy who was also one of those grifters."

"Seems like they should tell people, you know, warn them," Jillian said.

"They want to give the students the best possible chance for success. The hope is they'll blend in and adapt. Harvey says the program's very successful. There are students placed in universities all over the world."

Nana Jo tapped info into her iPad.

We waited until our server finished taking

our orders. When all the orders were placed, I told them what I'd learned on campus. Emma and Jillian helped fill in the gaps. I told them about my conversation with the athletic director and plan to talk to the team later.

When I was done reporting, I turned to Nana Jo.

"Freddie's son, Mark, found out that our friend Virgil Russell, spent time in prison for fraud, embezzlement, and" — she paused — "manslaughter."

Everyone sat up in their chairs and fired questions at the same time.

"Hold your horses. Virgil was convicted of murdering his partner, a man named . . ." She scrolled her iPad. "Here it is, Max Simpson."

I gasped. "Simpson, that's Melody's last name."

Nana Jo nodded. "Yep. Max had a daughter."

"Elizabeth Mae Simpson," we all said together.

She nodded.

Dawson looked shocked. "But that's . . ." He shook his head. "That's just wrong. He had his hands all over her."

I didn't understand that either. "If he went to jail for murdering her father, it seems odd she'd be having a relationship with him."

We talked until our food arrived, and then we put aside talk of murder until we finished eating. Irma hadn't been able to clean her teeth, so she drank her dinner and had her food placed in a take-out container. She was pretty tipsy and abandoned our group to flirt with a couple of men at the bar.

Jenna looked amazed by all of the activity and whispered to me, "Are they like this all the time?"

Dorothy had joined Irma at the bar and both were drinking like fish. Emma and Jillian looked amused.

I looked at Dorothy and Irma. "This is nothing. You should see them when they really get revved up."

Jenna looked as though her eyes would pop out of her head. "Seriously?"

I nodded. "They can be a handful, but they're also amazing at using their connections to collect information."

Jenna nodded. "I was impressed. They've found out a lot of information in a short period of time. Today is Thursday. It's only been four days."

I thought about that. Had it only been four days? It sure felt like a lot longer. "Well, Nana Jo gave us a deadline."

Jenna frowned. "Deadline?"

I hid my smile. "Yeah. She said we needed to have this figured out before next Saturday's game."

CHAPTER 11

Dorothy and Irma were too drunk to get home alone. Zaq volunteered to make sure Emma and Jillian arrived safely back on campus. I suspected Zaq had his own motives behind volunteering for taxi service. He and Emma were hitting it off well. I wasn't going to look a gift horse in the mouth, especially when it freed me up to get the girls back to the retirement village safely. Before they left, Jillian and Emma hugged me.

"Thank you for dinner and for including us in your investigation," Jillian said.

I hugged them both. "Thank you both. You were very helpful."

Jillian looked as though she was working up the courage to speak.

Emma poked her in the ribs. "Ask her."

"Ask me what?"

"We wondered if it would be okay if . . .

well, we were hoping maybe —" Jillian stammered.

"We wanted to know if we could continue to help investigate," Emma finished.

I was surprised. "Well, I'm not sure."

"Please," they begged.

"We really want to help," Emma said. "After all, even though I didn't like her, she was still my roommate."

"And neither one of us believe Dawson killed her," Jillian said.

I'd noticed a few looks between Dawson and Jillian while we were eating. Was something developing? However, I couldn't allow sentimental feelings to influence my judgment. "Girls, I truly appreciate your willingness to help."

"Why do I sense a 'but' is coming?" Emma asked.

"But this may seem like fun and games, but it's serious. Someone killed Melody. The killer may be on campus. If someone thinks you girls are asking questions and suspects you might figure this thing out, you might be in danger." I shuddered at the memory of what it felt like to be held at gunpoint during the summer. "It's too risky, and I can't take the chance you might get hurt."

"But we'll be very careful. There has to be something we can do to help," Jillian said.

I thought about it. "Okay. Here's how you can help." I looked seriously at the girls and tried to help them see the gravity of the situation. I turned to Emma. "As her roommate, maybe you could check with the university to see if anyone will be claiming her things. See if she has any family. Offer to pack up her belongings."

Emma nodded eagerly. "I can do that."

I turned to Jillian. "You can help by organizing a memorial."

Jillian frowned. "A memorial?"

I nodded. "Yes. Talk to the administration and put up flyers. Maybe a vigil of some sort."

"But I don't see . . ."

"Once the memorial is scheduled, then we'll come and observe the people who show up. It's a long shot, but worth a try."

Jillian's face lit up. "I get it. You're hoping the murderer will show up."

"Something like that. Actually, I'm hoping we'll run into people who knew her so we can talk to them." I looked at both girls. "Can you do that?"

They nodded eagerly.

"Good. But please be careful. This is very serious, and I don't want the killer to get suspicious."

They gave me their solemn promises to be

careful and left with Zaq. I still felt nervous and wondered if I was doing the right thing by involving them. However, something in the back of my mind told me if I didn't give them a job to do, they might go out on their own, which could be more dangerous. This way I hoped to control and protect them, if needed. I shook off the doubt and began the process of corralling the girls. Irma took a bit of persuasion, but we finally convinced her.

As we were leaving, the manager returned. "I hope you all enjoyed yourselves."

"Yes. Thank you. The food was very good," I said.

"I'm glad you liked it. I hope you'll come back again soon."

Even though I was standing with Nana Jo and Jenna, he stared directly at me.

Heat climbed up my neck. "I'm sure we will. You're so close."

For some reason, I found it hard to make eye contact and focused on pretty much everything except his eyes.

"Hi. My name is Josephine Thomas." Nana Jo stuck out her hand.

"Frank Patterson." He shook it.

"Frank, we're glad to meet you. This is my granddaughter Jenna Rutherford, and my other granddaughter Samantha Washington."

We shook.

"Sam owns Market Street Mysteries down the street. You should swing by sometime and check it out." Nana Jo was clearly matchmaking, and the heat in my face intensified.

"Nana Jo! Everyone doesn't read mysteries," I said.

Nana Jo smiled. "Do you like mysteries, Mr. Patterson?"

He smiled. "Actually, I do. I just haven't had much time to read, with opening the restaurant. I hope that changes soon."

"Perhaps your wife might enjoy mysteries?" Jenna asked with a coy smile.

Subtlety wasn't my family's strong suit. I tried to give Jenna a discreet pinch and prayed the ground would open up and swallow me whole.

Frank Patterson laughed. "I'm not married."

"Really? A nice-looking man like you? How on earth did you manage to escape?" Nana Jo joked.

Frank smiled. "I guess I've been too busy to settle down."

"Sam here is single too. What a coincidence."

"Widow. I'm widowed. I'm sure Mr.

Patterson doesn't want to hear about this. Oh my, look at the time." I grabbed my grandmother and sister by the arms and propelled them toward the door. "Thanks for everything. We'll see you around."

Outside on the street, I scowled at both of them. "What exactly do you two think you're doing?"

They smirked. "Who, us?"

"Yes. You."

Nana Jo smiled. "We're just being neighborly."

I huffed and stomped off toward the bookstore and ignored the laughter I heard from behind.

At the bookstore, the girls picked up a couple more books in the Mrs. Pollifax series, which they'd started reading over the summer. I was happy they enjoyed the series and decided to continue reading it. Although, Irma preferred more sex in her books and had also started reading J. D. Robb's In Death series. I preferred cozy mysteries, which tended not to have sex, violence, or bad language. Knowing J. D. Robb was the pseudonym for romance writer Nora Roberts, I thought there might be enough sex mixed in with the mystery to satisfy Irma. So far, she seemed pretty happy with my recommendation.

After their purchases were made, I drove the girls back to the retirement village and headed back to MISU to talk to the football team.

MISU wasn't a large university, so you wouldn't expect the athletic facility to be large either. However, you'd be wrong. The athletic and convocation center was a large facility which hosted not only athletic events for the university but was also a venue for concerts and other entertainment for the community. I remembered coming there as a child to see the circus. The main auditorium had more than five thousand seats. It wasn't as large as JAMU's stadium, which could hold almost ten thousand, but it was still bigger than Carnegie Hall.

Behind the main facility was another smaller building, which was where the security guard directed me to go after I showed my note and driver's license. I parked and followed the signs to the media room.

The media room looked like a small movie theatre with a large screen that covered an entire wall, a projector, and about one hundred seats. Nearly every seat was taken when I entered. I was at the front of the room and felt like all eyes were directed at me. The lights were low, so I took a minute for my eyes to adjust and then hurried up the stairs to find a seat near the back. I was spotted just as I started to climb.

"Mrs. Washington?" a voice boomed from the ceiling.

I froze and looked around but couldn't tell where the voice originated. The lights suddenly came up, and at the top of the theatre, there was a glass booth, just like at the movie theatre. Peter Castleton was waving at me behind the glass and motioned to indicate he was coming down.

I waited where I was until he and Coach Phillips came through a small door and descended the stairs. When they reached me, Peter Castleton did the introductions. "Samantha Washington, you know Coach Phillips."

We nodded and shook hands.

Coach Phillips was a little taller than me. I estimated his weight at one hundred fifty. I knew from the news that at thirty-seven, he was one of the youngest head football coaches in his division, but given MISU's success during his first season as head coach, he was getting a lot of attention. He always wore a baseball cap, which he tipped when we were introduced. I suspected the cap was an attempt to hide his receding hairline.

The players watched us in relative silence. Peter Castleton faced the group. "Guys, this is Mrs. Washington. She's Dawson's friend and has been trying to help clear him. She'd like to ask you all some questions. I know Coach Phillips and I would really appreciate any help you can provide."

Coach Phillips and Castleton left, along with some other older men I assumed were assistant coaches. I was facing a room full of large men and for a moment, I felt awkward. However, I took a deep breath and reminded myself of the many years, as a high school teacher, when I spoke to students who were a lot more dangerous and probably a lot less interested in what I had to say.

Before I could speak, a large guy who looked like a small tank raised his hand. He was at least four hundred pounds.

"Yes?"

"How's Dawg?"

I scowled. "Dog? You want to know about my dogs?" Surely this guy wasn't asking about Snickers and Oreo.

The group laughed.

"No. Daaawg? You know, Dawson."

Reality dawned. "Oh, I get it. Dawson

is . . . hanging in there."

He beat his chest with his fist twice and then repeated the gesture. "Tell him to stay strong. I don't believe he killed nobody." The small tank took his seat.

"I'm really glad to hear you say that. I don't believe he killed *anyone* either." The English teacher in me couldn't let the grammatical error slide, but it was really the least of my problems. "That's why I'm here. I'm hoping one of you can tell me something that might help prove he didn't kill her."

They looked around at each other, but no one volunteered any information. Finally, my tank friend raised his hand again. "How you gonna do that?"

"Well, right now, I'm just looking for any information you can tell me about Melody or anyone that might have a reason to want to hurt her."

A guy who was smaller than my tank friend, but bigger than a Volkswagen Beetle, said, "Dat girl was a honey trap. Dawg should a stayed clear."

"Did everyone feel like she was a honey trap?"

The guys mumbled amongst themselves. Most nodded.

The Beetle said, "She should a stuck with B Ball."

Several guys laughed

"What do you mean?" I asked.

"She started with the basketball team but got clocked. Guess she decided basketball was too dangerous."

They laughed.

"Wait. Are you saying she used to date a basketball player?"

"Yeah."

One guy who was sitting near the front said, "Man, I forgot 'bout that." He laughed. "She got whipped."

I cringed but quickly wiped all judgment from my face. If I wanted them to be open and honest, I had to create an environment where they felt free to share openly. "What happened?"

Several guys started talking at once, so I held up a hand. "One at a time."

Tank said, "Well, it must a been right after the winter basketball tournament. The men's team won the tournament and then the honeys started sniffing round. Next thing you know, Melody is hooked up with the star forward, Trammel Braxton."

I pulled out a notepad and took notes as quickly as I could.

"So, I heard one day, Trammel and Melody were out at a party when Tray's girlfriend comes up and coldcocks Melody."

"Girlfriend? I thought Melody was his girlfriend?" I said.

Tank laughed. "Apparently, so did she. Unfortunately, Trammel forgot to tell his baby mama."

The players laughed.

"So, this other girl shows up and hits Melody?"

He snorted. "She beat Melody. She beat Trammel. She beat everybody who tried to stop her from beating Trammel and Melody."

Tank was an excellent storyteller, with great facial expressions and body movements to go along with his tale. He burst into laughter at one point. When he pulled himself together, he said, "Man, I ain't never seen no woman fight like that. She whooped them like Muhammad Ali whooped Joe Frazier in the Thrilla in Manilla."

Inside I cringed at the violence. "Anybody know this slugger's name?"

They shook their heads. Tank responded, "Nahw. You gonna need to get that from Trammel."

"Where might I find this Trammel Braxton?" I asked.

"He was staying in those fancy apartments on the lake, but now his girl and baby

183

moved up here, and they're staying in off-campus housing."

One young man who had been relatively quiet throughout most of the conversation finally spoke up. "I can tell you where he lives." He was probably two hundred fifty pounds and about six feet. Compared to the other players, he looked like a shrimp.

I asked a few more questions, but no one had any other suggestions of possible murderers. I wrote my name and e-mail address on a white board near the front of the room. The guys filed out and most sent a message to Dawson to *hang tough, stay strong,* or some other manly message as they left. Some simply pounded their chest like the tank had earlier in a Tarzan gesture.

The shrimp stayed until everyone left. He provided directions to Trammel's apartment.

By the time I got home, it was dark and I felt exhausted. However, I wanted to get some writing done, which would allow my subconscious to sift through the information I'd learned today.

Thompkins had mastered the art of silently entering and leaving rooms. He entered the servants' hall and watched Millie and Flossie unobserved for several minutes. Flossie could barely contain herself as she told Millie what she'd seen.

Thompkins had heard rumors for years about Lord Charles. He knew Lord Charles was a man given to excess. He ate in excess, drank in excess, and pursued women in excess. However, when he was seen by the maid leaving the room of the Duchess of Windsor in the early morning, this was excessive, even for him.

"Gawd, you don't say?"

Millie's shock and surprised expression were everything Flossie could have hoped.

"And that weren't all." Flossie looked around to make sure Mrs. McDuffie wasn't around. "He was wearing pants, but his shirt was unbuttoned, and he was barefoot and carrying his shoes. He was skulking around like a thief in the night."

Millie stared openmouthed. "Oh my, poor Edward. I wonder if he knows."

Thompkins had heard enough. He moved forward and coughed.

Both girls were so engrossed in their conversation they failed to notice his approach.

"Knows what?"

His question caused the girls to jump.

"Nothing, sir," Flossie said.

"Nonsense. If there's something going on, you need to tell me at once."

Thompkins had long ago learned the importance of a stern look. He applied it to good use. Flossie shared what she'd seen with the butler.

He frowned. "You will not discuss what you've seen with anyone. What happens in this house stays in this house. Do you understand?"

"Yes, sir," both girls said.

"Now, get back to work."

The girls turned and returned to their duties.

Thompkins went in search of Mrs. McDuffie. He didn't have to search long. As he passed the small room he used as an office, he heard the distinct voice of the housekeeper.

"Bloomin' 'ell that American upstart has a nerve."

Thompkins sighed, knocked briefly on the door, and then entered.

"Your ladyship. I'm sorry. I didn't realize." Thompkins started to back out.

"Good, Thompkins, I'm so glad you're here. Please come in," Lady Elizabeth said.

The butler entered and closed the door behind him and then stood near the wall.

"I was just sharing with Mrs. McDuffie the changes the Duchess of Windsor has requested."

"Changes, m'lady?"

"Perhaps I should read the request." Lady

186

Elizabeth sighed and picked up a sheet of stationary. " 'My dearest Elizabeth.' "

Mrs. McDuffie snorted.

" 'You've been a real doll for opening your home for my little gathering. As you can see from the guest list, there's a lot at stake, so I know you won't be offended if I make a few small changes.' " Lady Elizabeth scanned the pages and then passed them to Mrs. McDuffie. "Perhaps you had better read them yourself."

Mrs. McDuffie picked up the pages and read. "She wants everyone's rooms changed." She scanned on. "What bloody cheek. She wants that little tart of a maid moved to the blue room what looks out over the back garden." Mrs. McDuffie slammed the paper down. "Well, I'll not do it. I'll not move 'Is Grace out of 'is large room for the likes of that little French strumpet."

Thompkins coughed gently. "May I?" He picked up the pages and read them. Then he gently placed the pages on the table and pulled out his handkerchief and wiped his hands. He turned to Lady Elizabeth and coughed. "If that is what your ladyship would like done, then, of course, we will honor your wishes, but . . ."

"Yes, Thompkins?"

"Well, in addition to the duke's room being slightly larger than the other rooms, it is also closest to the stairs. It is a large help to the staff not to have to carry His Grace's luggage down the hall." Thompkins's lips twitched. "I'm not as young as I used to be."

Lady Elizabeth smiled. "Thank you, Thompkins. I appreciate what you're trying to do." Lady Elizabeth sighed. "I'm okay with permitting the maid to stay near the duchess, if that's what she wants. Do you think the other servants will mind?"

Mrs. McDuffie snorted. "No one will be missing that uppity little piece of baggage. You'd think she's the ruddy duchess, the way she carries on." Mrs. McDuffie stuck her nose in the air and looked down it.

Lady Elizabeth smiled at the housekeeper. She looked at the letter again, and her smile vanished. "Well, that's good, but I agree James shouldn't have to sacrifice his room. He's practically family. I don't really care about the others."

"But it's highly unusual to have women in rooms immediately next to the men, especially when there are connecting doors," Thompkins said.

"I expect having men and women in separate wings is very old-fashioned," Lady Elizabeth said. "I suppose it's a sign of the changing times. We shall have to trust that everyone will behave themselves and there won't be any . . . inappropriate behavior."

Thompkins coughed discreetly and proceeded to tell Lady Elizabeth about the conversation he just had with the two housemaids.

Mrs. McDuffie stared openedmouthed. "Cor blimey."

Lady Elizabeth looked from the butler to the housekeeper. "Do you believe them?"

Mrs. McDuffie's chest heaved and Lady Elizabeth held up a hand to stem her ire. "I'm sure the girls are very honest and trustworthy. I just mean . . . It just seems so . . . I mean it isn't at all what I expected."

Mrs. McDuffie nodded. "I see what you mean. Lord Chitterly isn't the type of man a woman would risk wrecking 'er marriage for?"

"Something like that," Lady Elizabeth said.

Mrs. McDuffie nodded. "Agreed. You mark my words that one isn't about to risk a king for the likes of tubby Lord Chitterly."

Lady Elizabeth suppressed a smile. "I agree with your assessment." She picked up the letter and reread it. "I won't move James. I'll come up with some excuse, but I see no good reason why we shouldn't do the other moves she requested. However, I want to talk to James before we do anything." Lady Elizabeth stood. "So please hold off on the moves until I've had a chance to talk to him."

Lady Elizabeth found James in the library.

He read the note and scowled. "Well, I don't see how it can do any harm, and I'll be happy to move if it —"

She held up her hand. "Please don't feel you have to move. Actually, my housekeeper has flatly refused to move you out of the larger bedroom in favor of . . . 'that French tart.'"

James laughed. "I'll bet that got a reaction out of old Thompkins."

Lady Elizabeth smiled. "Almost, but he maintained his composure. For the peace of my household staff, I shall have to insist you retain your bedroom."

"I want you to know how much I appreciate you agreeing to do this." James hesitated for a moment. "I think you can see how important this is, not only for Great Britain but for the entire world."

"I can, but . . . well, I have to admit I'm slightly confused. I can't believe the king and Parliament are in favor of this . . . gathering."

James was silent for several minutes and then stood. "If you're asking if this assembly is being done at the king's request, the answer is no."

"But then why?"

"Britain's still a free country. We can't prevent people from attending house parties. The country's still recovering from the war and no one wants another one. If there is a peaceful way to prevent it, all the better."

"But you don't believe there is?"

James thought for a moment and then shook his head. "No. I don't. But, there are people like Mary Astor and the 'Cliveden set' who have been trying to negotiate peace."

"Peace, but at what cost?"

"Exactly. Britain can't stand by helplessly with her hands behind her back while Hitler ravages Europe." James smoked. "Plus, word is starting to trickle down about Hitler's true intentions."

Lady Elizabeth waited for him to continue, but he seemed far away. When he finally returned, he shook himself. "But I hope you understand why this is so important. We needed to find out what was going on. That's why . . ."

"That's why you needed them to come here."

"They never would have come to my estate. I'm a bit too close to the throne, I'm afraid. When we heard the duchess was planning this gathering, we needed it to be at a place where we could have access without seeming to condone it. We had heard Lady Emerald Cunard was looking for a country estate for the occasion, but thankfully, she was unable to secure it in time."

"I see. We have a large estate and we're cousins, so we're family, but not too close."

James nodded. "Exactly."

"Plus, William isn't overly involved in politics, which means the duchess can take all of the . . . credit should a deal be made."

Lady Elizabeth folded the letter from the duchess. "I had better instruct the staff to move forward with moving the guests' bedrooms. Everything should be done by the time you all return from shooting." She stood and headed to the door. One hand on the door, she turned back. "James, please be careful. I have a bad feeling about this."

Eventually, the shooting party left. There were twelve in all. Geoffrey Fordham-Baker elected to remain in the library with a bottle of scotch. Lady Elizabeth and Lady Penelope also chose to forego the shooting. Thompkins brought the tea tray into the library. Geoffrey Fordham-Baker snored in a chair in the corner while the ladies drank tea.

"I am rather surprised Daphne chose to go shooting," Penelope said.

Lady Elizabeth sipped her tea. "Well, she is rather a good shot."

"I know. She was always a much better shot than me, but she never really seemed to enjoy the cold, the mud, or anything else about it."

Lady Elizabeth smiled. "I know what you

192

mean. She did buy a new outfit, and James hasn't seen how well she can shoot."

Penelope smiled. "True. You know, she isn't really as vain and frivolous as she seems."

"Well, she may be vain, but she has brains and I think she's found a reason to use them."

"What do you mean?"

Lady Elizabeth set down her cup and took out her knitting. "Well, I believe she is truly in love for the first time, and I think she realizes that a duke needs a wife who can be a credit to him in his career. James isn't just part of the idle rich. He's an important person with political aspirations, and I think she realizes his wife will need to do more than host tea parties and look pretty."

Penelope stared at her aunt. "I think you're right. I really do hope things work out between them."

Lady Elizabeth paused in her knitting. "I just hope this weekend doesn't backfire."

"I've had an awful feeling about this whole thing. I know Victor is worried too. He thinks —"

Lady Penelope never got an opportunity to say what Victor thought because, at that minute, Thompkins abruptly entered the library.

"Excuse me, your ladyship, but there has been a terrible accident."

"What kind of accident?" Lady Elizabeth asked.

"Someone's been shot."

All color left Penelope's face. "Victor?"

"No, m'lady. I believe it's the Duchess of Windsor."

CHAPTER 12

I stayed up late writing and my brain wasn't functioning on all cylinders, even after two cups of coffee. At least that was my excuse. If I'd been well rested when my sister called and asked what I was doing today, I would have asked *why* before responding. I'd learned to be cautious with Jenna over the years. When the twins were younger, that question would have been followed up with a request to babysit while she went to the movies, a concert, or shopping. Rarely did the question *what are you doing* include an invitation to the interesting activity. Of course, now the twins were adults, her previous requests for babysitting were now replaced with requests to take her place with unpleasant activities she had committed to do with our mom; *I have a really important court case I have to prep for and was wondering if you could take Mom to the license bureau/dentist/podiatrist/etc.* My sleep-deprived state was the reason I was now sitting at the police station. Part of her negotiations to get me to come included a large turtle caramel nut latte and a glazed donut from a gourmet coffee shop.

I sipped my expensive coffee in the same room Nana Jo and I had sat in just five days earlier. "I'm not sure why you need me here."

"I've never met this A-squared person. You have a relationship with him."

I nearly choked. "A relationship? He broke into my store and got into a fight with Dawson. I hardly call that a relationship."

"It's more interaction than I've had." She sipped her tea. "Besides, he looks sleazy."

I stared at her. "You're at the police station. He's not likely to attack you."

"I'm not worried about him attacking me. I can take care of myself. I just don't want to be alone with him."

"If you're looking for a bodyguard, you should have invited Nana Jo. She's the one who's packing heat."

We both grinned.

A police officer escorted A-squared into the conference room. "You want me to stay?"

Jenna shook her head. "No, you can leave."

He nodded. "You know the drill. Call if you need us."

Alex Alexander, or A-squared, looked the same as he did on television. He was dirty. His clothes and hair were greasy. He smelled like a distillery, sweat, and vomit, which made the room seem even smaller.

"So, what can I do for you?" He propped his feet on the table and leaned back in his chair with his hands behind his head. The maneuver released a musk which had been trapped under his armpits, and I fought the desire to gag.

"The first thing you can do is put your arms down. You stink," Jenna said.

A-squared laughed and I thought he wasn't going to do it. I gave him my sternest schoolmarm stare, which did wonders with derelicts and delinquents. Jenna might not have been a teacher, but she had a fierce lawyer stare that caused criminals to cower in their boots. At least it made me want to cower. The combination seemed to work because he lowered his arms and chair and removed his feet.

"Thank you," Jenna said.

"Who're you?"

"My name is Jenna Rutherford. I'm the lawyer representing your son. He asked me to talk to you."

"Yeah? What about?"

"Well, he's concerned about you. He saw you on television and —"

"He saw that?" He laughed. "I was pretty good, huh? I'm a movie star. I saw him on television last night too. Not too flattering to his ole man, but . . ." He shrugged. "Everybody needs fifteen minutes of fame."

"Mr. Alexander, I —"

"Call me A-squared. Everybody does. Alex Alexander. Get it? A-squared."

Jenna was frustrated. "Okay. A-squared, your son is concerned because you implied you know who murdered Melody."

"Yep."

"You need to tell the police. This is a dangerous game you're playing," she said.

He smiled. "I'll be happy to tell the police everything." He paused and leaned forward. "But there has to be somethin' in it for me."

"Mr. . . . ah, A-squared. If you know who killed Melody Hardwick, you need to tell someone. It's illegal to withhold information about a felony."

He shook himself. "Oooh, I'm shakin' in my boots. What're they gonna do, arrest me?"

"The police are *not* going to pay you to tell them who killed Melody Hardwick. What they're going to do is throw your butt in jail and leave you there."

"Won't be the first time." He stretched. "Three hots and a cot."

Jenna's face could be very expressive. She stared at me with a "can you believe this idiot" look.

I tried to get through to him. "You have to see this is a dangerous business you're playing at. There's a killer out there who thinks you know who he or she is. You could be in danger."

"I can take care of myself. Been doin' it my whole life."

"The police believe Dawson killed her. If you don't tell them what you know, he could get convicted for murder." I doubted he possessed any parental emotions, especially considering how he'd beaten Dawson, but he was definitely concerned about money. "And, if he's convicted for murder, there goes all hope of a professional football career."

He shook his head. "Never happen. I'll never let my boy get hooked for a crime he didn't commit. That's why I went on TV. Besides, he's got you." He pointed toward Jenna. "It's your job to get him off."

Jenna stared at him as though she'd like nothing better than to leap over that table and throttle him. Instead she said, "Even the best lawyers can't guarantee an acquittal."

"He's not goin' to jail." He tapped his chest. "I got a plan that'll set us up for the rest of our lives."

Jenna narrowed her eyes. "I hope you don't mean what I think you mean."

He laughed. "No idea what you're talkin' 'bout, but I think we're done with this little talk." He stood.

"Don't you want to know how your son is doing?" I asked.

A-squared turned to face me and grinned. "How could he be anything but great with you two lookin' after him. Besides, you would a told me if he weren't okay."

Jenna buzzed for the police and they came promptly and removed A-squared.

We sat for several moments and stared at each other. Then we spontaneously burst into laughter.

"If I hadn't seen this with my own eyes, I wouldn't believe it," Jenna said.

"He's like a caricature of a real human being."

"That's why I wanted you here. I'm an attorney and I've dealt with some real lowlifes over the years. But this guy takes the cake." She paused. "Let's get out of here."

We left the police station and went to a

nearby coffee shop. Jenna needed a tea refill. We sat at a small table near the window and picked up our conversation where we'd left off.

"I've been thinking about why A-squared bothers me so much. I think this whole thing bothers me more because of Dawson."

"I know what you mean. It's different when you know the people personally."

She nodded. "I can distance myself from my clients, but this is very different. Dawson is practically family. Heck, he is family."

I allowed myself a moment of misty-eyed sentimentality and then my phone buzzed. It was a text message from Jillian informing me she had coordinated a memorial service for Melody for tomorrow.

I told Jenna about the memorial service and immediately received another text. This one was from Emma. She'd received a text from a woman named Cassidy Logan claiming to be Melody's half sister.

I read the text to Jenna.

"Half sister? Nana Jo didn't mention anything about a half sister."

"I know. I don't think Emma should meet with anyone alone. I'm going to tell her to hold off before responding." I typed the response and received an *Okay*.

"This is odd. I don't —"

My phone vibrated again.

"You're awfully popular," Jenna said.

I looked at my phone and my heart skipped a beat. "I totally forgot."

"Forgot what?"

I paused and took a deep breath before responding. "I forgot I agreed to meet someone."

I'm not sure if it was the blood I could feel rushing up my neck or the fact I was struggling to make eye contact that gave me away.

"Who did you agree to meet?" Jenna asked with a smirk.

"Just a professor I met on campus yesterday." I hurried to add, "He was one of Melody's professors, and I questioned him about her. He's British. So, I thought maybe he could help me with some of the details for my book. It's always good if I can add real details," I babbled.

"Hmm, a British professor. Interesting." Jenna grinned and sipped her tea.

"I barely know the guy. It's just research. That's all."

" 'The lady doth protest too much, methinks.' " Jenna quoted Shakespeare and took another sip of her tea.

I stuck out my tongue.

She laughed but then leaned forward and

stared. "Where is he taking you for this . . . ah . . . research?"

I looked at my phone. "I don't know."

"I hope you're going to do something about your hair."

"What's wrong with my hair?"

"Do you want it straight or sugarcoated?"

I stared at my sister. "Sugarcoated."

"Well, it's dull and lifeless. You've got split ends and the style does nothing for your face. Your eyebrows need to be arched. Most people have two. Yours are so thick and bushy you look like Oscar the Grouch. Plus, your makeup needs to come into the twenty-first century."

"If that's the sugarcoated version, I'd hate to hear it straight."

"The truth will set you free."

"The King James Version says 'the truth will MAKE you free,' *not* set."

"Whatever."

My feelings were hurt by Jenna's comments, but my sister was honest if nothing else — brutally honest. I wanted to lash out and say something critical about the way she looked, but I couldn't. Her hair and makeup were always flawless. Jenna never wore much makeup, but she always looked polished and professional. With no way to relieve the sting of her words, I resorted to sulking. "It's not a date."

"It doesn't matter whether it's a date or not. You don't have to do your hair and makeup to impress a man. You should do it for yourself. You used to dress better and take care of yourself, but ever since Leon died, you've just let yourself go."

"You've been talking to Mom."

"Doesn't mean it isn't true." She smiled kindly. "Look, your birthday is coming up and I was going to suggest we do a spa day. Why don't we do things a little early and see if we can get a little pampering. My treat."

"Geez. I must really look bad if you want to send me on a spa day."

"I'm pleading the fifth."

Jenna picked up her phone and made a few calls. She got us both in for manicures and pedicures, plus a hair and makeup session for me and a massage for herself.

North Harbor Spa was a beautifully relaxing facility located atop the North Harbor Inn. North Harbor only had fifteen thousand people. The location on the shores of Lake Michigan and the addition of the new senior professional golf course had made the town a popular summer vacation spot, despite its economically depressed condition. Small boutique hotels dotted the coastline. North Harbor Inn was a newer building and this was my first time going inside.

On a rare instance when I splurged for a manicure, I went to a small beauty college. The technicians weren't licensed, but prices were low. Results weren't optimal, but I didn't expect much for five dollars. According to Jenna, the experience of being pampered was worth the extra money. Here, soft music played in the background. No televisions were tuned to soap operas or Jerry Springer, and the pedicure chairs weren't lined up against the wall like suspects in a police lineup.

Jenna exaggerated when she accused me of having the Oscar the Grouch unibrow, but it had been a long time since I'd last arched them. My brows were thick and in need of pruning.

Jenna introduced me to her hairdresser and gave her carte blanche to make me beautiful.

Marika laughed at the look of terror in my eyes. "Don't worry. I take good care of you. I won't do anything to you I wouldn't do to myself."

I was even more terrified since her hair was electric blue and cut into an asymmetrical bob and shaved on one side. I decided to trust her. Jenna's hair looked nice. Marika permed, colored, conditioned, cut the split ends, and styled my hair. The dye hid my gray and she used caramel highlights. Between the brow waxing and hair change, my eyes looked huge. I barely recognized myself in the mirror and couldn't help smiling. My hair had bounce and shine and was so soft I kept touching it.

By the time the makeup artist came by, I was excited. She asked me a few questions about my daily makeup routine and then went to work. She explained everything as she went along and by the time she'd finished, I looked ten years younger. Neutral foundation and lip gloss with a smoky eye shadow that made my brown eyes pop.

I looked like me, only better. Best of all, I felt beautiful. Both Jenna and I were pleased with the final results.

"You look awesome."

I was in danger of bursting into tears, so I hugged my sister and whispered, "Thank you."

She smiled. "Happy birthday. Now, you're ready for your not-a-date research dinner."

I felt guilty for taking a half day on pampering, but I kept looking at myself in the mirror and smiling as I drove to MISU.

Emma and I were scheduled to meet at the student union. I found her sitting at a table by the window.

"Wow. You look amazing. I almost didn't recognize you."

I laughed. "Thank you." I sat down. "I think."

"I'm sorry. I didn't mean to imply that you —"

I held up my hand. "No need to apologize. Now, tell me about this half sister, Cassidy Logan."

"I'm afraid I don't know much." Emma pulled out her phone. "I did what you suggested and reached out to the university about her belongings. They gave her my number and she sent me a text." Emma pulled up the text message on her phone.

I read the string. "Doesn't sound like she and Melody were very close." I scrolled back and reread it, trying not to read tone into the sparse words.

"Nope. Sure doesn't. I mean if my sister was murdered, I'd be a basket case. I don't think I'd be asking for an inventory of her belongings so I can determine if it's worth my while to come pick them up."

"Well, she is a half sister," I said weakly.

Emma shrugged. "So."

"She said they weren't close."

"What do you want me to do?" she asked.

I pondered the question. "She's in Chicago. That's only an hour and a half away. Tell her you have a friend who will bring the items to her if she'll send you the address."

Emma picked up her phone and sent the message. We didn't have to wait long for the reply.

"She sent her address." Emma forwarded the message to me.

We went back to her dorm room and packed away Melody's few belongings. It seemed sad that all of her worldly goods fit into an old backpack Emma said she didn't need any longer. I thought about Melody and wondered where she kept her other belongings. Each time I'd seen her, she had on a different outfit and a lot of makeup. I put the backpack in my car. Since I was on campus, I decided to swing by the off-campus housing and pay a visit to Trammel Braxton.

Construction at MISU was never ending. Buildings were erected, renovated, or remodeled constantly. A few years ago, the off-campus housing for married couples and graduate students looked like a smaller version of Chicago's Cabrini-Green housing projects during the 1970s. The last of those buildings were demolished in 2011 and the MISU buildings met the same fate a couple of years ago. The new buildings looked like East Coast brownstone row houses with brick fronts and porches.

I found the one I wanted, parked, and tried to come up with a plausible cover story. I finally came up with something and got out of the car. I was so focused on the story running through in my head I was oblivious to everything else. As I got to the sidewalk, I was blindsided by a child on a Big Wheel being chased by a golden retriever and a very pregnant woman.

I avoided falling over by holding onto the Big Wheel. I held on until the child's mother caught up.

She was breathing heavily from hurrying down the street. "I'm so sorry. I hope he didn't hurt you. He just broke away from me and in my condition, I couldn't catch him." She looked extremely young, not more than eighteen with a dark olive complexion and dark hair and eyes.

"No harm done." I smiled. "He's adorable."

The boy was extremely cute. He had dark skin and jet-black curly hair, dark eyes, and chubby cheeks.

She smiled. "Thank you." She turned to

the boy. "Now it's nap time."

He let out a howl and would have taken off again if I hadn't bent down and scooped him up.

"You're going to be a good boy for your mama," I said in a soothing voice, which might have worked if the mother hadn't reached to take him.

He immediately started to kick and squirm.

I gasped, afraid he'd kick her stomach, but she must have been accustomed to this behavior because she turned to avoid a direct frontal kick just in time. She grabbed him by the waist and pulled, but my new companion must have also known what was coming because he wrapped both hands tightly around my neck and refused to let go, regardless of how much the mother pulled.

I winced as he grasped my hair in addition to my neck. "Maybe it would be better if I carried him in for you?" I suggested. "You seem to have your hands full, and I think two heads are better than one in this situation."

The little mother looked at me tentatively. However, I must have passed her scrutiny of not being a crazed child-napping serial killer because she nodded and gave a polite smile.

"If you're sure you don't mind?" She reached down and picked up the golden's leash and the Big Wheel while she balanced a large diaper bag on her other shoulder.

"I don't mind at all." I looked around. "Just lead the way." I stepped aside to allow her to get in front. I hid my surprise when she went to the wrought iron fence in front of me and walked up the stairs. This was the home of Trammel Braxton, just where I wanted to go.

She unlocked the door and stepped aside for me to enter. The living room was sparsely furnished with a cheap sofa in front of the window, two foldaway chairs, and a massive flat panel television with cords and controllers hanging off like tentacles on an octopus.

She put down the Big Wheel and released the dog from his leash and then tried again to get her son away from me. However, he still wasn't ready to let go and let out a bloodcurdling scream, which would have the neighbors believing a murder was occurring.

An embarrassed flush rose up her neck and she had a determined set to her eyes and chin which wouldn't bode well for the little guy if he didn't release me soon.

"Perhaps you'll let me put him to bed. I could read him a story." I tried to pull away far enough to look into his eyes. "Would you like me to read you a story?"

"Yes." He sniffed.

She nodded and led the way upstairs to a small nursery.

The nursery was decorated in a superhero theme with Superman soaring overhead through clouds which had been painted onto the ceiling. The room had a crib, dresser, rocker, and large rug. The floor was littered with toys. One wall had a small bookshelf and there were several books I remembered reading to my nephews when they were small. I turned sideways so my new appendage could see the books. "Which book do you want me to read?"

He looked up and pointed to a book which looked to have seen a lot of wear if the frayed corners and crayon marks were any indication.

"*Panda Bear's Paint Box.* I remember reading this to my nephews when they were little boys, just like you." I picked up the book and walked over to the rocker. I sat down. My companion turned so he could sit and see the pages of the book. He stuck his thumb in his mouth and leaned back against my chest as I read.

If the mother had hesitations about me, I think they evaporated as she watched me rock and read to her son. He was asleep before I finished the last page and I quietly got up and walked to the crib. I gently placed him in the crib and pulled the covers up over him.

"He's out like a light," I whispered.

She looked at her son and smiled. "He'll sleep like the dead now," she said in her normal tone. She turned to me. "Thank you."

"It was my pleasure."

We left the room and went downstairs.

"He's normally so good, but lately, he has fits and tantrums." She rubbed her belly. "Especially now he knows I'm slower and can't react as fast as before." She looked at me. "I do appreciate your help. I don't even know your name."

"My name's Samantha Washington, but, please, call me Sam."

She smiled. "Thank you, Sam. I'm Mariana Braxton."

She walked to the door to let me out. "I hope we didn't keep you."

"Actually, I was coming to see you and your husband, Trammel, that is."

She stopped and stared. "Do we know you?"

"No. I was hoping you could help me."

She looked skeptical and folded her arms across her chest. "Well, Trammel isn't here at the moment. Maybe you'd prefer to come back when he is." Her voice and body language indicated all barriers were now up and in place, and if I didn't do something quick, I'd be outside in less than two seconds.

"Mrs. Braxton, could I sit down for one moment? I just want to ask you a few questions and then I'll leave. I promise."

Whether it was the sincerity in my eyes or memories of me holding her son, it worked. She nodded and indicated I could sit on the sofa. She pulled over a folding chair and sat.

"Would you prefer —"

She waved away my protest. "It's a lot easier for me to get up and down on this chair than it is on that sofa." She patted her stomach. "Now, what questions do you want to ask me?"

I settled back down. "Well, I'm a friend of Dawson Alexander."

She had a vacant look on her face that indicated she had no idea who Dawson Alexander was.

"He's the football player accused of killing Melody Hardwick."

Based on the way she pursed her lips and rolled her eyes, it was clear she recognized Melody's name. "What do you want from me, a medal?"

"He didn't do it. Dawson didn't kill her. I was hoping you could help me figure out who might want her dead."

"Other than me, you mean?" She rose from her chair. "If you think I killed that gold digger, you've got another think coming."

"Please, Mrs. Braxton. I'm not accusing you of killing her." I pointed to her stomach. "It's pretty clear that would be impossible in your condition."

That settled her down and she returned to her seat. I wasn't so naive as to believe a pregnant woman couldn't have killed someone, but Melody was in pretty good shape and would have put up a struggle.

"Well, I don't know how you think I can help."

"Just tell me what you know about Melody. I'm trying to understand her character and so few people know anything about her. No one was really close to her. I was hoping you . . ." I looked down. "Or your husband might be able to tell me something that might help prevent an innocent man from paying for a crime he didn't commit."

She settled back. "I only saw her once. If you're here, someone told you what happened."

I nodded. "Yes, but I'd like to hear your side of the story, if you don't mind sharing."

She took a deep breath. "Trammel and I dated in high school. That's when I got pregnant with our son. Tray was a star basketball player, the best in the state. He got offers all over the country, but he came to MISU because it was close by. I was two years behind him in school and my parents wanted me to finish high school. He came home to see me almost every weekend when he didn't have a game, especially after the baby was born. He loved little Tray." She smiled. "We were going to get married as soon as he graduated. But his sophomore year he stopped calling and didn't visit as much. I got suspicious. He *said* everything was fine. He was just tired or studying. But he was never that into books. All he ever wanted was to play ball. So, I came to see for myself." She paused. "At first his roommate didn't want to tell me where he was, but he finally did. They were together and she was all over him." Her face hardened.

"I snapped. I tried to beat the crap out of her. How dare she think she was gonna come and take my man." She took several seconds to recapture her composure. "I'd invested years into that man. He wasn't about to leave me and our son for some no-account gold digger. Oh, no." Her chest heaved and her eyes flashed. "So, yeah, I tried to kill her. It took Trammel and two other men to pull me off her."

"What happened next?"

"I told Trammel if he thought he was about to leave me and our son for her, then he was next. I was so angry."

"I can understand that."

"Trammel apologized. He had a good thing and if he didn't want to lose me, he better straighten up and fly right." She smiled.

"That's when you moved here?"

"He said he didn't want anyone but me, and we got married a couple weeks later. I figured it would be better if I was here on campus in case anyone else tried to get their claws on my man."

"And you never saw Melody again?"

She shook her head. "Probably a good thing too."

I hesitated but decided I needed the truth. "Do you know if Trammel saw her again?"

She shook her head. "I don't think so. I told him if I heard he so much as looked at her again, I'd beat both of them next time." She giggled.

"Do you know of anyone else that might have wanted to kill her?"

She thought for a minute. "Not unless she tried to take somebody else's man."

I thanked Mrs. Braxton for her help and left. It was getting late and I still needed to get dressed for my non-date.

When I returned to the bookstore, Chris and Zaq were closing up for the day.

Nana Jo stopped sweeping and stared. "Sam. You look amazing. I love the hair."

Chris and Zaq seconded the compliments, which gave a huge boost to my ego.

There was only one customer in the store. When he turned around, I saw it was Frank Patterson, the owner of the restaurant down the street.

"Sam, you remember Frank." Nana Jo smiled as she guided Mr. Patterson toward me. "Doesn't Sam look beautiful?"

I tried to kill my grandmother with my eyes, but I hadn't yet mastered that trick. So, I scowled at her and then plastered a fake smile on my face.

He had a hand full of books and juggled them to shake hands. "Yes. She looks lovely."

"Are you a mystery lover, Mr. Patterson?"

"Please, call me Frank," he said. "Well, I don't know if I'd say I like mysteries as much as thrillers. Are those the same?"

"Not always, although they can be. Every mystery doesn't have to be a thriller, but it can be."

"I tend to go for spy stories. I like Ian Fleming and John Le Carré."

I indicated the pile of books in his arms. "I see Nana Jo has introduced you to a few new authors." I glanced at the titles of the books in his arms. "Have you read Marc Cameron? I think you might like him."

We spent a little time talking about thrillers, and he purchased his books. Frank Patterson was a nice man. If I were interested in dating, I would consider him. However, I wasn't dating, so the point was moot. When he was gone and the store locked up, I hurried upstairs and quickly went through practically everything in my closet trying to find something to wear to my non-date. The restaurant Professor Quin had selected wasn't super fancy but it was nicer than most of my clothes. Jeans and a nice shirt would be appropriate or a dress. But, a dress might imply I was looking at this as more than just a research non-date opportunity. I didn't want to look too eager, nor did I want to look slovenly. My new hair and makeup made my clothes look shabby. However, I did have one nice pair of jeans, a gift from Jenna two birthdays ago. They fit beautifully, but I rarely wore them. I could tell they were expensive and I'd saved them for special occasions. Tonight qualified.

I also had a pair of nice wedge shoes I loved because they were comfortable with a peep toe, which would show just enough of my pedicure and also raised me high enough that my jeans didn't drag the ground. My bottom half was set, but my shirts were faded out or stained. I was just about to give up and change to a dress when I noticed the pink bag at the back of my closet. I dug it out and found the cashmere sweater my mother shamed me into buying. I pulled the white cashmere sweater on and looked at myself in the mirror. The sweater looked fantastic with the dark-washed jeans and wedges. It was soft and felt like silk against my skin. It hugged my curves without being too tight and landed at just the right place on my hips.

I went into the kitchen. Nana Jo and Dawson sat at the table. When Dawson came to live with me, he had been on academic probation. As a former mathematics teacher, Nana Jo tutored him in math while I tutored him in English.

Nana Jo whistled like a New Yorker hailing a cab. "Wow, you look great. I don't think I've ever seen you wear that sweater before. Is it new?"

"Yeah. Mom talked me into getting it last Sunday." Was it only a week ago that I'd gone shopping with my mom? A lot had happened in a short period of time.

"Well, she was right. That sweater looks divine. Is that cashmere?" She rubbed it. "Yep. You can always tell the real stuff."

"You look amazing Mrs. W," Dawson said.

The compliments boosted my courage. I left with a smile and headed to my non-date research dinner.

Lake Michigan Grill was a South Harbor restaurant located near the beach. It was only about a mile from my building. We'd agreed to meet at the restaurant and he was there when I arrived.

"You look lovely," he said. "I like your hair."

"Thank you. My sister thought I needed a makeover."

"Well, I like both versions." He smiled.

The hostess showed us to our table.

He ordered a glass of wine when the waitress came by. I wasn't much of a wine drinker, but Lake Michigan Grill served one of the local wines made just up the road. The climate and soil on the southwestern shore of Lake Michigan made it an ideal location for winemaking. One of our local wines was even served at the White House. I ordered the Classic Demi-sec.

"Professor Quin, I really appreciate your agreeing to help me with my research."

"Please, call me Harley." He smiled.

I was thankful the lighting was dim because my face became heated. Thirty-something-year-old women shouldn't blush when they went out on non-dates.

"Thank you, Harley. Please call me Sam." I pulled a small notebook out of my purse. "Now, I've been thinking about what questions to ask you."

"Certainly. Perhaps you should start by telling me a little about the book you're writing."

So I did. He asked a lot of questions and I found myself doing the majority of the talking. The waitress came and took our orders and he asked more questions. Normally, I didn't talk about my writing. It was still very private, but Harley asked the right types of questions. He knew a lot about mysteries and was an Agatha Christie fan. I could talk about mysteries for hours and found that I had. Several hours later, I looked over and noticed we were the last people in the restaurant and the staff was waiting patiently for us to leave.

"What time is it?"

He looked at his watch. "Eleven thirty."

"They close at eleven. I didn't realize how quickly the time passed."

He reached for the check, but I was quicker. "This is on me. After all, you're helping me with my research. This is the least I can do."

He smiled. "I'm glad to help."

I pulled out my credit card and our waitress immediately came to take care of the check. I'm sure she wasn't allowed to leave until we left and was probably anxious to see the back of us. She returned promptly and I left a generous tip to compensate for her time.

Outside, Harley walked me to my car.

"I very much enjoyed talking to you. I'm not sure I answered all of your questions, though. Perhaps we should try again," he said with a sly smile.

I laughed. "Perhaps we should."

He took my hand, bowed low, and kissed it.

My knees started to buckle the tiniest bit as I got into the car. I was grateful he didn't try to kiss me. I'd enjoyed the evening, but kissing a man other than Leon was something I wasn't quite ready for yet. Although, as I drove home, I thought maybe there might be a time in the near future when I might be ready.

Once I got home, I was still very excited. Maybe there was room for a James Bond who looked like Sean Connery in 1938 England. I decided a little writing would help me settle down before I went to sleep.

Lady Elizabeth and Penelope stared at the butler in shock.

James hurried past the butler into the library and closed the doors behind him. "Quickly, there's very little time. I've already called the police. Has anyone else come by here?"

Both ladies shook their heads.

He turned to Thompkins. "Make sure no one leaves this house."

The butler nodded, turned, and left.

"Oh, James. What are we going to do? Someone has to break the news to David. He's going to be devastated. Is she going to live?"

James looked surprised. "David?"

"Yes, her husband, Edward the VIII," Lady Elizabeth said with a slight frown. "I thought you knew all the family call him David."

"I know, but Wallis isn't the one who's been shot. It was her maid, Rebecca."

Lady Elizabeth and Penelope stared at each other. "Thompkins just told us it was the duchess who'd been shot." She sighed. "I know I shouldn't be relieved, but I must confess I am. I certainly didn't fancy having to explain to the king his sister-in-law was shot at my home."

Penelope stared. "I wonder how Thompkins got things so wrong."

"Easy to do. The maid was wearing the duchess's clothes. Apparently she didn't have appropriate clothing for shooting, so the duchess gave her some of her things. They were dressed almost exactly alike. It wasn't until we got a close look at the body that we discovered the mistake."

Lady Elizabeth gasped. "Will the maid be alright?"

James looked grim. "I'm afraid not. She's dead."

The local constables arrived to secure the scene and wait for Scotland Yard. The shooting party returned in groups. Daphne and Lord Charles and Lady Abigail Chitterly came back together. Lord Charles seemed to be especially shaken up and required a stiff drink immediately upon arrival. Lady Abigail was remarkably well composed and sat quietly in the library.

Daphne looked a little pale, but she walked straight to the sofa where Penelope and Lady Elizabeth were seated. When she reached her aunt, she whispered, "The duchess was so distraught she fainted and had to be carried in by Count Rudolph."

Lady Elizabeth rose immediately and left the room.

Victor, Virginia Hall, and the Polish ambassador, Józef Lipski, were the next to arrive. They stood quietly near the window and whispered.

Lord William was the last to arrive as he had stayed to talk to the gamekeeper and the police, but quickly left.

The gathering in the library was grim. Lady Penelope looked to Victor. He caught her eye and smiled.

Daphne took her aunt's place on the sofa next to her sister.

Penelope took her sister's hand. "Are you okay?"

Daphne nodded. "I'm fine. I mean, it's not as though I knew her, but it's awful that it happened here, again."

Penelope nodded. She shuddered at the recollection of stumbling across Charles Parker's body, six months ago. Parker had been brutally stabbed. "Was it horrible?"

"No. It wasn't like . . . like before. She was shot in the back."

The sisters sat quietly for several seconds before Penelope asked the unspoken question on everyone's minds. "It was an accident, wasn't it?"

Daphne paused before responding. "I don't know. But, I wonder . . ."

"What?"

"I wonder if it was an accident, what kind of accident it was."

Penelope scowled. "I don't understand."

"Was the accident that a woman was shot? Or was the accident that the wrong woman was shot?"

"I see. James did tell us she was wearing Wallis's clothes. But surely it was merely an honest mistake. Accidents happen during shooting parties. It could have been a bad shot."

Daphne stared at her sister. "True. Accidents do happen, but if it was an accident, why is no one stepping forward? No one would blame them."

"Do you mean no one knows who shot her?"

Daphne nodded.

"But surely loaders or the beaters saw who . . ."

Daphne shook her head. "No one claims to have seen anything."

Penelope stared aghast. "That's impossible. You were all paired off, right? Surely someone was with her."

"She was paired off with Wallis, Count Rudolph, and Brasseur. They claim she said she was cold and wet and was heading back to the house."

"But where was she found?"

"In the marsh."

Penelope stared openmouthed. "But that's the total opposite direction from the house. It's not surprising she was shot if she was in the marsh. That's the direction everyone would be shooting. Why, that's suicide."

Daphne nodded. "They said she started walking toward the house. No one knows why she changed direction or why she went toward the shooting. It's awful."

James entered the library and stood for a few moments. He looked around, made eye contact with Daphne, and then strode purposely toward her. "Where's your aunt?"

Penelope rose to leave but James motioned for her to stay.

"She's seeing to the duchess. She fainted."

He looked around impatiently. "Look, I've got to run up to London."

"What about the police?" Daphne asked.

"If I wait to talk to the police, it'll be hours before I can go. I'm not sure . . . ."

Daphne stared at him for several seconds. "If you go down the back stairs, you can get out by the servants' entrance."

"Cut through the back to our house, and Victor's car is in the garage. He keeps the keys in the visor," Penelope added. "I know he won't mind."

James squeezed Penelope's hand in thanks and absentmindedly kissed Daphne's forehead before hurrying out.

Moments later, Lord William entered the library with a constable.

The constable stood at the door to the library. "We appreciate everyone's patience. However, I'm going to need to ask you all to bear with us a little longer. Someone from the Yard will be here shortly to take your statements. Thank you."

A low murmur started as guests whispered to each other.

Lord William walked over to his nieces. "Bloody bureaucratic falderal. Chap won't tell me what's happening in my own house."

Daphne and Penelope smiled at their uncle.

Daphne stood. "Would you like a glass of port? I think you deserve it."

Lord William smiled fondly. "I could use a bit of a drink. Thank you, dear."

He looked around. His favorite chair was occupied by Fordham-Baker, who was nodding off with a nearly empty bottle of his best scotch on the table nearby.

Daphne returned and handed the glass to her uncle.

"Thank you." He gulped down the liquid.

Thompkins entered the room with a tea cart. He looked around briefly and then rolled the cart to Daphne and Penelope. "Her ladyship thought everyone might like some tea and sandwiches."

Daphne and Penelope poured tea and offered sandwiches. Lord Charles looked as though he couldn't stomach the idea of eating but accepted a glass of port in lieu of tea. Lady Abigail, however, said she was famished and ate enough sandwiches and scones for both she and her husband.

The other guests declined food but accepted the tea graciously.

The atmosphere was strained and Penelope was just about to see if her aunt needed help with the duchess when the door finally opened. The constable returned with a tall man, who was lean and gangly with thick curly hair.

"Good afternoon. My name is Detective Inspector Covington from Scotland Yard." He looked around the room. He hurried over to Lord William, smiled big, and shook his hand. "Lord William, I came as soon as I heard."

"It's good to see you again, although, well, I don't mean with another murder, but . . . oh, dash it all, man. This is bad timing."

Detective Inspector Covington nodded. "Quite. Quite. Where's the Duchess of Windsor now?"

"Upstairs in her room. Fainted when she heard about her maid."

"Can you take me to her?" He followed Lord William upstairs.

Lady Elizabeth came out of the bedroom and saw Lord William and Detective Inspector Covington.

"Detective Inspector Covington, how nice to see you again."

"I wish it were under better circumstances." The detective suppressed a smile and looked around cautiously. "How is she?"

"She's had a shock. Dr. Haygood just arrived. I believe he's given her a sedative. She'll rest and I'm sure she'll be fine."

Detective Inspector Covington's shoulders relaxed and he released a sigh. "Well, that's certainly good news." He looked around again. "We don't have much time. Someone from the Home Office is coming down to handle this case personally. Is there any chance the maid was the intended victim?"

Lord William pondered the question and shrugged. "I don't know."

Another constable hurried down the hall to the small group. "Sir, take a look at this."

Detective Inspector Covington unfolded the sheet of stationery and read. When he finished, his eyes were large and his hands had a slight tremor.

Before the detective could say anything, Thompkins walked in, in a quiet, yet determined manner. He stopped at the group and said to Lady Elizabeth, "Telephone, your ladyship. It's the king."

Detective Inspector Covington's eyes looked as though they would pop out of his head. "Sweet mother of God."

CHAPTER 13

It is a truth universally acknowledged that anyone who owns a pet and thinks they will get to sleep later on the weekend than on weekdays must be delusional, especially if said pet is a twelve-year-old pampered poodle. For some reason, ever since daylight savings kicked in, Oreo now woke at three every morning to go outside. Despite the fact I'd only gone to bed about an hour earlier, I got up and opened his crate and made the trek downstairs. Snickers's bladder wasn't on the same schedule. She slept through this excursion.

He found his favorite spot near the fence line and did his business and then trotted back up the stairs and was snoring by the time I got back in bed.

Sleep evaded me. I tossed and turned and turned and tossed and finally gave up trying. I wasn't in a mood for more writing, so I pulled out a notebook and tried to make sense of all of the information we'd collected about Melody Hardwick.

I rolled the conversation with Mariana over and over in my mind. She was definitely a passionate individual. She'd gotten in a physical fistfight with Melody, so I knew she was capable of violence. However, I just wasn't sure her violent streak extended to murder. Maybe if she felt her family was in jeopardy, she might murder, but I doubted she would plan a cold-blooded murder. Of course, I could be wrong. She might have been lying. Maybe the relationship between Trammel and Melody wasn't over. However, my gut told me she was telling the truth, but I wasn't willing to bet Dawson's future on it.

Virgil Russell was a slimy lowlife. He was, according to Dawson, in an intimate relationship with the daughter of the man he'd murdered. That was weird. Although, based on what Ruby Mae said, he had been guilty of sexual extortion. His relationship with Melody could have been extortion rather than consensual.

Melody's half sister was another strange cog in the wheel. Where did she come from? No one knew anything about her, and she seemed to have popped out of nowhere. Chicago was only ninety miles away from

North Harbor. Their relationship didn't seem that close, based on the tone of her text messages with Emma. Although, it wasn't fair to read tone into a text message. Maybe she was just a curt texter. I would assess her veracity more after our meeting in a few hours.

Finally, did A-squared really know who the murderer was? He wasn't a reliable source. What was the likelihood he was in the exact location when the murder was committed, unless . . . unless he actually murdered Melody? I pondered the question, but my mind kept rejecting it. As much as I disliked him, I couldn't see him actually murdering her. Well, maybe I could. If he thought she would prevent him from reaping benefits from Dawson's professional football career, he certainly would kill her. But, would he let Dawson take the blame for it? Getting convicted of murder would prevent Dawson from making millions in the NFL. A-squared wasn't someone who thought things through to the end. His comment yesterday that Dawson was in good hands might imply he didn't worry about Dawson because he knew we would work to clear him. Surely he couldn't be that cold-blooded. Maybe if Dawson spoke to him? I wasn't sure Dawson and his father were on speaking terms, but he might know if his father was telling the truth or not. When Dawson was telling us about seeing Virgil with Melody, I got the feeling he was holding something back. What if he saw someone else there too, his father? I made a note to ask him.

I reread my notes but none of it made any more sense at four than it had at three. I turned out my light and settled down. I lay perfectly still and took deep, relaxing breaths and meditated on the suspects in the hope a clear plan of action would reveal itself. Unfortunately, my mind refused to cooperate and kept intertwining Melody with my British cozy. I kept seeing Melody wearing a French maid's uniform while a tweed-clad Professor Harley Quin smoked a pipe near the fireplace and cleaned his shotgun. A sleazy character in polyester with lots of gold chains stood ominously over Melody's body while A-squared, who surprisingly still had on greasy blue jeans and a T-shirt, drank scotch and laughed.

I awoke two hours later to the doorbell. It was barely six and I calculated I had gotten about three hours of sleep total. I looked around my room and Oreo and Snickers were still asleep.

"Some watch poodles you two turned out

to be." I pulled on the jeans I'd worn the night before and grabbed a T-shirt from the hamper and slid it over my head.

I hurried to the kitchen and looked over the rail and saw two uniformed police officers standing at my door. I was instantly awake. My heart raced and I hurried downstairs and opened the door.

"What's wrong?"

"Does Dawson Alexander live here?" one of the policemen asked.

I tried to take deep breaths to slow down my heart. "Yes," I whispered.

"May we speak to him?" the same policeman asked.

I closed my eyes and nodded. "Follow me."

I led them inside the garage. They seemed a bit hesitant about entering and looked around tentatively. I turned on the light and hurried to the door. I knocked loudly.

It took several minutes of me knocking to wake Dawson, who came downstairs wearing a MISU T-shirt, sweat pants, and flip-flops. He had bed hair and yawned when he opened the door.

A look of terror crossed his face at the sight of me with two police officers. The blood drained from his face. His eyes had the startled "deer in the headlights" look that reflected the internal anguish he was feeling. He must have thought they were there to arrest him, again.

"Dawson Alexander?" the officer asked.

He nodded.

"Your dad was involved in a car accident and was seriously injured. He's been flown to River Bend Memorial Hospital by Life Force."

I didn't think he could get much paler, but he did.

He gulped. "Is he gonna be okay?"

"Unfortunately, all we know is his injuries are severe. You'll have to talk to the doctors."

The other officer had been quiet up until this point. "Do you have someone who can take you to the hospital?"

I stepped forward. "I can take him."

The officers looked at me and then back at Dawson, who nodded his acceptance.

They turned to leave, but before they got out the door, one of the officers turned back and said, "I watched you play ball a couple of weeks ago. You're really good. I hope you get beyond all this."

We got in the car. I made the forty-mile drive in less than thirty minutes and dropped Dawson at the emergency room door. It wasn't until I pulled into the parking garage that I realized I'd left my purse and money at home.

Thankfully, I'd grabbed my cell phone and I called Jenna and asked her to swing by the house and grab my purse.

Two hours later, Jenna and Nana Jo walked down the hallway with my purse and a carrier from a nearby fast-food restaurant with four large beverages and a bag filled with greasy sausage biscuits. My mouth watered and my stomach growled at the sight of the coffee. Both Jenna and Nana Jo stared at me, but neither said a word as I snatched the coffee from the carrier and took a swig.

Jenna sat next to me. "How is he?" Jenna whispered as she glanced at Dawson, who was pacing up and down the hallway.

I shrugged. "Not good. A-squared's in intensive care. They let Dawson in for about ten minutes earlier but then alarms started going off and they kicked him out of the room. An army of doctors and nurses rushed in the room. A doctor eventually came out and said he'd gone into cardiac arrest. He's still alive, but . . . I don't think the outlook is good."

Nana Jo tsked. "That poor kid. He's been through a lifetime of misery in a short period of time."

"We let the dogs out before we left, and Chris and Zaq said they'd take care of things at the store." Jenna sipped her hot tea.

I was blessed to have my family. They were annoying and would result in my need for therapy, but they were here for me. I looked at Dawson and tried to guess how he must be feeling.

Jenna stared at Dawson and leaned close to me and whispered, "I talked to Stinky Pitt this morning."

I watched to make sure Dawson wasn't in listening distance. "Did he say how it happened?"

"Apparently A-Squared made two telephone calls. One was to Virgil Russell, who came and posted bail. They don't know who the other call was to."

"Virgil?"

She nodded. "A few hours later, they got a call someone was laying on the railroad tracks by Eden Springs trailer park."

"The railroad tracks?" I shivered.

"Some kids were walking around out there and thought it was a heap of clothes on the rails. He'd been hit by a car and moved to the tracks."

"Oh my. Do the police have any ideas? Did they question Virgil Russell?"

She paused as Dawson walked by before continuing. "He claimed he dropped him at a liquor store near the HOD. A-squared said he needed to use the phone. He says that's the last time he saw him, but the police are getting a warrant for his car. They'll go over it with a fine-tooth comb."

Jenna turned to stare at me and then took several sniffs. "Did you shower today?"

"No. I didn't have time. Why?"

"You stink."

I lifted my armpit and took a whiff.

"Plus, your hair is sticking straight up in the back." She pulled a compact out of her purse and handed it to me.

She was right. My hair was sticking straight up in the back as though held up by electric current. I had crusts at the corners of my eyes and a dried trail of drool from one corner of my mouth. "I can't believe no one said anything to me." I finger combed my hair into submission.

Memorial Hospital was the biggest hospital in the area. It was a huge facility that had been added onto many times over the years and was now a winding maze with lots of twists and turns. Thankfully, someone thought to color code the building. The multi-striped legend was painted on the walls. I followed the blue stripe down hallways to the elevator and down to the gift shop. It always felt like a major accomplishment whenever I visited someone here and managed to make it out without stopping to ask for directions, and today was no exception.

The hospital gift shop had been renovated since the last time I was here. Instead of being a small closet containing flowers, get well cards, and overpriced snacks, it was now a shop that would give any downtown boutique a run for its money. I browsed the aisles until I found the toiletries. I bought a kit that included toothbrush, toothpaste, comb and brush, soap, deodorant, mouthwash, and shaving kit. I also bought underwear and a T-shirt. Since I was there, I also ordered flowers for A-squared.

At the intensive care nurses' station, I asked if there was a place where I could clean up. They provided me a washcloth and towel and took me down a back hall to the nurses' fitness area. There were showers and I cleaned up.

When I returned, I felt better. Amazing what clean underwear and toothpaste could do. It was getting close to noon and Jenna said she needed to get home.

"You don't have to stay here with me. I'll be okay," Dawson said.

"I know I don't, but I want to stay."

Dawson paused. "There's nothing you can do. I know you have things you need to do." He looked down.

"Is there something you need me to do?"

"Yeah. I need you to find out who killed Melody and . . . who tried to kill my dad."

CHAPTER 14

"The girls hated missing out on our trip to Chicago, so I told them to take the South Shore and we'd meet them at the outlet mall later." Nana Jo looked sheepish. "I also told them we'd swing by The Boat."

The South Shore commuter train ran between River Bend, Indiana, and Chicago. For less than ten dollars, the South Shore transported people from the airport in River Bend to downtown Chicago, without the stress of traffic or parking. I knew people who made the two-hour-and-twenty-minute trip daily for work. I'd taken the South Shore downtown to go to Cubs games, museums, or shopping. The train didn't go through Michigan, but North Harbor residents drove thirty minutes to Michigan City, Indiana, to get on the train.

Michigan City was a small town on the Lake Michigan shoreline with nice beaches. It had a designer outlet mall, and The Boat.

For most of my life, land-based gambling was illegal in the state of Indiana. Eventually, some creative developer came up with a work-around by turning a boat into a casino. When The Boat first opened, it cruised up and down Lake Michigan. Guests entered every two hours. Eventually, lawmakers abandoned the requirement for the boat to move and people boarded or disembarked at will. A trip to The Boat meant I might not get home until the wee hours of the morning. Given that I'd only had a few hours of sleep, I wasn't happy.

I followed the directions Cassidy Logan had sent to the West Inglenook area of Chicago. North Harbor was an economically depressed area with abandoned buildings, high unemployment, and crime. West Inglenook, at fifteen miles wide with three times the North Harbor population, took economic depression to another level. Most buildings were boarded up and covered with gang graffiti. The few shops still open had uninviting iron bars covering every piece of glass and brick walls which reminded me of a prison.

I pulled up in front of an old brownstone with crumbling bricks, broken glass, and a tired-looking floral sofa from the seventies with no legs and sagging cushions in the yard. In the alley next to the house, a group of men were shooting craps. A couple of teenage boys with jeans down to their knees and bandanas tied around their heads hung on the porch.

I turned to Nana Jo. "Do you think my car is going to be safe here?"

She looked at me like she'd never seen me before and then patted my knee. "Honey, you can't be serious? This car is twelve years old and has close to two hundred thousand miles on it. The turn signal is attached to the steering column with duct tape and if you hit a bump, the lights turn off and on. The only thing of value is the radio, and it doesn't have any knobs."

"I have all of the knobs." I opened the ashtray and showed all of the knobs for the radio and air-conditioning, along with a pair of pliers I used to change channels. "Besides, you'll hurt her feelings."

Nana Jo rolled her eyes. "If I were you, I'd pay those guys fifty dollars to dispose of the car so the police don't find it."

"Don't listen to her, Martha." I patted the dashboard.

We got out of the car. I opened the hatch and picked up Melody's meager belongings. We walked toward the building. One of the young kids who looked to be about thirteen stared at me as though I were a piece of meat and then made a rude remark to his friend in Spanish. I always found it amusing when people thought you couldn't understand their language. When I responded in Spanish, the smirk immediately left his face. All outward signs indicated I should be afraid of this hooligan, but something in my gut told me not to be afraid. Years teaching in the public school system provided what I called a sixth sense. It had never failed me, so I trusted my gut.

"Would you keep an eye on my car?" I asked.

He looked at my Honda CRV and laughed. "That piece of junk? Lady, you'd have to pay somebody to take that piece of crap."

Two insults in less than five minutes was too much. I lifted my head and marched around him. Nana Jo came up behind me. Just as she climbed the porch, the kid came up on Nana Jo in a threatening manner. "But you can give me your purse, old lady." He reached out his hand as if he thought she would just hand it over.

I don't know if it was the idea of a thirteen-year-old boy trying to take her purse or the fact he called her "old lady." Nana Jo spread her legs, crouched low in her aikido stance, and dipped her shoulder. She reached out, grabbed his outstretched hand with both of hers, twisted, and dropped to her knee in one motion. The kid was flipped onto his back and Nana Jo put her knee in his chest and held his arm in the air.

He yelled obscenities while he lay on the ground.

His friend stood openmouthed.

After a few seconds, Nana Jo released the kid's arm and stood. "Better watch who you're calling an 'old lady,' " she said as she marched up the stairs.

There was no front door, so we walked into the building and headed up the stairs.

We walked up three flights of stairs in silence. When we got to the top floor, Nana Jo stepped aside for me to knock.

I looked at her. "You okay?"

"Yep. That was just a basic throw down."

"Okay, Bruce Lee. Maybe you shouldn't antagonize the locals."

She smiled. "Then the locals better stop provoking me."

I knocked on the door.

"Come in."

We opened the door and walked inside.

The apartment was small and cramped, with oversized leather furniture that looked as though it had seen better days. One wall was dominated by the largest television I'd ever seen. It was massive and similar to the one I'd seen at Trammel Braxton's home with cords hanging down to video games. There was a playpen in the middle of the room with two toddlers inside wearing nothing but diapers. Sitting in a chair, smoking a cigarette, was a small woman. She was a petite Caucasian, fair-skinned, with thin red hair and green eyes. She was also about six months pregnant.

"You must be from that school?"

"Well, actually, I'm just a friend of Emma's, your sister's roommate."

"Half sister." She took a long drag from her cigarette. "You can drop the stuff anywhere."

If I didn't talk fast, we'd be out of here in less than two seconds. "Sure, but let me introduce myself. My name is Samantha Washington and this is my grandmother, Mrs. Josephine Thomas."

Nana Jo frowned. "You know smoking when you're pregnant can lead to birth defects."

She stared at Nana Jo and exhaled slowly. "Thanks for the public service announcement."

This wasn't going well. "May we sit for a

few moments? Those stairs were a killer." I didn't wait for a response and plopped down on the sofa.

Using two fingers, Nana Jo removed some clothing and sat.

"Whew. Thank you so much." I tried to think of a way to ask my questions before she threw us out.

Nana Jo walked to the playpen. One of the kids was asleep. The other, a curly-haired boy, looked at her and immediately held up both arms to be picked up.

Nana Jo looked at Cassidy. "Do you mind if I hold him?"

Cassidy shrugged.

Nana Jo reached down and picked up the baby, who immediately threw back his head and laughed and reached for her earrings. Nana Jo had a way with babies, and she returned to her seat. The baby stood straight up. Nana Jo sang "Row, Row, Row Your Boat." With each "row," she rocked the youngster forward and back. He laughed hilariously each time he went backward.

I watched them for several moments. "Cassidy, when's the last time you saw your sister . . . ah, half sister?"

She smoked silently for so long I thought she wasn't going to answer. "It's been years. We weren't close."

"You both have the same father?"

"Mother."

Nana Jo stopped singing long enough to ask, "Did you know what your sister was involved in?"

Cassidy smiled. "She was always up to something." She finished her cigarette and put the butt out. "That's how she ended up in that program. Go to jail or go to college." She laughed. "Mel thought that was hilarious. She had access to an entirely new pool of marks."

"Did you know what scam she was running?" I asked.

Cassidy looked at me suspiciously. "You've got a lot of questions."

"We want to find out who killed her. We thought you might be able to help us."

"Why would I want to do that?"

"Because she was your sister," I said

She shrugged. "Everybody's gotta die of something."

"Maybe because, in spite of your attitude, you're basically a good person and want to do the right thing," Nana Jo said.

I stared at my grandmother, who seemed determined to get us thrown out before we got information, and then turned and looked at Cassidy.

Cassidy was staring at Nana Jo but didn't

say anything. Eventually, she wiped a tear from her eye. "Look. I haven't seen Mel in years. She sent text messages sometimes. The last one was a month ago."

"Do you still have it?" I asked.

She shook her head. "Nawh. She was running a scam. Said if things worked out, she'd be set for life." She looked at her sleeping baby and the one on Nana Jo's lap. Then she looked at her stomach. "Said she would get us out of this place." She wiped away an errant tear and got another cigarette out of the pack on the table and lit up. "She talked a lot of crap."

"Did she mention anyone that wanted to hurt her?" I asked.

Cassidy took a long drag of her cigarette and then she sat up. "She didn't mention any names. But she said someone was trying to muscle in on her, but she had his number."

We asked a few other questions, but Cassidy didn't have any more answers. The sleeping baby woke up and started screaming. She hoisted herself out of her seat and picked him up. He looked exactly like the boy Nana Jo was bouncing on her lap.

"Twins?" I asked.

She nodded.

She had her hands full, and it didn't seem

as though we'd learn anything more. So, we rose to leave. Nana Jo handed over the baby.

Before we left, Nana Jo turned and asked, "Did you know Virgil Russell?"

Cassidy was jiggling a baby on each hip. "Yeah. I know him. Why?"

"It seemed strange to us that Melody was . . . involved with him," I said.

"Mel was always pretty close to Virgil. He taught her practically everything she knew about conning people. Virgil taught her how to dress and talk and act so she got richer marks."

"But he killed your father?" Nana Jo said.

Cassidy shrugged. "Her father, not mine. Besides, that wasn't a big loss. He was a drunk who beat all of us every chance he got. That's how he died. He beat Mel so bad we thought he'd kill her. Virgil tried to stop him. He pushed him. He hit his head on the end of the table." She lowered the toddlers back into the playpen. "He and Mel got closer after that."

"Any chance he was the man trying to muscle onto her scam?" I asked.

Cassidy shook her head. "I doubt it. They worked together."

We left Cassidy and walked down the narrow stairway. Once outside, we saw the youngster Nana Jo had tossed earlier. He stood in the middle of the sidewalk in a threatening manner.

"Maybe I should call the police," I whispered to Nana Jo.

"No need." She stepped forward. "You want a piece of me?" she asked the kid.

The boy snarled. "I've got something for you this time, old lady." He reached into his pocket and pulled out a switchblade, which he held up with his right hand.

Nana Jo smiled and reached into her purse and pulled out her gun and pointed it. She squinted, closed one eye, and fired. The bullet hit the blade of the knife and ricocheted off.

The startled hooligan dropped the knife, turned, and ran.

There was a loud burst of laughter from the gamblers in the alley. Five young men in jeans with tattoos and piercings whistled and laughed. One of the men walked forward. "Hey, I've got two hundred dollars that says you can't hit that billboard?" He held up several bills and grinned. Each of the other men also held up money.

Nana Jo looked at the billboard that stood above the building across the street and within an arm's distance of the elevated train track.

"Oh, no," I pleaded with my grandmother.

The grin on her face and the gleam in her eyes told me I was wasting my time.

Nana Jo extended her arm and pointed her gun at the billboard. She cocked her head to the side and pulled the trigger.

We all looked at the billboard. There was a large picture of a popular insurance company's spokesperson wearing a white apron with her black hair pulled back with a headband. The woman had a large smile on her face and a perfectly round hole in the center of her forehead.

The men hooped and laughed. One of them even bowed to Nana Jo as they all came and handed her their money.

CHAPTER 15

I hustled my grandmother into my intact vehicle and hurried away.

Nana Jo laughed as she fanned herself with her money. "Easiest thousand dollars I've ever made."

"You could have gotten in trouble. What if you'd missed?"

She looked at me. "I was Lauderdale County's sharpshooter three years in a row. Besides, that billboard was huge. You'd have to be blind to miss it."

I gave up trying to shame my grandmother into reform and headed east. We drove in relative silence the forty minutes to the outlet mall in Michigan City. I found a parking space near one of the larger anchor stores.

Before I got out, Nana Jo took half of her winnings and handed it to me. "Happy Birthday, Sam."

I looked at the wad of cash with my mouth

open. "I can't take that."

"Why not?"

"It's too much. Besides, you won the money fair and square. You should spend it on yourself."

"I intend to splurge and enjoy myself. However, I wouldn't have had the opportunity to win the money if it wasn't for you. Besides, I want you to get yourself some nice clothes. You never know when you might get another date or non-date."

"But really, I don't need —"

She waved her hand. "Sam, will you please just take the money and say thank you?"

I reached over and gave my grandmother a big hug. "Thank you."

The title outlet mall implied incredibly low prices, but discounted prices could be a relative term. Lighthouse Place Mall was a designer outlet mall. While the prices were discounted from what you paid in a regular mall, they were still higher than discount retail stores. In the past, I'd limited myself to three or four stores known for ridiculously low prices where I bought blue jeans for less than five dollars. Today I walked into the stores with the designers' names on the front. I bought several really good pairs of jeans, silk blouses, and even a few dresses.

Nana Jo bought new tennis shoes and workout attire and then splurged on a lovely dress with a plunging neckline. Laden down with shopping bags, we made our way to the car several hours later. The girls' train was due to arrive in a few minutes. I needed to pick them up from the train station. There was a trolley that took visitors from the train station to the outlet mall, but the girls preferred spending their money at The Boat.

They were waiting at the depot when I arrived. No need to park, I pulled up to the platform and loaded them in. I then headed for The Boat.

I let everyone out at the front of the casino and parked. By the time I got to the lobby, I was tired. Lack of sleep and tons of walking at the outlet mall hit me at the same time. We'd agreed to eat first, so I went to the buffet and looked around until I found them.

Normally we went to the Four Feathers Casino, which was closer to North Harbor. Trips to The Boat were rare, which meant the girls hadn't racked up enough perks for free food. One thing remained constant, regardless of where we went. Ruby Mae always ran into someone she knew. Today was no exception. When I sat down at the restaurant, she was being hugged by one of the chefs, and a waitress was nearby, awaiting her turn. The chef turned out to be a godson and the waitress was a great-niece. Ruby Mae's connections resulted in free dinner vouchers and dessert take-out boxes, which were usually prohibited at buffets. When we finished, I took the boxes to the car. By the time I walked back to the lobby, I had moved beyond tired to exhausted. We agreed to meet in two hours, so I found a comfy wingback chair in a quiet, cozy corner and took a nap. I set the alarm on my phone to wake me after an hour and a half. When I awoke and felt my face, the pattern of the chair's fabric was imprinted on the side of my face and there was a large wet stain on the chair's wing from drool. I was amazed how refreshed and energized I felt after my power nap.

I walked around the casino and grabbed a coffee from a beverage station. I still had fifteen minutes before our meeting, so I put twenty dollars into a machine with a picture of Tarzan on the front. I only played penny slots and I was normally very conservative, but I tossed caution to the wind and bet the maximum, a dollar fifty. After only two spins, I went into a bonus. I was relatively new to slot machines, so I didn't know exactly what had happened, but the next thing I knew, Tarzan yodeled and swung across my screen. There was a lot going on. Wheels spun, Tarzan pounded gorillas, and drums beat. After the third spin, lights flashed, bells rang, my chair vibrated, and my screen was almost completely full of wilds. Coins started flying on the screen and the lady next to me started screaming and hitting me in the arm. A crowd of people gathered around my machine.

Two of the casino staff made their way through the crowd to my machine. One of them inserted a card into the machine, which stopped the flashing lights. The other one smiled and pulled out a clipboard. "Congratulations. Can I see your driver's license, please?"

I was dazed and couldn't grasp what had happened. "What just happened?"

He smiled. "You just won a lot of money." He took the driver's license I handed him and began copying information.

"How much did I win?"

He looked up at the machine. "You just won fifty-four thousand dollars."

I nearly passed out. "No way!"

The casino worker smiled. "Yes. Way!"

I stared at him with my mouth open. "I

think I need to go someplace so I can throw up."

He looked startled but helped me rise. I started to walk away but then turned back to the machine.

The other casino worker took me by the arm. "It's okay. I'll take care of everything." He looked back at his coworker. "I'll take her to the office."

I followed the casino worker until we came to a small door behind a cash machine that I wouldn't even have noticed. He opened the door and we went inside. There was a desk, two guest chairs, and a small love seat. I sat and put my head between my legs.

"Can I get you some water?"

I nodded.

He left and came back with a bottle of water.

I tried to open the lid, but my hands were shaking so badly I had to get the casino worker to open it for me. He untwisted the lid and gave me the bottle, and I took a long sip. My phone vibrated. Nana Jo and the girls must be wondering where I was. I couldn't get my phone out of my pants pocket fast enough. When I tried to dial, my hands shook so badly I kept missing her name. I turned to the casino worker. "My grandmother and three other ladies are in the lobby waiting for me. Can you please get them? I have no idea how to get to them from here."

He said he'd be happy to go. I took deep breaths and tried to process the fact I had just won fifty-four thousand dollars. Every time I thought about the dollar amount, I felt lightheaded and had to put my head back between my knees until the dizziness passed.

Several minutes later Nana Jo and the girls came into the room.

"What happened? Are you okay?" Nana Jo asked.

"Didn't he tell you?" I pointed at the casino worker.

"He didn't tell us anything. He just said you weren't feeling well."

The room was small and with six people, it was claustrophobic. I looked at the casino worker.

He struggled to hide a smile. "I thought you might prefer to tell them yourself."

Nana Jo's brow was wrinkled and a vein was pulsing on the side of her head. She was getting angry. "Tell us what?"

I pointed at the casino worker. "He said I won fifty-four thousand dollars."

There was dead silence for several seconds and then Nana Jo sank down onto a chair.

"Sweet mother of God."

Irma's response was not holy and resulted in a sharp reprimand from the others before she burst into a coughing fit.

Dorothy and Ruby Mae congratulated me.

The worker slid out of the room and returned with more waters, which he passed around. Nana Jo sat next to me. Irma and Ruby Mae were in the guest chairs, and Dorothy propped on the desk.

"Son, can you prop that door open a bit." Nana Jo fanned herself. "Either I'm having a hot flash or I'm going to pass out."

He propped the door open.

The casino worker who took my driver's license entered with a security guard. We were now packed like sardines in that room. He returned my driver's license and handed me some forms to fill out. "These are for the IRS. Do you want us to subtract taxes or do you want to pay them yourself?"

I filled in the paperwork. "Please subtract the taxes."

When I was done, I handed the papers back.

"How do you want the money?"

"Excuse me?"

The casino worker smiled. "Do you want a check? Cash? Or a combination of both?"

Nana Jo whistled. "Cash? You mean people

actually want cash?"

The woman nodded. "You'd be surprised."

I looked at the sheet she handed me, which indicated after taxes I would get over forty thousand dollars. "Can I get five checks?"

She smiled. "You can have anything you want."

"I need five checks. One made out to each of us." I pointed around the room.

The girls began to protest. "Oh, no. This is too much —"

I held up my hand. "We have a system. We always split the winnings. This is no different."

We argued for several moments, but ultimately I overruled them and made the arrangements with the casino. We would each get about eight thousand dollars. It took close to an hour for the casino to get all of the arrangements made.

Irma asked for a whiskey. Our friendly casino worker took orders and brought drinks.

Nana Jo asked if someone could find our car and bring it to the door for us.

I handed over my keys, along with directions on where I'd parked. By the time we were all settled out, the car was waiting at the front.

I was still dazed but ecstatic to share this windfall with my grandmother and her friends.

The ride home was spent talking about how we'd each spend our money. Irma wanted plastic surgery to lift everything that had sagged over the years. Dorothy suggested she do something about her chronic coughing instead, but that suggestion fell on deaf ears.

Dorothy wanted to go on a cruise. Ruby Mae's church was going on a trip to the Holy Land and she wanted to go. Now she could. Nana Jo was very vague and refused to say what she planned to do.

I didn't have plans for spending my share, but the girls were very vocal on how they thought I should spend it. The unanimous decision was I should use my share to buy a new car. I knew Nana Jo's views on my CRV, but the girls had never complained.

"Beggars can't be choosy," Irma said.

"Those newer cars have Wi-Fi and I would love to use my iPad or watch a movie," Dorothy said.

"My daughter has a Lexus and the ride is so smooth. You can barely tell the motor is running," Ruby Mae yelled from the back seat.

" 'Et tu, Brute?' " I looked at her in the rearview mirror.

Ruby Mae laughed. "One thing I can say for this car is that my prayer life has improved since I've been riding in it."

I stuck out my tongue.

They all laughed. I knew the joking was all in good fun. The girls weren't complainers. My CRV was old and loud and there were a number of aesthetic problems. But the engine was solid and the car was reliable. It had four-wheel drive and performed wonderfully in the snow.

I dropped the girls at the retirement village and they asked me to get out of the car, which was unusual.

I got out and each one of them hugged and thanked me. They had tears in their eyes, which made me cry too.

I got back in the car and Nana Jo and I drove back to the store. When I pulled into the garage, Nana Jo stopped me.

"I want to thank you too, Sam. That was a very nice thing you did. You didn't have to. No one would have blamed you. That is a lot of money."

"I know, but I wanted to."

She nodded. "I know you really love this car. It's served you well for more than a decade. However, I do think you should consider an upgrade. Not because the CRV is unreliable, but because you've been through so much over the years and I think it would be nice to treat yourself."

I started to protest, but she held up her hand. "You don't have to defend your decision. I just wanted to explain why you should do this. It's okay to have nice things, and it's not frivolous to spend money on yourself. You're a hard worker and you deserve nice clothes and a nice car. You're always thinking about others, and I want you to know it's okay to think about yourself too." She patted my hand and got out of the car.

I sat in the car for several minutes and let the tears stream down my face. Leon and I had worked hard our whole lives, and we never had eight thousand dollars at one time. That was more money than we put down on our house. I was accustomed to scrimping and saving and making every dollar stretch as far as it could go. I wasn't good at spending money on things that weren't essential. I drove cars until they were basically no longer drivable. I looked at Martha and patted the dashboard. "You've served me well, old friend, but maybe it's time for a change."

I had been on an emotional roller coaster

and felt tired. I finally got out of the car and went upstairs. Dawson had sent several text messages throughout the day. His dad was still in intensive care, but he was stable. The doctors had put him in a medically induced coma to decrease brain swelling. The twins had packed a bag for Dawson and took it to him at the hospital. They also had taken Oreo and Snickers home with them, which meant the house was quiet.

One pleasant surprise was a large vase of flowers on my kitchen counter. The card indicated they were from Professor Quin. I was glad Nana Jo was in her room because I couldn't stop smiling. The worst thing about trips to the casino was the smell of smoke that clung to your clothes and hair. I took a long hot shower and got ready for bed. Not surprisingly, I was too excited to sleep. Instead, I spent a couple hours looking at cars online. Eventually I decided writing therapy would be useful.

"Blasted doctor." Lord William beat his fist on the bed but winced as his leg teetered and nearly fell of the pillow where he had it propped.

Lady Elizabeth sat in a straight-back chair near her husband's side. "Now, dear, you know it isn't Doctor Haygood's fault your gout

268

flared up. You have nobody to blame but yourself."

"You'd think he could do more than say, 'keep your leg elevated and watch your diet.' My God, it's the twentieth century. Medicine should have a cure for this by now. I'm surprised he didn't pull out leeches. It's archaic."

Lady Elizabeth smiled. She was familiar with her husband's rants and knew he was in a great amount of pain.

Penelope paced. "When the king called, did he say how he expected us to keep this out of the newspapers?"

Daphne looked up from her seat at the window. "Especially with the editor of the *London Times* here in the house."

Victor leaned against a large armoire. "I doubt if Fordham-Baker even knows what day of the week it is. The man's been plastered all day."

Lady Elizabeth looked at Victor and then mumbled, "I wonder . . ."

"Maybe we can keep him that way," Penelope said.

Lady Elizabeth looked at her niece. "That might not be a bad idea." She took a deep breath. "The king wants us to solve this murder, like we did with Charles Parker's."

Penelope stopped pacing and turned to

stare at her aunt. "But that was different. We were trying to save a friend."

Elizabeth sighed. "Now we're trying to save a member of our family."

Penelope looked sheepish. "You're right. Whether we like it or not, Wallis is married to our cousin. She's family."

Daphne sighed. "Alright then, where do we begin? Remember, I wasn't involved in your other investigation."

"That's right. I'd forgotten." Lady Elizabeth frowned. "Well, I think we divide and conquer. First, let's go through what we know and then we can come up with our plan of attack."

Lord William saluted his wife. "Aye, captain."

Lady Elizabeth smiled.

Penelope paced. "We know she was shot in the marsh, but we don't know what she was doing there."

"Yes we do." Lord William sat up straight. "In all the excitement and pain" — he patted his leg — "I nearly forgot. When I was talking to Detective Inspector Covington, one of the constables brought him a note." Lord William's lips twitched as he struggled to hold back a smile. "I managed to get a look at the note when he was distracted."

"Well done," Lady Elizabeth said with pride and saluted her husband.

He beamed. "The note was from Lord

Charles, asking her to meet him in the trees by the marsh."

"That's very odd. I wonder why he chose that location," Lady Elizabeth mused.

"I think Detective Inspector Covington was going to find out," Lord William continued. "He was heading to talk to Charles but got distracted by the call from the king and then the call from the chief inspector."

"Now that was odd," Penelope said. "Why do you suppose he was called back to London?"

Lady Elizabeth reflected, "I suspect Bertie might have applied a little royal pressure. I think he's asked the Yard to back off for a few days to buy us time to figure this thing out."

Penelope stared. "And they listened?"

"The king carries a lot of weight. There used to be a time when the aristocracy ruled supreme." Lord William shook his head. "Those days are gone now."

"And rightly so," Lady Elizabeth said. "Justice shouldn't be reserved for the nobility."

"So, we need to find out from Lord Charles why he wanted to meet with Rebecca," Lady Elizabeth said.

Daphne smiled. "I can tell you why he wanted to meet with her. It's because he's a dirty old man and was most likely having a fling with her, right under his wife's nose."

Everyone stared.

"I think Lady Abigail was well aware of what Lord Charles was up to," Penelope added. "I sat next to her the other night, and she may look like a mouse, but I could tell she was bothered."

"Bothered enough to kill?" Victor asked.

Penelope shrugged. "I don't know."

"If she was, she certainly had the skill to do it," Daphne said. "I heard her say she was a crack shot in America. Apparently she won an Annie Oakley shooting trophy in the States when she was a young girl."

"Very interesting." Lady Elizabeth turned to her husband. "Do you feel up to doing a little investigating?"

Lord William nodded. "I can't go tramping around the grounds, but I can talk, and Charles and I are friendly enough."

Lady Elizabeth nodded. "Wonderful. You talk to Lord Charles and see what you can find out." She turned to Daphne. "Daphne, I'd like you to figure out who had the opportunity to shoot her. Where was everyone at the time of the shooting?"

Daphne frowned. "You want to know who was unaccounted for?"

Lady Elizabeth nodded. "Yes. That's it exactly. Do you think you can do that?"

She nodded.

"What would you like us to do?" Penelope asked.

Lady Elizabeth looked at Victor. "I know Bertie may want us to keep the police out of this, but there are things we need to know. I want you to work with Detective Inspector Covington to find out as much as you can about the gun that was used."

Victor nodded.

"What about me?" Penelope asked.

"I'd like you to talk to the servants. I'm sure they can tell you plenty about what was going on, plus, they've probably spent more time with Rebecca than anyone else."

Penelope nodded. "What are you going to do?"

Lady Elizabeth hesitated. "I'm going to try and make sense of this. If you stop and think about it, it really doesn't make any sense. Why would anyone want to kill the maid?"

"You think the duchess was the intended victim?" Victor asked.

Lady Elizabeth shook her head. "I don't know. This whole thing seems like an elaborate charade."

Daphne leaned forward. "I know what you mean. There are diplomats from all over the world staying under one roof. The world is on the brink of war and the tension is thick enough to cut with a knife and the only

273

casualty is a French maid."

"Exactly." Lady Elizabeth was surprised at her niece's perception. "I feel this whole thing has been staged."

"But the duchess arranged the whole thing. Surely she must be the puppeteer behind the scenes," Victor said.

Lady Elizabeth frowned. "Maybe. Wallis certainly has her own motives, but I'm not sure she is . . . well, to be completely honest, I don't think she's smart enough to be the mastermind behind this."

"Who then?" Victor asked.

"I don't know, but I'm going to find out."

CHAPTER 16

I woke up bright and early Sunday morning. Despite getting less than eight hours of sleep, I felt happy and alert. My good mood could have been attributed to the eight-thousand-dollar check in my purse. Or it could be related to the fact the twins had Snickers and Oreo and I was able to sleep past three. A night without my dogs was nice, but awkward. It felt weird not to have to look under my feet before I stood up or went down a flight of stairs, to make sure I didn't step on or trip over a lounging poodle.

I showered and put on one of my new outfits, a denim dress that was fitted at the top and flared at the bottom. I had a cup of coffee and sniffed my flowers, which made me smile. I picked up my cell and sent a thank-you text message.

"What are you grinning at?" Nana Jo

came into the kitchen and hopped on a bar-stool.

"Nothing. I'm just very thankful."

She sipped the coffee I handed her. "Well, I suppose you have eight thousand reasons to be."

"I got a text from Dawson. He said his dad is still in the coma. He's going to stay there with him."

She nodded. "Maybe we can take him something to eat later today."

"That's a great idea." I looked at the time. "You should come to church with Mom and me today. I'll treat you to dinner and we can pick up the girls and head to MISU for the memorial service. Afterward, we'll go check on Dawson."

Nana Jo agreed and got dressed.

My mom attended a large church located in downtown South Harbor. The building was brick but painted white with stained glass, a steeple, and bells. The church was one hundred and twelve years old and from the outside, nothing much had changed over the years. The changes were more noticeable inside. It still had a large pipe organ, but there was also a keyboard, a synthesizer, and drums. The pastor who baptized me and my sister as children died a few years ago. The new minister was very young. The congregation had grown substantially since Pastor Andy Timmons was installed. His messages were contemporary, as was the music. This change caused dissatisfaction from the older members, who were steeped in the traditional hymns and messages from decades gone by. To his credit, Pastor Timmons had done a fine job of finding the middle ground. The church now had two services. The first was traditional, with hymns and organ music. The second service was much more contemporary, with upbeat music.

Normally, I found the traditional hymns boring and dreary. Today I felt comfort in the ritual of tradition and sang songs of thanks with a glad heart.

Afterward, I treated Nana Jo and my mom to brunch at the Boulevard Hotel, one of the oldest and nicest hotels in South Harbor. When my mom learned we were going to River Bend to see Dawson, she insisted on picking up flowers for us to take with us. Nana Jo and I picked up extra flowers to take to the memorial service for Melody. We invited Mom to go along, but she declined with a vague excuse. I dropped her at home and headed to the retirement village and picked up the girls.

As arranged, I met Jillian and Emma at

the student union. I was surprised to see Zaq there too, although I gathered he was there for Emma and not Melody. The memorial service was to be held at the campus chapel, a quaint building in the center of campus. The chapel had wooden pews, stained glass windows, and an ornately carved altar of dark mahogany. The building was small and only held about one hundred people, which didn't seem to be a problem. Only about twenty people showed up, despite the flyers Jillian placed all over campus and the announcement she put in the school newspaper.

We mingled among the few guests, but with a crowd this small, there wasn't much to find out. When I bought the flowers, I also picked up a memorial book for signatures. I planned to send it to Cassidy when this was over.

I was disappointed by the low turnout until I saw Professor Harley Quin walk in. I smiled as he approached. I was glad I had on one of my new dresses.

"Hello, beautiful. You look amazing."

"What a lovely greeting," I said.

"I'll bet you say that to all the girls." Nana Jo smiled.

"Nana Jo, this is a friend, Professor Harley Quin. He's helping with my book." I turned to Harley. "This is my grandmother, Nana Jo."

Normally, Nana Jo was super friendly, but there was an edge to her voice. She held out her hand. "Nice to meet you." She shook his hand. "Please, call me Josephine."

Heat rushed to my face. Harley raised an eyebrow but smiled.

An awkward silence followed. I struggled to think of something to fill the gap. I looked around. Virgil Russell had entered the chapel. "Isn't that Virgil Russell?"

Nana Jo looked but then turned back to Harley. "Professor Quin, weren't you Melody's teacher?"

"Quite so. Quite so. Although, I didn't know her. In fact, I'm not sure I actually ever met her personally. I gather she didn't attend many classes."

"But she was getting an A in your class. That's rather odd, don't you think?"

Nana Jo was staring at Harley as if he were one of the students in her class. She was tall and could be very intimidating when she wanted to, and apparently she wanted to be today.

"I asked Harley about that. It turns out it was all just an error with the computer system," I said.

"Hmm . . . convenient," Nana Jo mumbled

just loud enough for Harley to hear.

He laughed. "I have to admit, I'm not great with computers, and the system they use here in the States is different from the one I used back home in England."

"Where exactly are you from?" she asked.

"He's British," I said.

"I can tell by the accent." Nana Jo smiled. "I meant, where in Great Britain?"

He chuckled. "It's a very small village. I doubt if you've ever heard of it —"

"Try me."

"It's a small town . . . Deering Vale. Ever heard of it?"

Nana Jo hesitated. "It sounds vaguely familiar."

"One English village is much like another. Small thatched roof cottages, a church, a pub, and a lot of sheep." He laughed.

"What brings you to North Harbor?"

"I'm researching a book on the House of David. Fascinating stuff."

I stood behind Harley and caught Nana Jo's gaze. I raised my eyebrows and flicked my head to the side to indicate she should scram.

She looked at the door. "My God, it's Stinky Pitt."

I turned. Detective Pitt was standing against the wall.

Harley looked startled.

"Well, it's been a pleasure meeting you, Dr. Quin, but I've got to go and . . . talk to a friend. Please excuse me."

When Nana Jo left, I exhaled, and Harley looked at me and laughed. "Your grandmother is very protective." He pulled at his collar but smiled.

"I'm sorry. Usually she's very friendly."

He placed his arm around my back and whispered in my ear, "Maybe she hasn't felt like you needed protecting before."

My stomach fluttered. My face heated and I knew I had a silly grin on my face, but I couldn't stop myself. His breath caressed my neck and my heart pounded in my ears. I turned my head slightly and looked in his eyes and giggled like a schoolgirl.

He smiled but didn't remove his hand from my waist.

I was grateful when the minister stood and asked everyone to take their seats.

With his hand on my back, Harley steered me to a seat near the front of the small church on the opposite end of the pew from where Nana Jo was sitting with the girls.

We took our seats.

Jillian read a scripture from the Bible. Everyone recited the Lord's Prayer. The minister said a few words. It was clear he hadn't known Melody, but he talked about a young life taken too soon and the promise of eternity in heaven. He then asked if anyone wished to speak about Melody. No one moved, and I was concerned no one would get up. Imagine my surprise when Nana Jo rose and walked to the front.

"I only met Melody a couple of days before she died, but she was an intelligent girl who had experienced a great deal of trouble in her young life. Despite those obstacles, she found a way to escape. She knew a lot about people and mastered a number of skills in her young life. She used her skills and her assets to move ahead. She had tremendous plans. Unfortunately, someone thwarted her plans. I always feel it's such a shame when young people are taken from this earth without a chance to live and experience life."

I was thoroughly amazed. Everything she said was the truth, but there was definitely more behind her words, much would only have meaning to a small few. Nana Jo was brilliant.

Once Nana Jo got the ball rolling, several others rose and said nice things, including Emma and Jillian. The last to speak was Virgil Russell. He seemed genuinely grieved. He spoke of Melody's beauty and her strength. He pulled out a handkerchief and hurriedly sat down.

When no one else got up, the minister thanked everyone for coming and encouraged us to seek peace in the Word of God and then prayed and dismissed us. Irma immediately sidled up to Virgil Russell, while Nana Jo talked to Stinky Pitt. Dorothy talked to Jillian and a small group of students. Everyone was working and here I was, sitting with Harley. I felt guilty. My focus should be on finding Melody's killer.

"Thank you again for the flowers. They were lovely."

He leaned close and whispered, "They were really a bribe."

"A bribe?"

"I'm hoping you'll go out again with me."

"You don't have to bribe me to go out with you," I said. "All you have to do is ask."

"Good. How about dinner?"

"I'm sorry, I can't tonight. I have to check on Dawson. His dad's in the hospital."

Harley looked surprised. "Really? Is he going to be okay?"

"We don't know. He was hit by a car. He's in intensive care. It doesn't look good."

"I'm very sorry to hear that." He did look sorry too, really troubled. "Which hospital?"

"Memorial in River Bend. How about

tomorrow night?" I asked.

He shook his head. "Sorry. I can't tomorrow night. I've got a late class. Tuesday?"

I shook my head. "Tuesday night is girls' night. But I'm free Wednesday."

"Wednesday it is."

I thanked Jillian for all her hard work coordinating the memorial, and then we loaded into the car. We stopped once on the way to the hospital and picked up snacks for Dawson. There were several places to eat at the hospital, including a Subway and a River Bend Chocolate Factory. However, I'd seen him eat and knew it would be expensive for him. Nana Jo insisted on getting necessities like underwear, socks, orange juice, peanut butter, and Doritos; just the necessities.

On the ride to the hospital, Nana Jo filled us in on her conversation with Stinky Pitt. "He thinks Virgil killed Melody and tried to kill A-squared. He's still waiting for the report on Virgil's car to come back to see if there's any trace evidence from the hit-and-run. In the meantime, he's keeping a close eye on him."

"He seemed genuinely upset about Melody," I said.

Irma coughed. "He was upset alright. I know real grief when I see it." She coughed

284

again. "He knew Melody had other lovers, but he said they had a 'special bond.'"

"Yeah right. I'll bet they had a special bond. The dirty old coot," Nana Jo said.

"All I'm saying is he seemed sincere." Irma took a swig from her flask.

"Irma, are you sure that's what he said?" I asked.

Irma looked offended. "Of course I'm sure. I'm not senile." She coughed.

"I just meant, are you sure he said Melody had other lovers, plural. Not that she had another love?" I looked at her in the rearview mirror and saw the look of recognition in her eyes.

"He definitely said lovers, as in more than one." She coughed.

"But that could mean anything. Maybe he meant, through the years, she's had other lovers," Ruby Mae said. "Nowadays, it isn't uncommon for girls to have had multiple lovers."

"Well, I always had more than one," Irma bragged. "Sometimes it was hard to keep them straight, but boy was it fun." She laughed before breaking into a coughing fit.

Nana Jo stared at me. "You're thinking she had another lover, other than Dawson and Virgil."

"Could it have been that Trammel Braxton?" Dorothy asked.

I shook my head. "I really don't think so. I think that relationship was over."

I drove to the hospital and let the girls out at the front while I parked the car. By the time I made my way to intensive care, Nana Jo and the girls were flocked around Dawson and were mothering him. He was hugged, kissed, fed, and loved. All of them shoved money into his jacket at one time or another. That much concentrated attention could be overwhelming. When I noticed his eyes glaze over, I suggested the girls go down to the gift shop.

When they were gone, Dawson sat next to me and released a heavy sigh. "Thank you. They're amazing, but I was starting to feel a little smothered."

"They really care about you."

He nodded. "I know. I care about them too, but it's been pretty emotional. Nothing to do but think."

"You sleeping?"

He shook his head. "Some, but it's not easy. The nurses have been great. There's a nurses' lounge and they let me sleep in there. When he gets out of intensive care, then I can sleep on a cot in his room."

"Any idea when that will be?"

He shook his head.

We visited a little longer and then the girls and I headed back to Michigan. I dropped Nana Jo and the girls at the retirement village and then swung by Jenna's to pick up Oreo and Snickers. Jenna claimed she wasn't a big dog lover, but her husband, Tony, was especially fond of Snickers.

When I got to her house, Oreo was barking before I got to the front door. He met me at the door and barked nonstop until we left. Snickers, however, was curled up on the sofa with my brother-in-law, watching a football game and eating cheese crackers. She barely looked up to acknowledge my arrival. In fact, I had to pick her up and carry her to the car to get her to leave. Her affections were fickle and could be bought with snacks and belly rubs. She had received both from Tony.

At home, I let the dogs do their business before heading upstairs. The house felt very lonely without Nana Jo and Dawson. It was comforting to look outside and see a friendly light coming from his apartment. Nana Jo had her own house at the retirement village, but she had spent most nights here at the bookstore since the murder over the summer. I didn't realize how much I relied on her until she wasn't here.

I tried to sleep but something kept nagging at my brain, and I couldn't figure out what it was. I sifted through the information from the day and tried to catch the clue, but it remained elusive. The best I could do was to narrow it down to something that happened at the memorial. However, the harder I tried, the further away it flew. Eventually, I gave up and decided to focus on other things. I got out my laptop.

Lady Penelope went down the back stairs to the servants' hall. It had been quite some time since she'd been down here. As she turned the corner at the bottom of the stairs, she couldn't help but glance at the place where she'd fallen as a child. She busted her lip and nearly split her head open. That was probably the closest she'd ever come to seeing Thompkins befuddled. He hurried to fetch the doctor, stopping only long enough to scold the housemaid for waxing the floors to such a dangerous state. Mrs. McDuffie had been the calm one. She had picked up the crying girl and rocked her to sleep, while holding a towel to the cut to staunch the bleeding.

In the hall, Thompkins and the other servants were just finishing their meal but saw Lady Penelope and immediately stood at attention.

"I'm terribly sorry. I didn't mean to interrupt

your breakfast."

"Can we help you, Lady Carlston?" Thompkins asked.

Penelope had only been married a few months and still smiled every time she heard herself addressed as Lady Carlston. But she stifled the smile and looked at the servants. "I wanted to talk to you all. Won't you please sit down?" She took a seat at the large table, knowing the others would never sit while she stood.

The servants seemed confused and looked to Thompkins, who gave a slight nod indicating they could sit.

Penelope looked around the table. "I know you've all heard about the terrible accident yesterday."

Everyone nodded.

"Well, we were hoping you could help us."

Thompkins coughed discreetly. "We will, of course, be happy to assist in any way we can."

She looked around and saw confusion. "Perhaps you could tell me anything you saw that seemed unusual." Penelope sat back.

The servants looked at each other. One of the housemaids squirmed in her chair.

Mrs. McDuffie smiled at Penelope. "Well, I don't know much that'll 'elp. We didn't 'ave much to say to the little tart."

"Mrs. McDuffie," Thompkins said.

Penelope smiled and help up a hand. "It's okay, Thompkins. I hate to admit it, but we didn't like her very much either." She leaned toward Mrs. McDuffie. "Please go on."

"Well, we didn't really get to know much about 'er. Thought she was too good for the likes of us."

"How do you mean?" Penelope asked.

Flossie leaned forward. "It were the way she talked, ma'am." Flossie put her nose in the air and looked down it. "Zis is the way Her Royal Highness prefers her coffee."

The others snickered.

Jim, the footman, joined in, "I tried to talk to her when she first arrived, but she give me the cold shoulder and made it clear I wasn't good enough to shine her shoes."

"And our Jim is one of the best bowlers in England." Mrs. McDuffie sniffed.

Frank chuckled. "I don't think she cared much for cricket."

Flossie poked Gladys in the ribs and gave her a stern look.

Gladys looked up and took a deep breath. "I tried to talk to her too, just to be friendly. I offered to help her unpack her things, but she said she didn't need to unpack. Said she wouldn't be staying here long. She was going to be rich and moving into her own mansion where she would be the mistress and have her own servants."

"Pshaw." Mrs. McDuffie snorted.

"Did she really? I don't suppose she mentioned how she was planning to do this?" Penelope asked.

Gladys shook her head. "I'm sorry, m'lady. She didn't say how. She just said she'd been watching her mistress and copying her mannerisms. She —" Gladys's face flushed.

"It's okay, Gladys. You can tell me what she said." Penelope smiled.

"Well, she said if an American divorcée could snare a king, then she should at least be able to catch a lord," Gladys said.

Thompkins gasped.

Mrs. McDuffie snorted again.

"I don't suppose she mentioned which lord she had in mind?"

Gladys shook her head. "No, ma'am."

Flossie looked uncomfortable but took a deep breath. "I think I know, miss." She looked at Thompkins, who nodded. "Well, I told Mr. Thompkins about seeing Lord Chitterly coming out of the duchess's room."

"Yes. We know about that," Penelope said.

"But it weren't the duchess's room at all. It were her room, Rebecca. She and the duchess had switched rooms. I went in to clean and I saw her, Rebecca, I mean. She weren't

291

wearing no clothes."

Mrs. McDuffie gasped. "The little trollop."

"But I don't understand," Penelope said.

"She said the duchess wanted the room next to that German bloke, and her mistress didn't care that the other room was smaller. So, they switched."

"So Lord Chitterly had been with Rebecca and not the duchess?" Penelope asked.

Flossie nodded. "Yes, m'lady."

Penelope nodded. "Very interesting."

While Penelope was downstairs questioning the servants, Victor headed to Scotland Yard to talk to Detective Inspector Covington. He'd never been to Scotland Yard before and found the technology fascinating. Everywhere he looked there was something new and interesting. He made his way to the detective's desk.

They shook hands. "My God, man, I had no idea half this stuff existed. It's no wonder the Yard has the reputation they do."

Detective Inspector Covington smiled. "The twentieth century technology is good, but nothing beats good old-fashioned police work." He indicated Victor should sit.

Once both men were seated, he continued, "But I don't think you drove all the way out here just to check out the latest technology at the Yard."

On the drive from the country, Victor had

292

rehearsed several excuses to explain his presence. Face-to-face with the detective, none of them seemed believable. "Actually, old man, I wanted to know if you've determined which gun killed the maid."

Detective Inspector Covington looked around. "I'm not working on that case. I've been pulled to work on a case of poaching in Shrewsbury."

Victor stared. "Poaching?"

"Yes. Poaching. Serious business, poaching."

"But surely, murder takes precedence over poaching?" Victor couldn't hide the astonishment in his voice.

Detective Inspector Covington looked around again. He pulled a folder from a drawer and placed it on top of his desk. "Well, you know poaching is a hanging offense. It threatens the very seat of the British government." He winked. "Nothing more important than finding poachers." He tapped the folder and slid it toward him. "Care for a spot of tea?"

Victor nodded. "Yes. I believe I would."

Detective Inspector Covington stood. "Afraid the canteen is clear down to the other side of the building. It'll take me at least ten minutes to get the tea and get back. Think you'll be okay?"

Victor nodded.

Detective Inspector Covington ambled down the hall.

As soon as he was gone, Victor grabbed the folder and opened it.

Victor left before Detective Inspector Covington returned.

Wickfield Lodge was a large U-shaped mansion, with the Marsh family's bedrooms on one side of the U and the guest rooms on the other, with a long hallway in between. Lord William needed to talk to Lord Charles. In his present condition, there was no way he could make it to Chitterly's room. Daphne volunteered to help.

She stood in front of the guest room now occupied by the Chitterlys. Just as she raised her hand to knock, one of the nearby doors opened. She turned and saw James. Her first instinct was to smile until she remembered this wasn't the room set aside for the Duke of Kingfordshire. No, this wasn't his room. She thought for a moment and remembered the arrangements her aunt had shared. This was Virginia Hall's bedroom.

He saw her and had the decency to blush. "Daphne. What are you doing here?"

"Just getting Lord Charles. My uncle wants to talk to him." She knocked on the door.

"I can explain."

"No need."

Charles Chitterly opened the door. "Yes?"

"My uncle was hoping you would join him for tea. He's had an attack of gout and is confined to his bedroom at the moment, but if you don't mind following me, I'll be happy to lead the way."

Lord Charles smiled. "I would like nothing better, my dear."

Daphne nodded at James as she walked arm in arm with Lord Charles down the hall.

CHAPTER 17

Monday morning I had to get back to my routine. Fall break was over and the twins were back in school. Nana Jo promised to swing by at noon to give me a few hours break. The morning went by slowly, and I was soon missing both Nana Jo and Dawson a lot. Not just because of the help they provided, but they were also good company.

We'd gone through the stockpile of baked goods Dawson had left, so I ordered quite a few things from a South Harbor bakery that delivered. The baked goods were tasty but lacked the extra special oomph Dawson's had. Admittedly, I might be slightly biased.

Nana Jo arrived promptly at noon. I went to the bank and deposited the check I'd been carrying around all weekend. Then I swung by a fast-food restaurant and grabbed a sandwich. As I was driving back to the store, I spotted a bright red Ford Escape on the edge of the parking lot of a large car dealership. Before I realized what I was doing, I pulled into the lot. As soon as I got out of the car, salesmen swarmed around me like locusts. My personal feeling is there is a special level of hell where the inhabitants are continually haggling with salesmen and buying and selling cars. It's just above the level where your penance for a life of evil is spent buying and selling real estate.

Leon had taken care of things like haggling with car salesmen. However, I was a big girl and refused to be intimidated.

"I'm just looking!" I shouted. I pointed to one of the salesmen. "What's your name?"

"Bob." He stepped forward and reached out his hand. He opened his mouth to start his sales pitch but was halted when I held up my hand.

"Bob. I want to *look* at SUVs. I don't want to be bothered. Don't follow me. Don't help me. When I need you, I will come find you. Understood?" I looked around at all of the salesmen. They all nodded and backed away.

The new models were on one side of the lot and the other side had a variety of used cars. The red Escape was last year's model and had thirty thousand miles, but it had a sunroof, leather seats, and tons of other bells and whistles I didn't even know existed. I spotted Bob about three aisles over and waved for him to join me.

"You were waving for me, right?" he asked, out of breath from his quick jog.

"Yes. I have questions."

Bob answered all of my questions and went inside to get the keys so I could take a test drive. I showed him my driver's license, and he came back with a license plate, which he stuck in the back window and gave me a large key fob. I stared at it. There was no key.

Bob laughed and explained all I had to do was push a button and, as long as I had the fob within a certain range, the car would respond. The doors unlocked. The motor started. It was magic.

I drove the car in a big loop around the block, which included a short jaunt on Interstate 94. I was amazed at how quiet the car was and how smooth the ride. Bob talked the entire test drive, explaining every feature he thought would sell me on the car. Little did he know, I was sold at intermittent wipers and automatic lights. I would have been happy with lights that dinged when left on. These lights actually turned themselves on and off, like magic.

Back at the car lot, Bob asked if I had a trade-in. I escorted him to my SUV. I was insulted when he asked if I wanted to get it repaired before I got my trade-in estimate.

"If I wanted to get the car repaired, I wouldn't be buying a new one." I pointed out that all of the pieces were there and showed him the knobs in the ashtray.

I looked at my watch. I needed to get back to the bookstore. Bob did everything he could to get me to stay, including a suggestion that I put a deposit down on the vehicle to make sure no one bought it before I returned. I declined. If it was gone in a few hours, then it wasn't meant to be.

At the bookstore, Nana Jo took one look at me and knew something was up. I had planned to surprise her when I arrived with the car, but she always knew when something was going on with me.

"It's about time," she teased when I told her about the car. "You can go back. I can handle things here."

The store wasn't busy. In fact, she was reading an Agatha Christie collection of short stories, *The Mysterious Mr. Quin.* However, now that I'd told her, I wanted her to see it before I bought it. I wanted her approval.

The hours until closing passed very slowly. When it finally did arrive, we dashed off to the car lot. My red SUV was still parked where I'd left it, and I breathed a sigh of relief.

Nana Jo heartily approved. I'd completed some of the paperwork for financing before I left and when we returned, I learned the trade-in amount for my CRV and the rate the dealership offered for financing. If Bob thought I had been tough on him earlier, he learned I was a lightweight compared to Nana Jo. She pulled out her iPhone and went to a few websites. By the time she finished negotiating, I got the car for five thousand dollars less and 2 percent better interest rate. We transferred my belongings from the Honda, and my heart tugged the slightest bit as I took one last look. I smiled and gave her a pat. "You served me well."

I signed a ton of papers, shook hands with Bob, and drove my new SUV off the lot.

"Open the sunroof. Let's go pick up the girls and go for a spin," Nana Jo said.

Before we could head to the retirement village, I got a call from Dawson. The rings vibrated throughout the car's stereo system.

"What on earth . . ." I said.

Nana Jo laughed. "You have Bluetooth. I synched your phone with the car while you were talking to Bob. Touch that button there." She pointed.

I pushed the button and Dawson's voice

came through the speakers. "Someone just tried to kill my dad."

"Oh my God. Are you okay?"

"Yeah. I'm okay."

"Call the police. We'll be there in thirty minutes."

CHAPTER 18

I didn't remember parking the car at the hospital. After disconnecting with Dawson, my next memory was giving him a big hug. Dawson was about a foot taller than me and probably a hundred pounds heavier, but when I put my arms around him, he bent down, put his head on my shoulder, and wept. I held him with everything I had. A few minutes, hours, who knew how long that embrace lasted, but I knew at that moment Dawson Alexander would forever be a part of my family, and I would do anything to protect him.

When Dawson was composed, he straightened up and I got a good look at him. He looked haggard. There were dark circles under his eyes.

Nana Jo gave him a fierce hug, then pulled his face close. She stared into his eyes as though she were looking into his soul. "You look terrible. You need a good meal and sleep."

Dawson kissed her on the cheek. "I'm fine, Mrs. T."

"What happened?" I asked.

He ran his hand through his hair. "I was in the lounge, lying on a sofa watching television." He lowered his eyes. "I should have been watching him."

"You can't blame yourself for this." I rubbed his shoulders. I hoped he felt reassured, although I doubted it. I'd gone through similar feelings of guilt when my husband died in the middle of the night. I should have been there. I should have single-handedly fought back death. I should have stayed by his side and watched him night and day. I should have forced him to go to the doctor for regular checkups years earlier. Regret was the survivor's burden. Like cancer, it got in your mind and ate away your common sense and reason. "Your dad's still alive. Focus on that for now."

Dawson took a deep breath. "One of the nurses came in and said I had a package at the front desk."

"That's odd. Don't they bring packages up to the room?" I asked.

"I thought so too, but the nurse said he told her it was from you. He said the

303

volunteers were gone for the day. If I came down to the lobby, I could pick it up now. Otherwise, it would be delivered tomorrow. I thought it was another pizza like the one you sent last night."

I frowned. I hadn't sent Dawson a pizza, but apparently someone else had.

"I went down to the lobby. No one knew anything about a package." He looked up and pointed. "That's when I saw him."

We followed where he was pointing. That's when we noticed Virgil Russell sitting at a desk in a small room off the nurses' station. He was covered in blood and was holding a bloody towel to his nose with his head tilted back.

"Virgil Russell?" Nana Jo asked.

Dawson nodded. "He claimed I sent him a note, but I didn't. So we rushed back up here and all hell had broken loose. Lights and alarms were going off in my dad's room. There were tons of people in there working on him." He looked at his hands. "That's when I hit him."

"Good," Nana Jo said.

"Nana Jo, you shouldn't encourage violence."

She sniffed.

The elevator opened and Stinky Pitt and a uniformed policeman stepped out and walked toward us.

One of the doctors came out of the room and said a few words to the two officers. The officer took up his position in front of A-squared's door. Detective Pitt and the doctor joined us on the sofa.

"Your father had a really close call. If he hadn't been in a coma, he'd be dead now. In fact, I'm not sure why he isn't. He's a fighter. We'll know more in the next twenty-four hours. All we can do now is wait." The doctor left.

Detective Pitt wanted to know what happened. Dawson repeated what he'd said to us. He asked a few questions and then Detective Pitt went to talk to Virgil.

Nana Jo wandered near the nurses' station outside the room where Detective Pitt and Virgil were talking. When I saw what she was doing, I told Dawson to wait there and I joined her at the desk. Unfortunately, when Detective Pitt turned and saw us standing nearby, he closed the door.

One of the nurses who had been sitting behind the desk looked up. She had a sympathetic face, and I'd seen her before when I visited. She winked at me, put a finger to her lips, and motioned for us to follow her. She led us behind the nurses' station, around a corner. There was a small room, barely bigger than a closet. There was a refrigerator and microwave and a small sliding door, which looked like a concession stand opening. The door was slightly ajar and we could hear everything in the room where Detective Pitt and Virgil Russell were sitting. We mouthed the words *thank you*. Our friendly nurse smiled and quietly returned to her desk.

"Come back to finish the job, did you?" Detective Pitt asked.

"I never laid one hand on him," Virgil said in a muffled voice.

"What brought you here tonight?"

"I got a note from Dawson to meet him here. He said he wanted to talk about Melody."

Nana Jo and I exchanged a glance.

"What note?"

We heard fumbling and then the sound of a note being opened.

"Did you ask him about this?"

"I never got the chance."

We heard the sound of a door opening and hurried back around the nurses' station. We took a roundabout route back to the sofa where Dawson was sitting. Detective Pitt stood nearby.

"Where have you two been?" he asked.

"Ladies' room. I've got a weak bladder,"

Nana Jo said. "It comes with old age."

"You got a weak bladder too?" He looked at me.

"Do you *have* a weak bladder is the correct question." I stared at the detective. "And, the answer is no. I do not."

"Women tend to go to the bathroom in pairs," Nana Jo added. "Surely you've noticed, Stinky Pitt."

A slight rise of color went up the detective's neck. Whether it was anger for the grammar lesson or frustration with Nana Jo for using his childhood nickname, I couldn't hazard a guess.

He turned to Dawson and held up a note. "Did you send this?"

Dawson reached out a hand, but Detective Pitt held it out of reach. "Just look. Don't touch. Probably a slim chance we'll find any prints, but it's still evidence." He held the paper from the corners so Dawson could look.

I strained to read the note, but Nana Jo was quicker and pulled out her iPhone and snapped a picture before Detective Pitt knew what was happening. She stretched the photo, and I looked over her shoulder and read the note.

If you want to know what happened to Melody, come round to the surgery at nine.

The note was on hospital stationery but didn't have a signature. Something about the note struck me as off.

"What's wrong?" Nana Jo asked.

"I don't know. Something just seems . . . odd about that note."

"I know. I was thinking the same thing, but I can't figure out what it is."

"Well, I wish someone would tell me what it is," Detective Pitt muttered. "Did you write this?" He looked at Dawson.

He shook his head. "Never seen it before."

"When did he get it?" I asked.

Detective Pitt looked puzzled, then turned and walked to the room where Virgil sat. He said a few words to him and then returned.

"Said he found it on the windshield of his car."

"But, I haven't left the hospital since my dad was admitted," Dawson said.

"How did he know A-squared was here? I haven't seen it in the papers." Nana Jo asked.

"Did you tell anyone?" Detective Pitt asked Dawson.

"No. I haven't left the hospital." Dawson gritted his teeth.

"I might have mentioned it to a few people." I severely hoped I wasn't responsible for this attack.

"Who?" Detective Pitt didn't look at all sympathetic.

"Well, I told Jenna and Chris and Zaq. I'm pretty sure I told Emma and Jillian. The girls from the nursing home and Professor Quin."

"Why didn't you just put an ad in the newspaper? It would have been faster."

"Stop. Can't you see she feels bad enough as it is?" Nana Jo put a comforting arm around my shoulders.

Detective Pitt grunted. "Was Virgil Russell around when you told any of those people?"

I thought for a moment. "He might have overheard when I told Professor Quin at Melody's memorial service."

Detective Pitt asked a few more questions, then he got Virgil, and asked him to accompany him to the police station to answer questions. "You can even file a report against Mr. Alexander for assault, if you'd like."

Nana Jo scowled at Stinky Pitt. I held onto Dawson's hand.

Virgil Russell stared at Dawson, who

309

didn't look contrite or repentant in the least. In fact, he looked like he'd like nothing better than to take another swing at him if given the chance. He and Dawson stared at each other like two boxers sizing each other up before a fight. During that exchange, something happened. Maybe Virgil realized Dawson was younger, bigger, and stronger than him. "Nawh, I won't be filing no police report."

Stinky Pitt escorted Virgil to the elevator.

"What just happened there?" Nana Jo asked as the elevator closed behind the two men.

"I have no idea."

Nana Jo and I offered to stay at the hospital, but Dawson urged us to go home. I was prepared to camp out, despite his assurances he would be fine.

"I appreciate you both for driving all the way here, but I'm fine. No one can try anything now. The hospital is on alert. There's a cop standing guard, and I'm not going to be fooled into leaving again."

"But we want to help," I said.

Dawson looked very intense. "Then find out who killed Melody and who tried to kill my dad."

Nana Jo and I tried to figure out what was

bothering us about the note during the drive home. Neither of us could put our finger on it. She sent me the picture of Virgil's note so I could study it later. I tried to figure out what was nagging at my mind. Was it possible A-squared really knew who killed Melody? Whoever killed Melody tried to kill him. Why did he wait until now to make another attempt?

It was late or rather early morning by the time we made it home. Oreo and Snickers were knocked out. Not even turning on the lights woke them. I literally had to pick them up to take them out to take care of business. They immediately got back in their beds when they were done, but I didn't even try to sleep.

"Wallis claims she and Count Rudolph were talking all night." Lady Elizabeth pursed her lips as she continued knitting.

"Talking? Really, and they had to do this in his bedroom?" Penelope asked.

"That's what she claims, dear."

Something in her aunt's voice made Penelope stare at her in disbelief. "Don't tell me you believe her?"

Lady Elizabeth knitted a few stitches and then paused. "Actually, I do."

"But that's crazy. Why would she be in the

311

count's bedroom? If they wanted to talk, there are over a hundred rooms in this house where they could have 'talked.' "

"True, dear, but you have to remember, Wallis was trying to negotiate some type of agreement. They needed a place that was private." Lady Elizabeth looked at her family. "I'm not saying it was wise, but I did believe her when she said she wasn't having an affair with Count Rudolph."

"Despite the fact that she's practically thrown herself at him the entire time she's been here?" Penelope asked.

"Yes. Wallis isn't beautiful. She's a flirt and she knows how to use her sex appeal to attract men. But take a look at the type of men she attracts."

"I don't think I understand you, dear?" Lord William looked at his wife as he sat in his bed with his leg propped up on pillows.

"I think I know what you mean," Daphne said from her seat near the window. She had a large drawing pad on her lap and appeared to be sketching. "She seems to flirt with men who aren't very bright and who aren't . . . very manly."

"Exactly." Lady Elizabeth smiled at her niece. "Let's face it, David isn't exactly known for his brains. He's always been a bit spoiled," she said thoughtfully. "He liked women, dancing, drinking, and having fun. He was a playboy."

Victor stood against the wall and smoked. "He was the king. He could have had any woman he wanted."

Lady Elizabeth picked up her knitting. "And who does he choose? A married woman with two living husbands. There's no way he believed he would be allowed to reign as the head of the Church of England."

Daphne looked at her aunt. "You think he married her to escape being king?"

"Yes, I do."

"But why did she marry him?" Penelope asked.

Lady Elizabeth knitted. "I think Wallis is one of those women who's always attracted to the wrong type of men. She doesn't want a strong man. She wants a man she can manipulate and control, someone who will never love her, not in the real way a man loves a woman." Lady Elizabeth blushed slightly.

Lord William fumbled with his pipe. "Well, I'll be."

"In David, she found someone in need of a mother figure. In Count Rudolph . . . well, I suspect she has found someone who is struggling with his own sexuality."

"My word," Lord William said.

"He is a bit of a dandy," Victor said.

"That explains why he never made a pass at me," Daphne said. "Most men do, but Count Rudolph never did." She looked very serious.

Everyone stared at Daphne for several seconds until they noticed the slightest twitch around her mouth before she broke into a laugh.

Everyone laughed until a knock at the door caused them to stop and stare.

Penelope looked to her aunt, who gave her a slight nod. She walked to the door and opened it slightly. When she looked out, she smiled and opened the door wider. "James, at last. I thought you'd never get here."

The duke entered the room and Penelope closed the door behind him. Inside, he looked around. His eyes lingered longest on Daphne by the window. "Sorry I'm late. Have you figured out who the murderer is?"

"We were just waiting for Lady Elizabeth to tell us," Victor joked. "Take a seat."

Lady Elizabeth shook her head and continued to knit. "I have no idea who the murderer is. I can't even tell who the intended victim was."

Lady Penelope recapped her conversation with the servants.

"That goes along with what I learned from Lord Charles," Lord William said. "Darned fool admitted he had a fling with the maid. Called

314

it a bit of fun." He pursed his lips as though he had just tasted a bitter lemon. "Got a nasty shock the next morning. The girl wanted him to divorce his wife and marry her."

"You mean she tried to blackmail him?" Victor asked.

Lord William nodded. "That's about the size of it. Threatened to tell his wife." He chuckled.

"Well, I don't think that's funny at all." Lady Elizabeth frowned at her husband. "Looks like he had a motive to kill the girl."

"Except, Lord Charles had no intention of leaving his wife. She's got all the money."

Lady Elizabeth nodded. "I thought so. His family has that large estate in Sussex, but no money. He went to America and came back with an American heiress."

"He'd have to go to America to find someone who'd marry him," Daphne added. "His reputation in England was abominable."

"Yes. He was definitely a womanizer," Lady Elizabeth said.

"He could have killed her to keep his wife from finding out," Penelope said.

"She'd have to be deaf, dumb, and blind not to know her husband was a womanizer," Daphne said. "And I think Lady Abigail is a very intelligent woman."

Everyone stared at Daphne.

"I spent time with her after the shoot. She's

very intelligent. Graduated from Smith College in the States."

"If she's so smart, why'd she marry an old bore like Charles Chitterly?" Penelope frowned.

Lady Elizabeth smiled. "Well, she's not very attractive. Maybe she didn't have a lot of other options."

"Exactly," Daphne added. "She's very ambitious. I believe she plans to see that Lord Charles advances, politically."

"A woman with that type of ambition might not want to have her plans ruined by a French maid," James said.

"Didn't you say she was a crack shot who won shooting contests in the States?" Penelope asked.

Daphne nodded. "Yes, but I don't think it was her."

"Why not, dear?" Lady Elizabeth asked.

Daphne looked around as though looking for the right word. "I don't think she would shoot her in the marsh like that. She'd confront the girl and tell her to, pardon my language, bugger off."

Lady Elizabeth smiled at her niece. "I think you're right. That's the impression I have of her as well."

"Well, I had a conversation with Detective Inspector Covington today. You know he's been pulled from the case to find poachers?"

"Poachers?" Penelope stared at her husband. "You're joking, right?"

Everyone had a surprised look on their face, except James and Lady Elizabeth. "Why do I get the feeling the two of you already knew about this?"

Lady Elizabeth pulled yarn from a ball. "I can't say I knew anything about poachers; however, I did suspect Bertie would do something." She sighed. "The king doesn't want attention drawn to the case. I suspected he might use his considerable influence —"

"To delay justice," Penelope said.

"To buy us some time, dear," Lady Elizabeth said.

James stared at Lady Elizabeth with a look of respect. "Three days. I just talked to Budgy, ah . . . I mean Chief Inspector Buddington. That's how long we have to solve this before the Met comes in with everything they've got."

"I looked through a report Detective Inspector Covington had on his desk. The maid wasn't shot with any of the guns belonging to Lord William."

"Thank God," Lord William said.

"But if it wasn't one of our guns, then whose gun was it?" Lady Elizabeth asked.

"No idea. The constables were pulled off the case before they could search the place,"

Victor said.

"We could search for it," Penelope said.

"I'm afraid that gun will be long gone by now, dear," Lord William said.

"Agreed. I think it unlikely the killer would risk hanging onto the murder weapon." Lady Elizabeth shook her head. "Pity we didn't think to have the guests searched sooner. But there might be something . . . Yes, we might be able to find out who had a gun before the killing and doesn't have one now." She knitted for a few moments. "I'll have a word with Thompkins about it. Now, Daphne, were you able to make any progress on your assignment?"

Daphne walked over to her aunt, who was sitting in a chair next to her husband's bedside. Daphne stood in between her aunt and uncle and opened her drawing pad.

The others gathered close for a better view.

"I worked out who was where during the shoot." She pointed at the sketch pad, which had a timeline and circles indicating who was in each group at what time. "Józef Lipski and Virginia Hall are the only ones who are completely unaccounted for at the time the maid was shot."

They stared at the sketch pad and asked a few questions, which Daphne answered.

"Daphne, that's wonderful. You did a tremendous job." Lady Elizabeth smiled at her niece.

Everyone congratulated Daphne. The only person who seemed less than pleased was James. In a brooding silence, he walked to the window and stared out.

"James?" Lady Elizabeth asked. "What's wrong?"

"Nothing." James shook himself. "Virginia Hall is beyond reproach. I know she didn't kill that maid."

Daphne sniffed.

"How can you be sure?" Lady Elizabeth stared at James.

"I just know. I need you to trust me."

They looked at each other, everyone except Daphne, who refused to make eye contact.

"Well, of course we trust you," Lady Elizabeth said. "But can you tell us why you're so sure?"

James stared at Daphne as though willing her to make eye contact, but she merely folded up her sketch pad and returned to her seat by the window. James shook his head. "I'm afraid I can't at the moment, but I promise I'll explain soon."

"Well, if Miss Hall is out, that just leaves Lipski," Victor said.

The group agreed that Victor and James would question Józef Lipski immediately following tea.

James released a heavy sigh.

"What's the matter?" Penelope asked.

"Nothing. I was just thinking about what this will mean if it turns out Józef Lipski is indeed the murderer." James looked out the window for several minutes. "This incident could be twisted to justify German aggression toward the Pols and more German expansion in Europe. No one wants another war with Germany, but we won't be able to avoid it forever."

Everyone stared in shocked silence.

"You think war is inevitable?" Victor asked softly.

James nodded. "I do, and I'm not alone. Other prominent people believe Poland is critical in this political chess game Germany's playing."

Lord William puffed on his pipe. "Dash it all. I hope it doesn't come to that. I hope you're wrong. If it does, well . . . we beat the krauts once, we can do it again."

James lowered his head. "The last war took a terrible toll on England and her allies. A lot has changed since the Treaty of Versailles. Advancements. Advancements in weapons, airplanes, and submarines. Germany's stronger now." His eyes lingered on Daphne. "This could be the match that lights the flame of war. And once that flame is lit, England will never be the same."

CHAPTER 19

The fact I had yet to go to bed did not prevent Oreo from needing to go potty at three thirty in the morning. Sure, I'd let him out just two hours earlier when I got home, but his biological clock was set. Snickers rolled her eyes and growled when I suggested she join us. I couldn't say I blamed her, so I let her sleep in peace.

This time I was tired enough to sleep. I must have slept through my alarm clock because the next thing I remembered was an eight-pound weight landing on my chest. Snickers was fourteen, and I've had her since she was six weeks old. You'd think by now I would have learned not to open my mouth. Unfortunately, I was a slow learner.

"Eww." I rolled over and dislodged the poodle who'd just stuck her tongue in my mouth. I used the blanket to wipe out my mouth.

Snickers simply jumped off the bed and

sat by my bedroom door.

I glared at her. "Do you know what time it is?"

She yawned, stretched, and then began to lick herself.

Just when I thought nothing could make me feel dirtier than I did already. I put a pillow over my head and contemplated ignoring her, but my bladder wouldn't co-operate. I stretched and then got up.

I let the poodles out and then took care of business. By the time I got out of the shower, I got a whiff of my two favorite smells, coffee and bacon. My nana was my hero.

The day went by relatively quickly. We had a steady stream of customers and I didn't have much time to think about Virgil, A-squared, or Melody. Just before closing, Frank Patterson stopped by.

"Frank, what a pleasant surprise," Nana Jo said in a voice that sounded like she wasn't the least bit surprised.

I should have guessed she was up to something when I noticed the goofy smile on her face when she came back from lunch.

"Finish all those books already?" I asked.

"Not yet. I was wondering if maybe you'd be free for dinner."

I smiled. "Thank you, but I'm afraid I

can't. Tonight I'll be hanging out with the girls. It's ladies' night."

"Pishposh," Nana Jo interrupted. "Why don't you join us at the casino tonight?"

I stared at Nana Jo.

Frank Patterson intercepted the look. "Well, I don't want to interrupt."

"You won't be interrupting at all," Nana Jo said. "Meet us at the Four Feathers Casino at eight."

"If you're sure it's okay." Frank looked at me.

I smiled. "Of course it's alright. Why don't you meet us in the lobby in front of the large fireplace?"

Frank agreed and left.

I stared at Nana Jo, who seemed intent on dusting a bookshelf. "Why do I suspect you arranged that?"

"I have no idea what you're talking about." She turned to face me. "But if you didn't want him to come, you could have said something."

I smiled. "You're incorrigible."

Tuesdays was ladies' day at a lot of local shops. The girls liked to stock up on paper towels, vitamins, and whatever else they could get at bargain prices. I normally would have gotten a half-priced oil change and car wash, but since I'd just bought my car yesterday, I wouldn't need to take advantage of that discount yet. We often dined at Randy's Steak House on Tuesday and then hit the bars for half-priced drinks. However, in light of my recent windfall, the girls were anxious to try their luck at the casino.

The girls were surprised and gushed appropriately at my new wheels. The hands-free back door was a huge help when loading up after a day of ladies' day shopping.

"We're ridin' in style now," Ruby Mae said.

On the ride to the casino, we filled the girls in on the latest from Dawson and Virgil Russell.

Irma still doubted Virgil's guilt, but the others felt he was the most likely suspect.

I dropped the girls at the front of the casino and then drove to the back of the parking garage. I parked as far away from potential scratches as possible. When I arrived in the lobby, Frank Patterson was waiting. He had a single rose, which made me smile.

"Where's Nana Jo?"

"They said they'd get a table."

Frank had on a pair of dark wash jeans and a sweater. He looked freshly groomed and smelled of shampoo. I liked that he wasn't wearing cologne.

I was wearing one of my outlet mall finds, a silk blouse and bright red cardigan with jeans.

We walked to the buffet and I looked around until I spotted them. They were sitting at a small booth that could only hold four comfortably. The hostess was talking, but I was so surprised, I didn't hear a word she said. I made a beeline to their booth and stood looking at them.

Dorothy and Ruby Mae hopped up and hurried to the buffet. Irma said she needed a drink and flagged down a waiter. Nana Jo was suddenly really thirsty and drank an entire glass of water.

"Well?" I stared at my grandmother.

"Sorry, dear, they didn't have any larger tables. I guess you two will have to find a table alone."

I looked around at all of the empty tables and booths, which were clearly large enough for all six of us.

The hostess followed us and was at my side when I turned around.

"Come on." I followed the young girl to a table for two in a corner.

Once we were seated and beverage orders taken, I looked across at Frank.

His lips twitched and he did his best to

hide a smile. Eventually, our eyes met and we both burst into laughter.

"Your grandmother is an exceptional woman."

"If by exceptional you mean meddling busybody, then you're right."

We filled our plates at the buffet and talked for hours. I was surprised at how much we had in common. There wasn't an awkward moment. Frank had a knack for telling interesting stories. He'd retired from the military earlier this year and was living his dream of living in one place and running a bar. "Kind of like Cheers, a place where everyone knows your name."

It usually took a while before I opened up and shared about my personal life, but Frank was easy to talk to and he listened. He seemed interested in everything from Leon to Oreo and Snickers to Dawson.

"Your grandmother told me about your investigation. I'd like to help if I can."

I stared. "I'm not sure how you can. It looks like the police might have their killer." I shared what I knew about Virgil Russell and the incident at the hospital. Frank asked who knew about A-squared's accident and which hospital he was in.

"I have some friends who are very connected. Would you mind if I asked them to look up some of the names you gave me?"

"Of course not."

We talked about Melody being a grifter, the special program she was in, her sister Cassidy, Virgil, and the mysterious person Melody thought was trying to muscle in on her mark.

"And you said Virgil mentioned he knew Melody had other lovers?"

I stared. "You think the person who was trying to muscle in on her mark was her lover?"

Frank shrugged. "Beats me. But it seems odd. She didn't make many friends, not even with her roommate. How else would someone get close enough to her to find out about her scam?"

"That makes sense."

"What makes sense?"

I looked up.

Nana Jo was standing by our table. "Are you two still in here?"

I looked at my watch. "I can't believe it's almost midnight. Where's our bill?"

Frank smiled. "I've already taken care of it."

I started to protest, but he simply smiled. "I'm old-fashioned. A gentleman always takes care of the bill."

We met the girls in the lobby and I told

them I'd get the car and pick them up. I protested, but Frank escorted me to my vehicle and held the door open for me while I got in. He said he'd check with one of his buddies on some of the names I gave him, and he'd have something by tomorrow night.

I drove to the front of the casino and picked up Nana Jo and the girls, who were surprisingly quiet for the majority of the ride back to the retirement village. I expected a lot of teasing about Frank but was pleasantly amazed when none came.

Nana Jo stopped in the bookstore and picked up the Agatha Christie book she'd been reading earlier and then went to her room.

I let the poodles out, but something was nagging at my mind. When I went back upstairs, I got on the computer and tried to focus on the clues. I read an article about free writing, where you tried to turn off your conscious mind and let your subconscious write. However, with my eyes closed, my brain kept picturing Frank Patterson and my hands kept typing Quin and Deering Vale. Perhaps writing would help my subconscious grab hold of the elusive thread.

Everyone except the Duchess of Windsor and

Lord William assembled in the parlor for tea. Count Rudolph and Georges Brasseur stood near the fireplace.

"I have never come to understand the British obsession with tea," Brasseur said. "In France we drink wine, or cocoa, but tea . . . it is like drinking dishwater."

Lady Elizabeth blushed slightly. "How thoughtless of me. If you would prefer something else, I'll be more than happy to have the cook prepare you something. I'm sure she has cocoa."

Józef Lipski stood near the window. "Ah, but you have not tasted the cocoa until you have tasted Polish cocoa," he said proudly and puffed out his chest. "It is a special blend." He pulled a small box from his inside pocket. "Perhaps you would care to try some?"

Brasseur looked as though nothing would give him less pleasure than to try the Pol's special blend of cocoa.

"Thank you so much." Lady Elizabeth reached out her hand and Lipski brought the container to her.

She rang a buzzer that summoned the butler.

"Thompkins, would you please ask Cook to prepare a cup of cocoa for Monsieur Brasseur and . . . Mr. Lipski?"

Lipski shook his head. "No, I only drink

cocoa before bed."

Thompkins took the tin and left.

Lady Elizabeth continued pouring tea for the rest of the guests. Fordham-Baker declined. He was drinking what appeared to be a new bottle of scotch. The only way she could gauge was by noting the current bottle contained more liquid than the one she'd seen him with earlier. If she weren't trying to keep the maid's murder out of the newspapers, she would talk to Thompkins about restricting his alcohol. However, in light of the current situation, perhaps she should allow the man to continue drinking.

Within a relatively short period of time, the butler returned with a steaming hot mug, which he presented to the French diplomat.

Brasseur accepted the cup and nodded to Lipski. He placed the cup on the fireplace mantle and continued talking to Count Rudolph.

Józef Lipzki's face turned purple. It was clear Brasseur didn't intend to drink his cocoa.

Thompkins walked to Lipski and returned the tin.

Lipski took the tin and replaced it in his pocket and turned his back to the crowd and walked to the window.

Count Rudolph, normally very quiet and taciturn, surprised the group by speaking.

"Perhaps we can have more music, or is it not acceptable to play music during the British tea?" he asked in a very theatrical manner.

"Well, certainly, you may have music," Lady Elizabeth said.

Count Rudolph followed Daphne to the wireless. When she found a station playing music, he further surprised the group by asking her to waltz.

Count Rudolph bowed dramatically, clicked his heels, and then took Daphne by the waist and waltzed her around the room.

Everyone stared in shocked silence. Virginia Hall approached Lipski, who declined dancing.

The two stood in awkward silence.

When the dance was over, Rudolph bowed to Daphne and returned to his place next to Brasseur.

"Ah, Monsieur Brasseur, you have not drunk your Polish cocoa. You will offend Heir Lipski. You must taste it and tell us if the Polish cocoa is superior to that of the French."

Brasseur looked as though he would rather drink petrol; however, he picked up his cup and took a sip of the liquid. He pursed his lips and frowned. Within a few seconds, he was grasping at his throat and gasping for air. He fell to his knees and then lay prostrate on the ground.

James hurried to his side. He loosened his shirt and tie.

Everyone looked on in stunned silence.

The French diplomat was seized by convulsions for several seconds. He foamed at the mouth. After one exceptionally violent shake, he lay silent.

James felt for a pulse. He looked to the crowd which had gathered around. "He's dead."

CHAPTER 20

I woke from a dream where James Bond was running from all of Agatha Christie's protagonists. Harley Quin was leading a pack which included Hercule Poirot, Miss Marple, Tommy and Tuppence, and Parker Pyne through an English village. At the last minute, Captain America, who bore a striking resemblance to Frank Patterson, dropped from a plane and hog-tied James Bond. Apart from confusion, I felt like I'd run a marathon. Given the knot my sheets were in, I guess I had.

I showered and dressed with care. Tonight I was going on a date with Professor Quin. I had butterflies in the pit of my stomach and considered cancelling. Several times I actually picked up my phone to cancel but stopped myself. Nerves? Fear? Whatever the reason, it was time to put on my big girl panties and face my fears. Just as I made the decision to move forward, I got a call from Harley. His car was in the shop.

"Would you like to reschedule?"

"Actually, I was hoping you would pick me up. I have an opportunity to tour Purnell mansion and I'm really keen on going."

"Okay, sure."

We arranged for me to pick him up around six on campus.

Nana Jo listened nearby with her lips pursed.

I couldn't take the silence anymore. "What?"

"Nothing."

I refused to probe deeper and we worked in silence most of the day, ignoring the giant elephant in the room. Between Nana Jo's silence, a dream that wouldn't go away, first date insecurity, and the nagging question of whether or not Frank would call, I was a nervous wreck by noon. I had just decided to skip lunch when Frank arrived with a tray.

"I hope you two ladies haven't had lunch yet."

We acknowledged that we hadn't eaten.

"Great. I thought about flowers but decided food might be more practical."

The spread he brought looked delicious. There was clam chowder and chicken salad, two of my favorites, and a single rose.

"Hmm . . . clam chowder is my favorite. How did you know?"

He smiled. "You mentioned it last night. I had to get up early to get to the market to get the clams or I would have been by earlier."

"I can't believe you went to so much trouble."

"No trouble at all."

"But there are only two servings?"

He laughed. "How hungry are you?"

I smiled. "Aren't you going to join us?"

"I wish I could, but I've got to get back to the restaurant. Lunch is my busiest time and one of my cooks called out today." He looked disappointed. "Rain check?"

I smiled. "Definitely, and thank you."

He hurried off and Nana Jo and I ate in shifts. However, the arrival of the food helped to eliminate the tension between us.

The only event of note was a text message I received from Emma in the afternoon asking if I would be on campus anytime in the near future. I responded that I was going to be on campus by five thirty and arranged to meet her at the student union.

The rest of the afternoon we worked in a companionable silence. When it was time to leave, I gave Nana Jo a hug.

"What's that for?"

"Because I love you and I appreciate your help and everything you do."

She squeezed me. "I love you too and I'm proud of you, regardless of your taste in men."

"Why don't you like Harley?"

She shook her head. "I don't trust him. Something isn't right with him."

I thought about that for a moment. "I know. I feel it too, but then I'm not planning to marry him. We're just going to dinner and then touring the Purnell mansion."

"The Purnell mansion? You mean that mausoleum built by the House of David?"

I nodded. "I'm not excited about it either, but Harley's writing a book about the House of David and that's where he wants to go."

"Hmm . . . what about what you want?"

I laughed. "I thought you'd be glad I was actually going on a date."

"I am proud of you, but I also don't want to see you get hurt."

I gave her another squeeze. "Honestly, I don't care about him like that. I'm flattered, but . . . that's it. Besides, it's just one date. I'll be fine." I pulled my purse strap onto my shoulder. "I better get out of here. I'll see you later."

Driving my new SUV put a smile on my

face. I loved the light coming through the sunroof, the satellite radio, and the gauge that told me how many miles until empty. Today, I was disappointed by how quickly the drive to MISU was from downtown. I parked away from other vehicles and walked to the student union with a joyful heart.

Inside, Emma and Zaq sat together in a booth. They were sharing an order of onion rings and laughing with their heads together. I hesitated for a moment, not wanting to interrupt the moment.

Eventually, Emma looked up and smiled. "There you are."

I sat down and declined the onion rings they generously offered to share.

"I didn't want to bother you, but Zaq said I should tell you about a couple of weird things that happened."

"Of course you aren't bothering me. You can talk to me anytime," I said with sincerity. I learned long ago not to get attached to my nephews' girlfriends. Just when I got to know them, they were gone, but I liked Emma. I hoped we could be friends, regardless of what happened between her and Zaq.

She smiled. "Well, first someone broke into my dorm room."

"Are you okay? Was anything taken?"

"I wasn't there and the only thing missing

337

was my laptop, best I can figure. It happened on Sunday. Zaq and I went to the movies after the memorial."

"Did you call the police?"

"Campus police. They filed a report but said I'd probably never see it again. Good thing I back up everything. Plus, I paid for insurance, so I got a replacement." She patted her new MacBook.

"That's strange, but it isn't really that unusual. I think thefts are common on college campuses."

"The weird thing isn't that the laptop was stolen. The weird thing is that it was returned."

"Returned? You mean the thief brought your laptop back?"

"Not exactly. They tossed it in a dumpster. It was kind of insulting, really, like my laptop wasn't good enough for them or something."

Zaq smiled. "I don't think that's it." He looked at me. "I think they thought it was Melody's, but when they looked through it, they saw it wasn't."

"What makes you think that?"

Zaq shrugged. "They didn't take the television or the microwave or any of her jewelry. Plus, you guys had already packed up all of Melody's stuff, but whoever broke in, opened all her drawers and cut open the mattress."

"But only the one on Melody's side of the room," Emma added.

"Aunt Sammy, I think the burglar was looking for something."

Emma's phone vibrated. "That reminds me about the other thing." She held up her cell. "I got another text from Melody's sister."

I read the screen.

"I tried to forward, but it wouldn't let me. Zaq said she must have sent it so it couldn't be forwarded."

"Can someone do that?" I asked.

"Depends on their e-mail system, but yes. There are systems that prevent forwarding," Zaq said.

The text said she thought whoever was trying to get in on Mel's scam was someone she had been having an affair with.

"I guess this means Detective Pitt is right. It must be Virgil."

"Didn't Cassidy know Virgil? I thought you mentioned that at the memorial," Emma said.

I nodded. "She did know Virgil."

"Plus, Virgil was already in on the scam, wasn't he?" Zaq asked.

I didn't have answers. This was odd. I told

them what Virgil told us the other night at the hospital.

I looked at my watch. "I better go. I've got to pick up Harley . . . ah, Professor Quin."

Emma looked surprised. "Are you dating Professor Quin?"

"I wouldn't call it dating. He's helping me with some stuff for a book, being British and everything. How was your lab Monday night?" I asked.

"What lab?" Emma looked puzzled.

"I thought you had a lab Monday night for Professor Quin's class."

Emma shook her head. "Nope, in fact he cancelled class on Monday."

Something in the look that passed between Zaq and Emma made me stop. "Why? What's up?"

"Nothing." Emma was a horrible liar. Her face turned red and she couldn't make eye contact.

"You can tell me. I'm not in love with the guy. He's cute, but . . . oh, I don't know. There's just something odd about him."

Emma breathed a sigh of relief. "I'm so glad you aren't serious about him. I think the guy is kind of creepy. He hits on his students, and there was a rumor he was having an affair with one of them." Emma

340

paused before making up her mind. "I think it was Melody."

"Do you have any proof?"

"No."

"Accusing a professor of having an affair with a student is serious business. You wouldn't want to make an accusation like that without proof," I cautioned. "But maybe I can ask him some questions tonight."

"Be careful, Aunt Sammy," Zaq said.

"I will. Don't worry."

CHAPTER 21

I met Harley outside his office.

"Is this a new car?"

I smiled. "Yes. I've only had it for two days."

"You should have gotten one of those new Land Rovers. They have tons more room in the back." He proceeded to put his bicycle into the back of my new SUV. I tried not to grimace at the sight of the mud which dropped from the tires or the scratches he'd gotten on the molding.

"There's a really lovely vegan restaurant down the road. Why don't we grab a bite before we go to the mansion?" He tossed his backpack on the back seat and got in and fastened his seat belt.

I shook off the desire to tip my hat like a chauffeur and got in the car. I followed his directions and pulled into the parking lot of a very expensive restaurant which I'd heard mixed reviews about. The décor was extremely high-end. The service was awful. The food was beautifully plated, but the taste was average. Harley talked a lot and seemed very excited.

Near the end of the meal, he finally seemed to notice I hadn't said much. "You're very quiet tonight. Is anything the matter?"

I shook my head. "No. I'm fine."

The waiter brought the bill and Harley sat very still. I, too, sat still. After an awkward few minutes, he smiled and pulled out his wallet. "I'm afraid I didn't bring any cash with me."

I smiled. "It says on the window they take credit cards. You do take credit cards, don't you?" I asked the waiter.

He nodded.

Harley's smile seemed forced, but he kept it plastered on. He looked back in his wallet and pulled out a Diner's Club card.

The waiter frowned. "We take Visa, Master Card, Discover, and American Express. We don't take Diner's Club."

Harley looked at me. "I'm afraid that's the only card I have. Would you mind covering this one? The next meal is on me." He smiled.

I wondered briefly what would happen if I claimed to have forgotten my wallet. However, the waiter loomed over my shoulder and I wasn't up for making a mad dash to the car. Instead, I pulled out my credit card and promised myself this would be the last meal Professor Harley Quin would ever receive from me.

"Thanks, love." He smiled.

I stared back. I hadn't noticed before how crooked his teeth were.

Once the bill was taken care of, I drove to Purnell mansion. The mansion was over a hundred and ten years old and it looked every day of its age. I could imagine the building in its heyday was grand and beautiful, with a front porch that covered the entire front of the building, leaded glass windows, and ornately carved moldings. However, the paint had chipped away long ago. The floorboards of the porch sagged and there was evidence of termite damage around the outside.

Harley got out of the car and grabbed his backpack from the back seat and hurried up the sidewalk. He was halfway up on the porch before he seemed to realize I wasn't behind him. He turned and looked at me. "You coming?"

Perhaps it was too much to expect him to open my door, but I couldn't help comparing my experience with Frank Patterson. I don't *need* someone to open doors for me, but it sure felt nice when they did. I sighed and got out of the car.

An older gentleman with a long white beard and thick glasses waited for us on the porch. He said his name was Josiah Templeton.

"You that young fella that called?" Josiah stared long and hard at Harley.

"Yes. I'm Harley Quin, and this is Mrs. Washington."

I smiled and shook his hand. "I'm pleased to meet you."

He dragged his gaze away from Harley. He looked frail and his skin was almost translucent, but he smiled and patted my hand. "Don't get a chance to see many pretty women."

I smiled. "I'll bet you say that to all the women."

He laughed. "Don't get much chance to anymore. Just a handful of us left these days." He kept patting my hand. "I'll be a hundred on Christmas Day."

"You don't look it," I lied.

He stared at Harley again. "You look familiar. Have we met before?"

"I just have one of those faces." Harley's smile seemed strained. "Well, we appreciate you allowing us to tour the mansion, but . . ." He stared at Josiah with sympathy. "I'm afraid this tour might be a bit much for you, old boy. Look, why don't you just give me the key and we'll wander around and then I can lock everything up when I'm done."

My eyes narrowed and I would have berated him for insensitivity, but Josiah said he didn't mind and handed over the key. He pointed at a small building across the street. "I have a cottage over there to the right. Just drop the key in the mail slot."

Harley promised to do so and hurriedly unlocked the door. "You coming?" He turned to me.

"I'll be there in a few minutes. I'm going to make sure Josiah makes it home safely."

"Fine." Harley hurried inside.

I offered an arm to Josiah and, between me and his walking stick, he hoisted himself up.

"Thank you. If you just help me down to the bottom of the stairs, I'll be fine from there. These old joints need a little boost to get going, but once I'm moving, you just watch my steam."

We walked down the stairs slowly and I mentally cursed Harley for dragging this nice man out here just to tour an old house. At the bottom of the stairs, Josiah refused further assistance. I continued talking and made sure he made it safely to his cottage.

Once inside, he thanked me and I turned and made my way back to the mansion. I contemplated not entering, but I knew my defiant gesture would be wasted. Instead, I went inside.

"Hello? Harley, where are you?" I yelled from the foyer.

"I'm down here."

I followed the voice past the elaborately carved staircase, high ceilings, and tapestries to a door that lead downstairs to the cellar. I was surprised, but thankful, the old house still looked relatively sturdy, although the cobwebs and musty smell indicated it had been many years since the house had been opened and aired.

In the cellar, I looked around and tried to ignore the creepy feeling there were more than spiders crawling around down there.

Harley was on his knees with a flashlight, studying the cinder block walls.

"What are you looking for down here?"

He continued scanning the walls. "Legend has it there were secret tunnels under this building."

"You mean the tunnels where Benjamin Purnell allegedly abused young girls and conducted satanic rituals and where the

347

commune stored his body in a hermetically sealed glass coffin?"

Growing up in North Harbor, these rumors were spread widely among North Harbor children, especially around Halloween.

Harley continued his search. I couldn't see his face, but I could hear the glee in his voice. "Tunnels full of buried treasure."

"Oh my God. You're a treasure hunter." I didn't even try to keep the scorn out of my voice. This guy was a nutcase. I made up my mind to leave him there when my cell phone rang. It was Nana Jo. I'd barely gotten a word out when she started.

"Sam, you've gotta get away from that guy. He's not what he claims to be. Frank had one of his friends at Scotland Yard investigate him, and he has a record. He was a grifter too. He lied about where he was from. There is no Deering Vale —"

I never got to hear what else she was going to say because Harley snatched the phone out of my hand. "Your grandmother has a big mouth."

I stared as Harley Quin turned off my cell phone and put it in his pocket. "Deering Vale . . . Oh my goodness. I can't believe I missed it. That's a fictitious town Agatha Christie made up for *The Mysterious Harley*

Quin." I hit myself on the head with my palm. "Harley Quin? Oh my God, I can't believe I missed that."

He smiled smugly and pulled a gun from his pocket. "Now, what am I going to do with you?"

Something inside told me insulting him was a bad idea, but I didn't listen. "You cheap murdering lowlife scumbag."

He hauled off and struck me across the face. The blow was so hard it sent me flying into the wall. I hit my head on the doorjamb and fell to the ground. I must have been knocked out for some time because when I came to, there was no light coming through the small basement windows.

I felt a kick in my side. "You awake?"

I groaned.

He leaned his face down within inches of mine. "Now, what am I going to do with you?"

I had a few ideas of what I wanted to do to him. He must have read my thoughts because he laughed. "You're a feisty one, aren't you? Too bad you had to be so smart. We could have had fun together." He leered and ran his finger along my cheek.

I swatted his hand away. If I'd had any saliva in my mouth, I would have spit in his face. Unfortunately, I think the tofu and black bean mush I'd eaten earlier had absorbed all the fluid in my body.

"Few people come down here anymore. It'll be a long time before anyone finds your body. You and Benjamin Purnell can rot down here together." He stood and pointed his gun at me. "Goodbye, Samantha."

I needed to keep him talking, buy myself some time. "Why did you do it? Why did you kill Melody?"

He smiled. "She got greedy. She had a good con going with that oaf Dawson, but she didn't want to cut me in." He sneered.

I wondered how I had ever thought him attractive. In this cold, damp dark basement, the only thing I felt when I looked at him was revulsion. "So it was about money?"

"It was always about the money."

"Maybe she really cared about Dawson."

He laughed. "You are so naive. She didn't care two bits for that dumb jock. He was just a mark. She said he was going to be her meal ticket out of the life." He paced. "I didn't care if she wanted to believe she could stop and go the straight and narrow, as long as she gave me my cut."

I shivered in spite of myself at the cold tone of his voice. "So you killed her. Just like that?"

350

He nodded. "Just like that." He raised his gun.

"What about A-squared?" I rushed to get in before he killed me.

"He saw us together at the HOD. Followed us." He shrugged. "The crazy old fool tried to blackmail me. Me?" He laughed. "Can you believe that? He saw me kill her in the parking lot at the HOD, and he thinks I'm going to pay him money not to tell the police?" He shook his head in disbelief. "Now, enough talk. I don't like loose ends and you're just another loose end." He pointed the gun at my head and stared.

I refused to close my eyes. Instead, I stared defiantly at him and awaited my fate.

Just then, I heard a thunderous sound as someone leapt down the stairs. Harley turned just as a huge shadow came barreling toward him and knocked him to the ground. I slid back against the wall and felt arms coming around.

"Sam, are you okay?" Nana Jo asked.

I leaned against her arms and rested my head. "I'll be fine. Who's that?" I pointed to the tousling shadows.

Just then, Dawson pulled Harley up by his shirt and punched him in the face. Harley went limp and Dawson reared back and hit him again. Dawson's face was red with fury. Just as he was about to hit him again, Zaq and Frank Patterson grabbed his arm and held onto him.

Tears streamed down Dawson's face. "He killed Melody and tried to kill my dad."

Frank put his arms around Dawson and held on to him. "I know, but it's over now."

Zaq came over to me. "You okay, Aunt Sammy?"

I nodded. "I'm fine now."

Sirens blared. Footsteps trampled overhead.

"We're down here!" Nana Jo yelled.

CHAPTER 22

The EMTs patched up my head. They wanted me to go to the hospital, but I declined. Nana Jo insisted I ride home with Frank, but I refused to leave my new car.

I looked at Dawson. "How did you get here?"

He nodded toward Zaq. "My dad came to. He told me it was Harley. He was taking a leak behind a bush at the HOD and he saw him kill her. They were kissing in the back seat of his car and then he strangled her, got in the front seat and drove away. He must have dumped her body by the river where the police found her." He looked sad. "He left her like a piece of trash by the side of the road." He took a deep breath. "My dad tried to get him to pay to keep quiet and he tried to kill him."

I hugged him. "Dawson, I'm so glad your dad is okay." I stared at him. "But, how did you get here?"

"Zaq and Emma came by to see me and I got a ride back with him."

I looked around. "Where's Emma?"

He smiled. "Zaq made her stay at the bookstore."

"Would you permit me to drive you home?" Frank asked.

We were outside and Zaq circled my new car. It was the first time he'd seen it. "Wow. Nice car, Aunt Sammy."

I smiled and handed Frank my key fob. He held the door for me and I got into the passenger seat. However, before he closed the door, I hopped out.

"What are you doing?" he asked.

I opened the back door and pulled Harley Quin's bicycle out of the back and tossed it to the ground. I brushed the caked mud out and slammed the door. Then I went back and got in and buckled my seat belt.

Frank drove Nana Jo and me home. Dawson rode with Zaq.

Detective Pitt came by the bookstore later to get my statement. We were upstairs in my loft. Snickers and Oreo must have sensed something was wrong. They hadn't left my side from the moment I got home. Christopher and Jenna had been assigned taxi service. Jenna was, according to her, ordered by Dorothy to get to the retirement village and pick them up. Christopher had picked up my mom and picked Jillian up from MISU when she asked.

Surrounded by friends, family, and Detective Stinky Pitt, I gave my statement.

"He's been singing like a canary," Detective Pitt said. "Doesn't want to be extradited back to England." He chuckled.

Jenna pulled out her tape recorder. "So Virgil and Melody were planning to get Dawson to go to the pros so they could try and hustle money from him. Is that right?"

I nodded. "I think Melody hoped to trap Dawson into marriage to strengthen her bond."

Dawson shook his head. "My dad knew about that. He thought he could get money out of me too."

"But Dawson broke up with her," I said. "Virgil said she was dating someone else."

Emma chimed in, "That was Professor Quin."

Nana Jo scoffed. "Professor, my big toe."

"He was the other person in that special program Dorothy told us about," I said.

"So if he wasn't a professor . . . ?" Emma asked.

I pointed to Frank.

Frank said, "He was a grifter. I have a friend who used to be in British intelligence.

355

I had him run his name." He avoided eye contact with me, and I thought I detected a small amount of color on his ears.

"So, he was a con man, too, and he and Melody ended up at the same university together. Convenient," Detective Pitt said.

"Well, there were only a few universities willing to take them. I think if you check around, you'll find Harley Quin was originally sent to another school. I think he must have been in contact with Melody, who told him pickings were good at MISU, so he came here. I think he heard the rumors about the House of David and created an identity for himself." I looked around. "That's why Melody didn't bother about classes. She knew she would get a good grade from Harley and just needed to hang around long enough to get an athlete with PEP." I glanced at Nana Jo.

"But what happened to Professor Quin? Or is there a real Professor Quin?" Emma asked.

"He made up the identity and lied to the university. You'd be surprised how few places take the time to check references."

"Good for us he used the alias before or I might not have found him," Frank said.

"Thanks to Irma, we learned that Virgil Russell knew Melody had another lover." I turned to her. "She found that out at the memorial."

Irma smiled broadly before breaking into a coughing fit.

"Everything came to a head at the memorial service Jillian arranged."

Jillian looked shocked. "Me?"

"If you hadn't gotten the memorial together, Quin wouldn't have found out that A-squared was still alive and in intensive care."

She smiled.

"But then he made another attempt on my dad's life," Dawson said.

"Yes, but that's how he trapped himself. If Stinky . . . ah . . . I mean Detective Pitt hadn't asked who I'd told about your dad being in the hospital, I might not have put it together. We were so focused on Virgil, but someone had to have put the note on his windshield."

"He could have faked the note." Detective Pitt looked condescendingly at me. "Real detectives would have thought of that."

Nana Jo grunted. "A real detective arrested the wrong man."

I chose to ignore Detective Pitt. "The note bothered me and it took a long time before I figured out why." I stared at Nana Jo.

She nodded. "It bothered me too."

"It was the language. It told Virgil to go to the surgery."

Detective Pitt stared.

"Americans would say hospital or doctor's office, not 'surgery.' "

"That's it? That was what tipped you off?" Detective Pitt looked skeptical.

I nodded. "Not at first. It just bothered me. But, thanks to Nana Jo for catching on to the Deering Vale reference."

Detective Pitt looked confused. "Deering Vale? What's Deering Vale?"

"It's one of the fictitious towns Agatha Christie created. That's where Quin said he was from when Nana Jo asked."

Nana Jo smiled. "Thought he was so smart that one. I knew I'd read that name before. So, I started rereading the Agatha Christie books until I found it. Darned fool."

Frank shook his head. "That was pretty stupid. He should know better than to use a name and a village in an Agatha Christie novel to women who own a mystery bookstore."

"Well, it is a bit obscure. If he'd used something more obvious, like St. Mary Mead, I'd have caught on immediately. Most people haven't even heard of the Harley Quin or Parker Payne short stories.

They aren't as famous as her other sleuths."

"Except to someone who owns a mystery bookstore," my nephews said simultaneously.

"It rang a bell, but it took me a while to place it."

"Why did he steal Emma's laptop?" Zaq asked.

"I can answer that," Detective Pitt said. "He thought it would help him find out what you were up to." He nodded toward me. "He thought she had notes."

We talked for hours after Detective Pitt left until I was so tired I could barely keep my eyes open.

I woke up when I smelled bacon and coffee. Nana Jo came in to check on me. I suspected she'd been in several times during the night because whenever I woke up, my blankets were always neat and Oreo never woke me to go potty. I looked around and didn't see them.

"I had Dawson keep them so you could sleep in peace." Nana Jo opened the curtains. "You feel up to breakfast?"

"Definitely."

I was stiff and sore and there was an ugly red-and-blue bruise on my forehead. Otherwise, I felt pretty good. Despite my good appetite and assurances I could work in the bookstore, Nana Jo would have none of it. She was going to keep things going at the bookstore, with a little help from my mom and the girls. The thought of Irma hitting on my male clients struck fear in my heart for a moment, but I supposed the store and the mystery reading men of North Harbor could survive one day with Irma.

I'd tried to go back to sleep, but it was hopeless. Eventually, I gave up and looked for other ways to occupy my mind.

"Dis is frame. Is Frame. *Jestem wrobiony.*"

Józef Lipski paced and alternated proclamations of innocence in broken English and Polish. Neither James nor Victor spoke Polish, but they were able to comprehend the gist of the diplomat's rants.

"Mr. Lipski, we aren't accusing you of murder. However, we do need to ask you some questions," James said.

"Questions. Questions. Always questions wit de English." Lipski's accent was thicker when he was emotional and made it difficult for Victor and James to understand him.

"Did you tell anyone about your special cocoa?" James asked.

"Of course. I talk about de cocoa. I tell dem Poland has best cocoa." He puffed out his chest with pride. "Is true."

"I'm sure it is," Victor said quietly as he looked around the room.

"Did you show the cocoa to anyone?" James tried again.

"Show it? I tell dem. I no show."

James rubbed the back of his neck. "The police are going to need to test the cocoa."

Lipski halted and turned to James. "Goot. Goot. Your police test." He handed the cocoa to James. "Test prove I did not kill."

"Can you think of anyone who would want to harm you?" Victor asked.

"Me?" Lipski stared. "You dink poison was for me?"

"We don't know."

Lipski was silent for several seconds. He walked to his bed and lifted a corner of the mattress, reached under, and pulled out a note. He took the note to James. "I give you dis."

James opened the note and read it. He looked up at Lipski. When he reread the note, he handed it to Victor.

Victor read the note and then stared at James.

"When did you get this?" James asked.

Lipski walked to the door and leaned down. "It appear on floor." He pointed down. "Day French woman shot."

"Meet me by the Marsh at three. W," James

read aloud. "Did you meet her?"

"No." Lipski paced. "I shoot wit de American." He stopped pacing and faced James and Victor. "We leave de shooting. But de leg. It get stuck in de mud." He pulled on his leg. "I pull and pull, but . . . de leg it not come out. She take de leg off. Only den am I able to pull it out of de mud."

James's lips twitched as he watched Lipski's demonstration.

"So, once you got her leg out of the mud, what did you do then? Did you go to the marsh?"

He shook his head vigorously. "No. I help de American to de house." He hopped on one leg. "I help. I not go to marsh. I not meet anyone. Later, she is killed."

"Why didn't you tell anyone?" Victor asked.

Lipski shrugged. "She is dead. Dat is how I know is frame. *Jestem wrobiony.*"

Victor joined the Marsh Family in Lord William's bedroom.

"What took so long?" Penelope asked. "And where's James?"

"We were on our way here when we got stopped by Thompkins. James was wanted on the telephone."

James and Detective Inspector Covington rushed into the room and closed the door.

"I'm sorry, I don't have much time. I've been

called back to London. I hope I haven't overstepped, but I invited Detective Inspector Covington. I think it'll be fastest if we just include him."

"How did you get here so quickly?" Lady Penelope asked.

"I called him after Brasseur died," James said.

Victor smiled. "What about the poachers?"

Detective Inspector Covington grinned. "I'm hot on their trail." Then he put his fingers to his lips and took a position near the window, where Daphne was seated.

Lady Elizabeth nodded. "Of course, you're very welcome."

The detective smiled his thanks and quietly sat with a notepad on his lap.

"What's happened?" Daphne stared at James.

"A German secretary, Ernst von Rath's, been assassinated in Paris."

"Good Lord. What's happening to the world?" Lady Elizabeth whispered.

James paced. "I'm afraid that's not all. A Polish teenager's been arrested for the murder."

The family looked shocked.

Lord William fumbled with his pipe. "Here we are on the brink of war and now this."

James nodded. "Exactly. And, somehow

word has leaked out to *The Week* that an attempt was made on the Duchess of Windsor's life.

Daphne looked pale. "What's *The Week*?"

It's an anti-fascist newsletter run by Claud Cockburn. The readership is small, but . . ."

"But it could still cause trouble?" she asked. James nodded.

"So if word got out the French Ambassador was murdered by a Polish Emissary . . ."

"It could be disastrous. I've got to run up to London. I'll be back as quick as I can." James hurried away, and the group sat in silence for a few moments.

Lady Elizabeth looked around. "Well, we better get busy."

They filled Detective Inspector Covington in on what they had learned so far, including Victor's conversation with Józef Lipski.

"So, Lipski couldn't possibly be responsible for the murder of the maid," Penelope said. "If he was with Virginia Hall, then he has an alibi. Did anyone check with her?"

Victor nodded. "Yes. As soon as we left Lipski, we questioned her. She confirmed everything he said."

"Do you trust her?" Daphne asked.

"Yes. She was very credible. Both James and I agreed."

"He also couldn't have poisoned the cocoa,"

Lady Elizabeth said.

"Really? How can you be certain?" Detective Inspector Covington asked.

"I talked to Mrs. Anderson."

"Who is Mrs. Anderson?"

"Mrs. Anderson is the cook," Lady Elizabeth said. "It took a bit of prodding to get her to admit it, but apparently, she was rather curious about this cocoa. She'd never had cocoa from Poland so . . . she made a couple of cups for herself and her daughter, Agnes."

"Well, I'll be," Lord William said.

"Yes. She said it tasted just like good old-fashioned English cocoa, and she and her daughter are perfectly fine."

Detective Inspector Covington perched on the end of his seat. "That's significant."

Lady Elizabeth nodded. "I know. It means the poison wasn't in the cocoa."

Lord William stared. "But how can that be? If the poison wasn't in the cocoa, how did the blasted fool get it?"

"The poison has to have been put into his cup," Lady Elizabeth said.

"That's not the worst of it." Daphne looked around at her family.

Penelope stopped pacing and stared at her sister. "What do you mean?"

"Unless you believe Thompkins or Mrs. Anderson put the poison in his cup, it had to

365

have been put there by someone in the room."

Penelope paled. "You mean one of us."

"Exactly," Lady Elizabeth said.

Detective Inspector Covington wrote furiously. "You all are very good, very thorough."

There was a tentative knock on the door.

"Come in," Lady Elizabeth said.

Thompkins entered the room and closed the door. He moved to a corner and stood erect.

"Great, Thompkins, did you finish your assignment?"

The butler coughed discreetly. "Yes, m'lady."

Lady Elizabeth looked around the room. "I asked Thompkins to come here and share the results from the search."

Detective Inspector Covington looked confused. "Excuse me, did you say search?"

Lady Elizabeth nodded. "Yes. We needed to find out if anyone had a gun, since none of the ones used in the murder belonged to us."

Detective Inspector Covington stared at Lady Elizabeth with awe. "Did you really? How did you get them to agree to a search?"

Lady Elizabeth smiled. "I didn't ask them."

Thompkins looked slightly uncomfortable but straightened his already straight back, pushed his shoulders backed, and lifted his head higher. "As your ladyship instructed, I asked the maids, Flossie, Millie, and Gladys. The only one who remembered seeing a weapon of any type was Millie. She said Count Rudolph had a gun, but she hasn't seen it since. Under my supervision, they searched the room again, and there was no gun."

Lady Elizabeth sighed. "That's what I was afraid of." She smiled at the butler. "Well done, Thompkins. Please tell the staff I said thank you."

Thompkins nodded. "Yes, m'lady." He paused for several moments.

"Is there anything else?" Lady Elizabeth asked.

Thompkins coughed. "There is just one other thing . . . I hesitate to bring it up, but you said you wanted to know about anything out of the ordinary."

Lady Elizabeth nodded. "Of course."

Everyone stared at the butler.

"Millie found this in the Duchess of Windsor's wastebasket." The butler held up a small piece of paper in the shape of a funnel. Everyone stared, but Detective Inspector Covington immediately hopped up and practically ran to the butler's side.

The detective grabbed the paper and stared at it and then whistled. "I need to have this tested." He wrapped the funnel in a handkerchief and placed it in his pocket.

Thompkins nodded. "I believe Her Grace is in the parlor with the rest of the guests."

Lady Elizabeth looked thoughtful.

"I know that look." Lord William sat up straight and stared at his wife. "You've figured it out."

Everyone stared at Lady Elizabeth. For several moments, she stared off into space. Eventually, she nodded and looked around and seemed to notice everyone was staring at her. "I'm sorry. Did you say something, dear?"

"You've figured out who the murderer is, haven't you?" Penelope walked over to her aunt. "Tell us."

Lady Elizabeth looked around at her family. "Well, I believe I have."

Detective Inspector Covington anxiously looked at her but stood very still.

"I'm afraid I've been terribly dense. I should have figured it out sooner. I believe Daphne commented on how 'theatrical' the murder seemed. I should have known then. Maybe that poor man wouldn't have died," Lady Elizabeth said softly. "But, well, at least we can give him justice."

"Who did it?" Detective Covington asked.

"Count Rudolph, of course. He used to be an actor before World War I. He even starred in some god-awful propaganda movie advocating the involuntary sterilization of the disabled and those with hereditary diseases."

She shivered. "He staged the murder. The setting, a British country home. The duchess, killed by the Polish ambassador."

Penelope stared at her aunt. "But the duchess wasn't killed."

"I think the count put the note in the duchess's pocket, sometime during the night when they were together. He wasn't to know she would have her maid wear her clothes."

"And Rebecca probably found the note in her pocket and thought the duchess wanted to meet her," Penelope said.

Victor looked confused. "But, Józef Lipski has an iron-tight alibi. There's no way he could have killed her."

Lady Elizabeth nodded. "But Count Rudolph wasn't to know about that. Virginia Hall is very casual about her wooden leg. She jokes and calls it Cuthbert, but I think she was embarrassed about getting it stuck in the mud. Neither she nor Lipski told anyone about the incident."

"But how did he kill her? Wouldn't he have been missed by the other members of his shooting party?" Penelope asked.

Lord William reddened. "Count Rudolph was with Georges Brasseur and Wallis. I suspect it would be pretty easy for a gentleman to . . . excuse himself for a few minutes and sneak off."

Daphne stared at her uncle. "Excuse him-self?"

Lord William squirmed uncomfortably.

Penelope smiled. "You mean to relieve himself?"

Lord William's face reddened and he puffed on his pipe.

"But surely someone would have mentioned it," Daphne added.

"At the time it probably seemed normal. Later, after they'd had time to think about it, they might have suspected. That's probably why he killed Brasseur," Victor said.

Lady Elizabeth nodded. "I suspect so."

"But surely the Duchess of Windsor would have said something," Daphne said.

Lady Elizabeth sighed. "Perhaps, but the duchess may have found herself in an awkward situation. Remember, she had been seen coming out of his bedroom. She isn't exactly well loved by the British public at the moment. That type of negative publicity would have been the last thing she wanted."

"Where is he?" Detective Inspector Covington asked.

"I believe Count Rudolph and the duchess are in the parlor," Thompkins said.

Detective Inspector Covington got a constable and went to confront the count. Victor went along.

As the detectives entered the parlor, Count Rudolph glanced up at the approaching officers. A glimmer of realization flashed in his eyes and was quickly followed by panic. Before the detectives knew what was happening, Count Rudolph made a mad dash toward the door. He pushed the detectives aside and quickly closed the door behind him and turned the lock.

When Detective Inspector Covington regained his feet, he pulled frantically at the doorknobs, but the heavy doors were locked.

Detective Covington threw his body against the doors in an effort to force them open, but the sturdy oak doors didn't budge.

Victor looked around for a way out. He glanced at the French doors. "Quickly, the window."

They quickly unlatched the windows and rushed out.

Outside, they split up. Detective Covington and Victor ran in one direction and the constable ran in the other.

Around the back of the house, Victor spotted Count Rudolph making a run for the garage. "There. He's going for the garage."

The footmen, Jim and Frank, were carrying a large basket of laundry outside for Gladys, who followed close behind.

"Stop him!" Victor yelled.

The footmen looked where Victor pointed and dropped the basket and took off after the count.

Frank caught up to Count Rudolph seconds before Jim. When they were mere feet from their target, both men took their stance, knees bent, feet about shoulder-width apart, back straight, and heads up. In a few quick steps, they closed the gap between them and the count. They lowered their shoulders and wrapped both arms around him and took him to the ground, just as they had been taught to tackle ball carriers on the rugby field.

Count Rudolph struggled briefly but quickly recognized the futility of his situation. Detective Covington arrived and relieved the footmen of their prey. "Well done!"

Frank and Jim looked at Victor, who nodded further approval.

The Duchess of Windsor was so upset when told by Lady Elizabeth of Count Rudolph's actions, she immediately left and returned to Fort Belvedere; poor plumbing notwithstanding.

Józef Lipski received a telegram recalling him to Poland. The assassination of the German ambassador and fear of escalating violence were cited as the reasons for his return. Lipski thanked the Marsh family profusely before leaving.

Lord and Lady Chitterly made discreet departures.

Fordham-Baker was one of the last to leave.

Lady Elizabeth waited in the hall to say goodbye.

"Thank you so much for the wonderful hospitality," Fordham-Baker said to Lady Elizabeth as he prepared to depart.

Lady Elizabeth smiled. "And thanks are due to you, too, I think."

He blinked and looked at Lady Elizabeth with surprise. "To me, your ladyship? I don't know what you mean?"

"I think you do." She smiled. "I think you were not as . . . indisposed as you pretended to be. I also think you are the one responsible for feeding information to Claud Cockburn."

He blinked. "I don't know . . ." He chuckled. "What gave me away?"

"You were quite convincing." Lady Elizabeth smiled. "But we were very concerned about your health. So, I had my butler substitute the scotch with a diluted mixture. Your reaction was the same to both."

"I should have guessed." He laughed. "I take back all the evil thoughts I had about the quality of your cellars." He laughed until he had to wipe tears from his eyes. "I find people are very reticent to speak freely in front of a newspaper editor unless he's in a drunken stupor.

Then you would be surprised what they will say."

Lady Elizabeth bid him farewell.

Virginia Hall looked for Lady Daphne before she left. She found her in the library, sitting on the window seat.

Daphne looked up at her. "Are you leaving? Well, it's been a pleasure meeting you," she said politely.

Virginia Hall smiled. "You British ladies are such well-bred liars. You haven't enjoyed meeting me at all."

Daphne looked shocked. "I don't know what you mean."

"Don't get your back up, dear. It's not your fault, and I don't blame you one little bit." She sat down on the window seat next to Daphne. "I blame that handsome man of yours."

Daphne's face heated and she looked down. "I don't know what you mean."

"Yes, you do. Lord James FitzAndrew Browning." Virginia looked around the room. "I told James he needed to come clean and explain everything to you, but he wouldn't do it."

Daphne stood up abruptly. "I don't know what you're talking about, but I don't think I want to hear it." She turned and took several steps away.

"There's nothing going on between James and me," Virginia said.

Daphne stopped. "What?"

Virginia got up and walked over to Daphne. "Look. He should have told you himself, but he just kept saying you should trust him." She huffed. "Men. They're impossible." She pulled a small card out of her purse and showed it to Daphne. "I work for the American Secret Service. I was sent here to keep an eye on Józef Lipski. The president believed the Germans might be up to some funny business and looks like he was right."

"You're a spy?" Daphne asked.

Virginia Hall nodded. "Pretty good cover, right? Who'd believe a one-legged woman could be a spy?" She patted her leg.

"Is that real?" She pointed to the leg.

"Yes. Cuthbert's real alright." She pulled up her skirt so Daphne could see the buckle. She put away her identification card and stared at Daphne. "He really does care about you."

Daphne shook her head. "If he did, why didn't he tell me the truth?"

"Because I was a fool," James said from the doorway.

Daphne turned at the sound of his voice.

Virginia Hall gave her a hug and whispered, "I think you and I could be great friends. I hope so."

Daphne squeezed her back and whispered, "Thank you."

Virginia nodded to James as she left.

Daphne returned to her seat, and James walked over and stood next to her.

"I'm terribly sorry, darling. I should have told you the truth from the beginning."

"No, I'm sorry. I was just . . . jealous." She laughed. "It's a new emotion for me. I don't think I've ever been jealous of anyone before."

James held her hand. "You don't have any reason to be. You have my heart totally and completely." He looked down. "I love you."

"I love you too," Daphne whispered.

James pulled Daphne toward him and kissed her passionately and thoroughly. Daphne couldn't have said whether they kissed for seconds or hours.

When they finally pulled apart, James held her close and whispered, "Darling, I plan to make an official request for your hand, but I have one favor to ask of you."

Daphne snuggled next to him like a kitten. "Anything."

"I would like to introduce you to my mother."

Daphne smiled. "I would like nothing better."

Lady Daphne had no idea how she would regret that remark.

"Hmmm. Maybe foreshadowing is a bit much here," I said aloud, even though there was no one to hear.

I better leave that part out. I deleted the last sentence and read the last few lines.

"I would like to introduce you to my mother." Daphne smiled. "I would like nothing better."

Chapter 23

The Sleuthing Seniors Book Club met on Thursdays. That was the only reason I came downstairs. The bruise on my forehead was now a deep purple and it looked like I was getting a black eye. However, after a day alone, I was tired of my own company.

Dawson had been busy baking most of the day. Tomorrow, he would be allowed back at school and back on the football team. One of my favorite desserts was carrot cake, so he'd made a delicious carrot cake with cream cheese icing. It was moist and tasty and I ate more than I should, but I enjoyed every bite.

"Have you ladies decided on your next book?" I asked.

"We're going for Raymond Chandler's *The Big Sleep*," Dorothy said.

"That's a good one," Nana Jo added.

"Is there sex in it?" Irma asked.

I thought back. "It's been a while since I

read it, but I don't think so."

Irma looked disappointed.

"I've got something for you." I went to the back office and came back with three books which I placed in front of Irma. "I ordered these for you."

She looked at them. They were romance novels by Brenda Jackson.

"*A Brother's Honor* is the first book in the series. *A Man's Promise* is the second, and *A Lover's Vow* is the third. Technically, they're romances, not mysteries, but there is definitely a mystery subplot. I thought you might enjoy them."

Irma coughed and gave me a hug. "Thank you, Sam. I can't wait to read them."

Frank Patterson entered with a bottle of champagne, followed by Dawson, who had a tray of glasses. Nana Jo came over to me with a sly smile on her face and a mysterious envelope in her hand. "Sam, I have a surprise for you."

I looked at Nana Jo and tried to imagine what the surprise might be. I looked around at the girls, and they seemed to be a mixture of happiness and nervous anxiety.

Nana Jo took a deep breath. "We know how . . . deeply private you are about your book and your writing. We all think it's wonderful."

I could feel the heat rush to my face. It had been difficult to allow the girls to read my book, but they were all very complimentary. However, they were my friends and I knew they would never say or do anything to hurt me.

Dorothy said, "Josephine, stop beating around the bush and tell the girl."

I looked from Dorothy to Nana Jo. "Tell me what?"

Nana Jo hesitated for a moment. "You know Ruby Mae has a second cousin whose daughter is a literary agent in New York."

I suddenly felt a huge weight in the pit of my stomach. "Yes."

"Well, we sent her a copy of your manuscript, and she loved it."

"You did what?" My head was dizzy and I felt like I needed to puke.

Nana Jo looked shocked. "We . . . I wanted to help."

I put my head between my knees for several moments. The room was completely quiet.

When I finally felt I could sit up without getting sick, I did. Tears streamed down my face.

Nana Jo hurried to my seat. "I'm so sorry, Sam." She put her arms around me to comfort me. "I never would have done it if

I'd known it would upset you this much."

I pulled away from her and stood. "Upset?" I stared at Nana Jo.

Her expression was one of disappointment and remorse. I looked around at the girls and each of them looked ashamed.

I took several deep breaths and collected myself. Then I threw both arms around my grandmother. "Thank you."

Nana Jo pushed me away to look in my face. Seeing I was okay, she pulled me close and hugged me tightly.

Irma took a swig from her flask. "Jesus Christ, you scared the living daylights out of me."

Dorothy and Ruby Mae came over and hugged me. Frank popped the cork and poured champagne into glasses.

"I'm just in shock. I'm sorry. I just can't believe it." I stared at the letter Nana Jo handed me.

"You'd better believe it." Nana Jo smiled at Sam. "I have one more surprise for you."

"I don't know if I can take any more."

"I decided how I want to spend my share of the casino winnings." She pulled an envelope out of her back pocket and handed it to me.

I opened the envelope. Inside were brochures and flyers for a trip to England. I looked at my grandmother with tears in my eyes. "Really?"

"I thought it would help with your research . . . for your next book."

I was dumbstruck. Tears streamed down my face. I grabbed Nana Jo and squeezed her. "Thank you."

"You deserve it." Nana Jo wiped away a tear and took a drink from the glass of champagne Dawson handed her. "Now, let's get this party started."

ABOUT THE AUTHOR

V. M. Burns was born and raised in South Bend, Indiana. She currently resides in Tennessee with her two poodles, Cash and Kenzie. Valerie is a member of Mystery Writers of America and a lifetime member of Sisters in Crime. Readers can visit her website at www.vmburns.com.

Author Residence: Chattanooga, TN

The employees of Thorndike Press hope you have enjoyed this Large Print book. All our Thorndike, Wheeler, and Kennebec Large Print titles are designed for easy reading, and all our books are made to last. Other Thorndike Press Large Print books are available at your library, through selected bookstores, or directly from us.

For information about titles, please call:
  (800) 223-1244

or visit our website at:
  gale.com/thorndike

To share your comments, please write:
  Publisher
  Thorndike Press
  10 Water St., Suite 310
  Waterville, ME 04901